"My life is very complicated, Mia."

"Because of your family situation?"

Jay squeezed his eyes shut, but not before Mia saw the flash of pain. When he opened them again, she felt a hitch in her chest. There was so much raw emotion there—pain, regret and a sadness that made her own heart ache. He searched her face. "I can't be what you need."

"How do you know what I need?" she managed to say.

A sad smile played on his lips. "As much as I'd love to find out, I'm not the man to give it to you, to give you anything."

"Jay, I'm not asking you for anything."

He lowered his gaze to her lips. "This is such a bad idea," he whispered.

"I know. That's what I'm trying to tell you."

"We're going to anyway, though, aren't we."

It wasn't a question, she realized, and knew he was right.

Dear Reader,

Like a lot of you out there, I'm an animal lover. I've always had pets: cats, dogs, bunnies, gerbils, hamsters, fish, goats. I spent a good portion of my childhood thinking I would be a veterinarian when I grew up. I held on to this dream until the day my cat "introduced" himself to my gerbil and I realized that I wouldn't be able to save them all. Fortunately, there are those selfless and insightful people out there who understand that being a veterinarian isn't all about them—it's about saving or comforting an injured or ill critter in whatever way they can.

Heroine and veterinarian Mia Frasier is this kind of person. She sees the bigger picture and she wants to make a difference, to leave the world a better place. Maybe a little too much sometimes.

A chaotic upbringing combined with years of supplying financial support to his younger siblings have left Jay Johnston focused on his family and confident that he can provide. But when his teenage brother and sister come to live with him, he soon finds life spiraling out of his control. Jay needs help. Mia knows he needs help. It's a tricky thing, though—help. It's not easy to ask for, it's difficult to admit that you need it, and offering it can often cause problems, too. Thankfully, an orphaned dog, a hellish tomcat and two troubled teens get Jay and Mia to finally learn to meet in the middle.

Thanks so much for reading!

Carol

HEARTWARMING

Summer at the Shore

———

USA TODAY Bestselling Author

Carol Ross

Recycling programs
for this product may
not exist in your area.

ISBN-13: 978-0-373-36840-2

Summer at the Shore

Printed in U.S.A.

www.Harlequin.com

Carol Ross lives in the Pacific Northwest with her husband and two dogs. She is a graduate of Washington State University. When not writing, or thinking about writing, she enjoys reading, running, hiking, skiing, traveling and making plans for the next adventure to subject her sometimes reluctant but always fun-loving family to. Carol can be contacted at www.carolrossauthor.com.

Books by Carol Ross

Harlequin Heartwarming

Christmas at the Cove

Seasons of Alaska

A Family Like Hannah's
If Not for a Bee
A Case for Forgiveness
Mountains Apart

For Dr. Katie, to whom I owe a giant debt of gratitude. Not just for meeting with me and answering all of my crazy questions, but especially for taking such wonderful care of our precious fur-babies for all of these years. Your kindness, compassion and generosity are so inspiring. Thank you.

CHAPTER ONE

WHOEVER SAID THAT your life flashes before your eyes right before you die must not have gone down in a plane crash. Because all Mia Frasier could think about was the life she *hadn't* yet lived. She glanced out the window at the brilliant blue sky and the sparkle of the sun reflecting off the Pacific Ocean below. It seemed wrong somehow to die when it was so gorgeous outside. The plane argued with a wild dip. She gritted her teeth as her stomach mimicked the action.

At this point she supposed some people might close their eyes and sit back, count their blessings, resign themselves to the inevitable, pray, make their peace, or whatever you call it when you give up and accept the inevitable end. Not Mia.

She had plans, things to accomplish before her time was up. Not huge news-making achievements; she didn't need the Nobel Peace Prize or anything. But she did want to make a difference in this world before she left it. She wanted to save some cats. Lucky Cats, her stray and feral cat reduction program, hadn't even gotten off the ground yet. And kids. She *really* wanted a family. A husband was right up there on the list, too. And a home. Not just a house either, but a home like she'd never had. One filled with that husband and kids, a couple dogs, and a bunch of rescued cats... Was this all too much to ask for? She didn't think so, because as it was she'd barely had a chance to enjoy her life, the life she was finally building in Pacific Cove.

It had only been a few months since Dr. Anthony made her a partner in his already-established veterinary practice. Not only was the position the opportunity of a lifetime and a dream come true, Dr. Anthony needed her. His wife, Sara, and precious daughter, McKenzie, needed her. She couldn't let him down by dying now. Not to mention all the animals who needed her help. Which reminded her of George. Her rescued bloodhound-mastiff mix could make the promo reel for the prevention of animal abuse. Sure, he was a bit of a handful. His massive size combined with his penchant for eating inedible non-food items made him more like two hands full. She'd only recently convinced him the furniture legs were off-limits. Who would take care of George with both her and her mom gone?

Mom. She loved her mom, Nora, so much. And finally, her mom was living the life she deserved, too. Doing all the things she hadn't been able to do when Mia's dad was alive. She glanced over at the seat next to her where her mom was gazing tranquilly out the side window as if they were on a sightseeing jaunt and not plummeting to their deaths. Even when Captain Shear had told them to make sure their seat belts were fastened good and tight, her mom had remained calm. Typical Nora Frasier: cheerful in the face of any adversity. Not even death scared her. Mia was pretty sure there wasn't anything the woman was afraid of.

Her mom must have sensed her fear, though, because she turned her head at that moment. Reaching for Mia's hand, she said, "I love you, honey." She couldn't really hear the words over the rumble and desperate sputtering of the plane's engine, but as she'd heard them from her mother nearly every day of her life, she knew the words when she saw them crossing her lips. They were finally together and living in the same town with no plans to ever move again. She'd thought that would mean years and years of being happy and settled. Mia felt a fresh wave of panic; they needed more time.

"I love you, too, Mom," she called out, managing a shaky smile as she proceeded to watch the final seconds of her paltry existence on this planet pass by the tiny airplane window.

She braced herself as the plane hit the surface of the ocean with a thunderous crash. Her body lurched forward, then back and sideways, her head smacking against the side window with a loud *crack*. Cool air rushed in around her. Not at all like the smooth-as-glass lakes she'd landed on in her previous floatplane experiences.

Of course, this wasn't a floatplane or a lake. A fact she was immediately reminded of as the ocean proceeded to assault the little plane. Wave after wave rolled into them, some battering the cabin and leaving the windows covered with drips of seawater and bits of foam. The fuselage groaned in response. Water was seeping in through the cracked window beside her. Droplets ran down her forehead, which struck her as odd because there didn't seem to be *that* much water getting inside. She reached up and swiped it away. Blood. A quick probing told her the wound was barely more than a scratch. No other injuries that she could feel or see.

And she was alive. Alive! As in not dead. Hope roared to life inside her.

"Mom!" she cried. "We're alive." She turned to find her mom slumped over in her seat. "Oh, please no…"

She shouted this time, "Mom?" No response. Terror flamed inside her again as she unbuckled her seat belt with shaking hands. Crouching between the seats, she felt her mom's wrist for a pulse—weak, but there. She couldn't see any visible signs of trauma, but as a doctor herself, she knew that often the worst injuries were the ones you couldn't immediately recognize.

She realized then that she'd been expecting the pilot to turn and say something, give them some kind of instructions, until she realized there was no movement from the cockpit, either. Did you call it a cockpit in a plane this small? As the plane pitched and rolled violently in the waves, she stumbled her way to the pilot's seat, praying he'd survived the impact. She reached over and searched for a pulse on his neck. Strong. Good. There was a lot of blood, though. She spotted a laceration on his forehead. Head wounds bleed a lot, so that could explain it. A soft moan escaped his lips when she touched the area to examine it. Even better.

Dropping to her hands and knees, she crawled toward the side of the plane to the emergency compartment. Even though he'd only carried two passengers this morning, Captain Shear hadn't neglected to give them a preflight safety chat. Hard to believe it had only been a few short hours since they'd taken off from Pacific Cove that morning. They'd flown up the coast to tiny Windsor Island in Washington's Puget Sound, where Mia had helped a pregnant mare in distress deliver a healthy foal. They'd only been a few miles from home when the plane's engine stalled and then continued to falter. Within seconds, Captain Shear had placed the Mayday call that they were going down.

Along with the first-aid kit and life jackets, she was relieved to find an inflatable raft. Slipping a life jacket on, she set two others aside. As she gathered what supplies she needed, she tried to figure out how she was going to load two unconscious people into a life raft. Because surely the plane would begin sinking soon? It was already tilting to one side. There was no way she was going to be able to stabilize any spines; she'd have to take her chances. Using a gauze pad, she wiped at her head and slapped a large bandage on it. She wasn't concerned about the wound, but she needed to keep the blood from dripping into her eyes so she could see and then somehow get them all out of here. No way was she going to survive a plane crash only to drown in this freezing cold ocean. Fate had given her this chance and she wasn't going to waste it.

On her way back to the captain, she stopped to check her mom's pulse again. No change. By the time she got back to Captain Shear he was coming around, mumbling incoherently.

"Captain Shear? Russell? Can you hear me?"

Holding a sterile pad to his head to slow the bleeding, she continued talking to him.

"We're alive." His voice was a hoarse whisper, but Mia was relieved by the sound.

"Yes! We are, thanks to your excellent piloting skills."

"How's Nora?"

"She's alive but unconscious." She had already liked what she knew of this man, but his questioning the condition of his passengers while in his current state solidified those feelings and then some.

"How are you?"

"I'm fine. Tiny cut on my head." She managed a small smile as she wrapped his head wound and secured it with some tape.

"How am I?" He winced as he asked, and she could tell he was in serious pain.

"My earlier cursory exam suggested you have a broken clavicle and arm, and possibly a fractured leg."

"That's why I can't move it. I was afraid I was paralyzed."

"That's right," she said, although she had no idea if it was the truth. She didn't know if he was talking about his arm or leg, and she didn't ask. The fact was, he could be paralyzed, but she certainly wasn't going to tell him that.

He tipped his chin up, eyes focused on the ceiling. "I hear them. Do you hear that?"

Oh no, she thought, was she losing him? "What do you hear, Captain?"

"It's all good." His lips curved up into a smile as his head lolled to one side. "We'll be fine now. We'll all be fine…" His lashes drooped to cover his eyes, but the remnants of his smile lingered.

Mia went still, holding her breath and concentrating on the sounds around her. She couldn't hear anything but the incessant pounding of the ocean's waves against the plane, the groaning and grinding sound of twisted metal. Terror made her heart race. Maybe he'd hit his head harder than she knew… She reached out to check his pulse again.

His eyelids popped open. "I'm not losing my marbles, Dr. Frasier." He added a chuckle. "Coast Guard helicopter. Go check on your mom. We'll be out of here before you know it."

PETTY OFFICER JAY JOHNSTON of Coast Guard Air Station Astoria was elbow-deep in a pile of chopped onions when the emergency call came in. Making chili wasn't part of a flight mechanic's normal duties, but it had sort of become one of his. His upbringing had ensured that he knew how to cook for a crowd and on a budget, which is how he often ended up here in the kitchen. An earlier transmission from an airplane en route to Pacific Cove had reported engine trouble. The second and last communication had just confirmed that the plane was going down.

Abandoning the chili pot, he hurried into his flight suit, grabbed his gear and ran to the Jayhawk helicopter. He was the first one there, but his teammate and friend Aubrey Wynn, the rescue swimmer on duty, was close behind him. Seconds later they were joined by

Lieutenant Commander Holmes, the pilot, and Lieutenant Reeves, the copilot.

Within minutes the team was taking off, heading toward the last known coordinates for the plane. They discussed the possible locations of the fuselage.

"I know Captain Shear," Jay said when he learned who was piloting the small fixed-wing aircraft. "Great guy. He was in the Air Force. Flew small planes and floatplanes for years in the Alaskan bush. He has skills. There's a very strong chance he managed to land it in one piece. I think the plane could be floating down there."

Lieutenant Commander Holmes was unsure. "There was so little time from the Mayday to the loss of communication. The chances of him managing a water landing are slim…"

On it went.

Jay glanced over at Aubrey, who was staring straight ahead. Her lips were moving, but no sound emerged, and he knew she was silently singing the words to Aretha Franklin's "Respect" over and over again. It was part of her ritual and hey, who was he to question the methods of the best rescue swimmer he'd ever had the pleasure of working beside? Jay felt confident that if there were survivors in the ocean, this crew would bring them safely on board.

As the flight mechanic, operating the hoist to lower the rescue swimmer into the water was part of his job. After locating the accident site, the RS would be attached to a cable whereupon he, along with the precision flying skills of the pilot, would lower the RS into the water or onto a ship as quickly and efficiently as possible. Sometimes the target could be as small as a few square feet. Barely enough room for a person meant there was no room for error. Jay knew he was good at his job, but that didn't stop the rush of adrenaline before every rescue. Lives were on the line—literally.

The voice of the copilot, Reeves, broke into his thoughts. "There it is!"

His gaze locked onto the location. The plane was floating on the surface like he'd hoped. Jay smiled. If anyone was alive inside, and he felt the possibility was strong, this could make the rescue go much more smoothly.

"Jay, what do you think?" Aubrey asked. "As close as you can on the starboard side?"

"Yes." They went over the maneuver while he prepared the cable. Aubrey removed her ICS, or onboard communications, while he slid open the door of the helo. At this point, they would rely on hand signals until she'd boarded the aircraft below. She positioned herself on the edge and within seconds he signaled to her with a tap on the chest.

Indicating she was good to go, he released the cable, hoisting her down into the ocean. He never took his eyes off her as she unhooked the cable from her harness and flashed the "swimmer away" signal. He retrieved the cable as she swam the short distance to the plane. She climbed inside while he and the rest of the crew waited for her assessment.

A short time later the communication line crackled and her voice came through: "Three survivors. One is in good shape, the other two are injured and incapacitated. I'm sending up the survivor without injury first."

A voice sounded in the background, loud and agitated. Jay was always amazed at both the bravery and cowardice that emerged from people in the midst of life-and-death situations. He'd seen the burliest, toughest-looking men cry like babies and demand to go first, while the most fragile of women refused to be taken until everyone else was gone. He'd seen men insist that their dogs be rescued before them, while he'd witnessed others charge forward ahead of their own children.

He wondered which case they were dealing with now.

MIA APPRECIATED THE rescue swimmer's confidence and take-charge demeanor. After climbing into the plane, she introduced herself, assessed the condition of each of them, talking to both her and Captain Shear the entire time. "Once the water reaches a certain level, the plane is going to start sinking faster. I'm calling my crew now to let them know how we're going to proceed." She clicked on the radio and outlined her plan, which Mia was fine with until she heard her say she was sending Mia up first.

"No!" Mia shouted. "I can't go first. Take my mom and Captain Shear. They need medical attention. My mom is unconscious and—"

"Mia!" Aubrey interrupted firmly. "I understand your opinion. I am aware of her condition. However, if the plane starts to sink then I'll essentially have to do three difficult rescues. Right now I have one simple rescue and two that are more challenging. We will save you all, but please don't make my job any more difficult."

"Oh… Right. I'm sorry."

"It's fine. I know you're worried," Aubrey assured her as she checked and tightened the straps on Mia's life jacket. "Your mom will go up right after you." She made her way to the door as Mia followed.

"The water is going to be really cold. Don't worry about swimming. Relax and float. I'll get us into position and then I'll signal to the helicopter. They will lower a basket, I'll help you get in and you'll be up in the helo in a couple minutes."

"Okay," she said. She wasn't worried about the water. Her dad had been an officer in the Navy and made sure she and her brother were strong swimmers. Aubrey jumped into the water and motioned for her to do the same. Mia followed, but despite her confidence and Aubrey's warning, the cold hit her like an electric shock. Because of the life jacket, she surfaced quickly but found that she was unable to inhale a breath. She felt as if she'd been flash-frozen and her lungs shrink-wrapped in the process.

She could hear Aubrey but all she could think about was air. Gasping and croaking, it seemed an eternity before the tension in her chest finally loosened enough to inhale. Unfortunately, the feeling didn't last; she sucked in a deep breath at the exact moment a wave rolled over her. Water invaded her lungs. Panic took hold as she thrashed around trying to figure out which way was up until finally, she realized she was floating. *I'd be dead without this flotation device*, she thought, coughing violently as she tried to calm down. This was so much more difficult than she'd anticipated. She thought about her brother, Kyle, who was a Navy SEAL. How did people do this? Why would they want to? But then suddenly, thankfully, Aubrey was right next to her.

"Lie back," she instructed. She did as she was told while Aubrey took a hold of her and propelled them away from the plane.

A large metal basket hit the water in front of them.

"Let's get you inside," Aubrey shouted in order to be heard above the scream of the helicopter, which had moved closer and was now hovering much lower in the sky above them. The powerful force of the rotor wash took her breath away. Again.

As Aubrey helped her into the basket, she wondered how in the world this woman was going to manage to get her unconscious mother and a seriously injured Captain Shear into it? She didn't have time to ask. Huddling into a ball as instructed, she closed her eyes as the basket lifted. Fear surged through her as cold air rushed in around her.

Next thing she knew, she was being pulled inside the helicopter. A man in an orange flight suit helped her out of the basket and told her his name was Jay. As he got her seated and dried her with a towel, he asked her name and how she was doing. He pointed at her head. Then warm fingers peeled away the bandage she'd applied.

His voice was calm and deep as he asked, "Any other injuries besides this one? That you're aware of?"

She shook her head, trying to answer through the shivers racking her body, but was pretty sure she was incomprehensible.

He looked her over thoroughly. "This should do for now," he said, smoothing a fresh dressing into place. He wrapped a blanket around her shoulders. Keeping one edge in each hand, he held it tight around her. "Hey," he said, shaking it gently until she looked up. His face only inches away now, earnest hazel-green eyes locked onto hers. "We got this, okay?"

For a few seconds, she stared back, frozen with fear. The sob she'd been keeping at bay welled up, taking her by surprise. "My mom…" was all she could manage to mutter.

"Your mom is down there?"

She nodded, hot tears burning the cold flesh of her cheeks.

"Not for long. Aubrey is the best rescue swimmer in the Coast Guard. And I'm the best hoist operator. We've also got the best pilot and copilot working with us today.

Which makes us the dream team of Coast Guard rescue." He reached out and squeezed her cold fingers. "Mia, look at me." She did. How could anyone refuse that gentle yet commanding voice? He seemed to ooze confidence. "I promise we will get your mom out of that airplane and we will do everything we can." A warm feeling she recognized as hope bubbled inside her. He added an encouraging smile. She gave him another nod and he moved back toward the open door of the helicopter.

Oddly enough, his words helped. Mia noticed and appreciated that he didn't promise that her mom would be fine. It was the same strategy she used with her patients' families. You could never guarantee that a patient would be okay, but you could promise that you would do everything in your power to try to make it so.

He arranged the basket in the doorway, studying the scene below, his lips moving again. Even though she couldn't hear what he was saying over the noise of the helicopter's motor, both the concentration and competence he displayed managed to keep her calm.

After positioning the basket, he slid it out the open door. It disappeared, but within minutes it appeared again, her mom tucked safely inside. *Please, please let her be alive.* He easily lifted her mom's petite form, arranging her on the litter he'd already prepared and covering her with a blanket. Looking up as Mia started to move forward, he gave her a quick thumbs-up before discouraging further movement from her with a palm up and out. Mia nodded, expelling a breath of relief as she sank back in her seat. She wanted to see for herself, but she also didn't want to get in the way.

It wasn't long before Captain Shear and the rescue swimmer Aubrey were on board as well. Aubrey examined the captain while Jay inserted an IV into her mom's arm. He checked her vitals again and then Mia watched, transfixed as he sat beside her unconscious mom, holding her hand and smoothing the hair away from her face. Within minutes they were safely on the landing pad of the hospital's roof. Mia was positive that she'd never been so grateful for another human being's kindness in her entire life.

CHAPTER TWO

UNLIKE HIS FRIEND AUBREY, Jay wasn't comfortable visiting survivors or their family members. He was always afraid that he was imposing. Or that the people would think he had shown up in order for them to express their gratitude. But he knew Captain Shear and, as it turned out, Aubrey knew Nora Frasier.

Nora taught yoga classes at the studio Aubrey frequented and she also worked part-time at the health food store in town where Aubrey shopped. When Aubrey said she was going to the hospital to visit both Nora and Captain Shear, it didn't seem odd for Jay to volunteer to tag along. Visiting a friend was different. Although it would be nice to see for himself that Nora Frasier was going to be okay. For some reason, Mia Frasier's terror-filled eyes full of concern for her mom kept flashing through his mind.

After arriving, they had a nice visit with Captain Shear, who was in high spirits after learning he was set to be released in a couple days. They spent some time talking about their Coast Guard service while he reminisced about his twenty years in the Air Force. They swapped stories until his daughter and grandkids showed up to visit.

On their way out, Aubrey asked the captain if he wanted anything. He requested ice cream. Before Jay could offer to go get it, Aubrey sent him to Nora Frasier's room while she ran down to the cafeteria to fetch his butterscotch sundae.

Jay found Nora's room at the end of the hall. He recognized Mia sitting in a chair beside the bed. Tapping lightly on the door frame, he felt a buzz of nerves. He hoped this wasn't a bad time.

"Hey, Mia? Hi. Do you remember me?"

When she looked up and smiled, he was struck with the thought that if it wasn't a bad time, then it was definitely a bad idea. Something about her, the earnest expression or the intensity in those striking blue eyes, made him want to both leave and stay at the same time. There was so much…emotion there. Outside of his family, he didn't do emotion, especially not with women he was attracted to.

"How could I forget? Hi. Officer Johnston, right?"

"Yes, but let's go with Jay, okay?"

"Sure. Come on in, Jay."

"Aubrey is here with me," he said as that awkwardness he was concerned about reared its ugly head. "She, uh, she went down to the cafeteria to get Captain Shear some ice cream." He pointed down the hall to where he kind of wanted to go. "She'll be here…soon."

"Please." She motioned with one hand. "Come in. It's so nice of you to stop by."

"Yeah, it's, uh," he muttered as he walked into the room, "it's a thing Aubrey likes to do, visiting survivors."

"Survivors," she repeated with a grin. "I really like that word."

He'd noticed she was pretty on the helicopter, but she'd also been freezing, soaking wet and terrified. Now, her black hair was dry and silky and settled around her shoulders. Her skin wasn't nearly as pale, either. She looked tired and very beautiful.

He lowered himself onto the chair next to hers. The space was small, and it took a conscious effort not to allow his long leg to brush against hers. He had no choice but to breathe in the scent of her, which made him think of wildflowers and soft music. Soft music? Clearly, he was tired, too.

Spreading his fingers, he splayed his clammy

palms over his knees and reminded himself he was a member of the United States military and a grown man. "How is your mom?"

"She's going to be fine. No permanent damage. And she's awake."

His mood lightened as he looked at the peacefully sleeping woman lying on the bed next to them. Nora had her head turned toward the wall and Jay could hear the comforting sound of her soft snore. For some reason, he couldn't resist teasing her. With a tip of his head toward the bed, he said drily, "I can see that."

Mia looked surprised for a second and then let out a chuckle. "Well, not *now*... Obviously. But she woke up. Finally. This morning her eyes popped open and she asked for a green tea smoothie and a vitamin B12 shot."

Jay grinned. "That's so great." He liked the way her cheeks blushed with color. Her unease somehow made his a little more bearable.

Nora stirred and murmured in her sleep, drawing both of their gazes.

He flipped a thumb toward the doorway. "Should I...? Are we going to wake her up?"

"I really don't think so. The meds are making her really sleepy. Even though she only wants turmeric, fish oil and cannabis tincture, the doctors insist on giving her actual medication."

He chuckled. "Aubrey knows your mom. She sounds like a character."

"You have no idea." She sighed and then added in a voice choked with emotion, "She's actually really amazing. I don't know what I'd do without her..." She sniffled. "I'm so sorry. I keep doing this." She pointed at her eyes, which were brimming with tears. "Having these little episodes. It's embarrassing."

"Don't be sorry. Trauma like you lived through can be really emotional, even when it has a positive outcome."

Tears glistened on her cheeks. She swiped them away. "I thought I had a pretty good handle on death. I'm a vet and I deal with animal deaths all the time. But when it's your own you're facing or someone that you love..." Her words trailed off and she exhaled a shaky breath. "I'm so grateful we're all alive." She surprised him by belting out a laugh. "I'm suddenly grateful for everything." She gestured around the room. "And not the obvious stuff like hospitals and doctors and antibiotics. But like *everything*— paper cups, liquid soap, dry-roasted peanuts, plastic wrap, tennis shoes and... And this is kind of a weird topic, huh? I think I might be over-sharing."

"No, it's perfectly fine," he said. "I understand."

"Do you?" she asked, her expression turning earnest. She went on before he could answer, "You must. Because I've been thinking about you a lot. I mean…" Another blush, and Jay found himself trying not to laugh and at the same time wanting to reach out and touch her, calm her down, comfort her. That wasn't his job at this point, he reminded himself. Under certain circumstances that might be okay, but something told him he might enjoy being close to her a little too much.

She added, "You and the rest of your crew, I mean. I'm embarrassed to admit this… My own brother is a Navy SEAL and I've never thought of it in this way before. I can't believe you guys do what you do. Risking your lives *all* the time. On purpose. For other people. It's so selfless and generous and brave."

Jay shifted in his seat, uncomfortable with her gratitude, reminding him of why he didn't like to visit survivors. "So others may live," he said.

"What?" Her brow scrunched.

"It's the motto for Coast Guard rescue swimmers—so others may live."

"Oh…right. Well, that's perfect."

He lifted a shoulder. "It's an honor, actually. It's the best feeling in the world to play a part in saving someone's life. Human life is the most precious thing on this planet." *Who was over-sharing now?* he asked himself, startled by his admission. He wasn't normally one to share anything with anyone outside of his family.

She narrowed her eyes thoughtfully. "I think I get that."

"Sure, yeah, saving animals must be re-warding, too." Her lips parted like she was going to comment, but then they stayed that way. Her eyes traveled over his face. He watched, riveted because he could almost feel the intensity radiating from her.

"It is," she finally agreed with a little nod.

He suspected that wasn't what she'd been about to say as her gaze flickered to his and then to her mom and back to him again. "Thank you," she added. "For saving me— us—especially my mom."

"You are welcome." His gaze traveled up to her left temple. He remembered how she'd had a bloody bandage stuck there when he'd pulled her into the helo, how she'd insisted it was nothing, how scared she'd been about her mom. A rush of tenderness coursed through him and he found himself reaching toward it. "How's your noggin?" He traced a thumb around the edge of the dressing. Yep, exactly as he'd expected, he liked the feel of her skin a little too much.

The quick intake of breath and the widening of her eyes confirmed his belief that she was feeling the chemistry between them, too. He reminded himself that on her part, some of that could be gratitude manifesting as attraction toward him. Which also meant he shouldn't be thinking about what a striking shade of blue her eyes were and how sweet she seemed. This woman with her compassion that already had him saying more than he liked to say could only mean trouble for him.

Removing his hand, he attempted to make light of his actions. "Do I need to take a look at it? Do these doctors know what they're doing around here?"

She laughed. "They seem competent."

He grinned. "It's difficult to set the job aside sometimes."

"I understand. I offered to stitch this up myself so the doctor could go help my mom. I, um, sort of demanded it, actually. She was already being treated at the time. It's possible I may have been a little, um, overly dis-traught?"

Aubrey had told him that she'd insisted her mom be taken up into the helicopter first. That was the commotion they'd heard on the radio. It was obvious this woman loved her mother. He wished he could relate. It wasn't that he didn't love his mom, it was just that circumstances didn't allow him to love her in this way.

"What does your mom do?"

"She's a retired teacher. A retired school-teacher, that is. She still teaches, though. These days it's yoga at Vela Studio and nu-tritional workshops at Clean and Green, the health food store here in town?"

"Aubrey told me that she knows your mom from yoga. She's also been to a couple of her health workshops. I think there's one about how bad sugar is for you?"

"Ah." Mia nodded. "The Sweet Life, Short Life classes? All about the dangers of sugar and how to break your addiction."

"That sounds right." He glanced toward the door and lowered his voice. "Aubrey seriously believes sugar is toxic."

"Mom, too. She tells me my addiction is 'out of control.' She's always making these sugar-free creations. The other day it was banana muffins with this natural alternative sweetener. I tried to eat them. I did. But I just…" She shuddered. "Thankfully, my dog, George, will literally eat anything and I was able to slip a couple to him. I had to stop at Bakery-by-the-Sea on my way to work and get a maple bar to get that taste out of my mouth."

He laughed and they discussed the glories of the bakery's treats for a moment.

"I know what you mean about those muffins. Aubrey makes these disgusting…" He watched Mia's lips curl into a smile that seemed to be on the verge of laughter. Then she flickered her eyes up and to the left. "Peanut butter–oatmeal–date blobs that—"

He jumped as Aubrey's voice sounded next to his ear. "They're called energy bites, Jay."

Mia let out a laugh. "I tried to warn you."

"Jeez, Wynn. I swear you're part cat. They give me energy all right—the energy to get as far away from them as possible. Did you deliver Captain Shear his poison?"

Aubrey chuckled. "I did. Along with a gentle lecture about the healthy protein-packed benefits of a Greek yogurt and fruit parfait versus an ice cream sundae."

"Eww," Mia drawled. "That stuff is the texture of wallpaper paste. Sorry, but who suddenly decided gummy, dried-out yogurt was a delicious treat? What's wrong with regular smooth and creamy yogurt?"

Aubrey peered at Mia. "Did he tell you to say that?" She glared at Jay. "Did you tell her to say that?"

Chuckling, he held his hands up, palms out. "No, I swear." He explained to Mia, "Aubrey and I had a conversation about this very topic yesterday morning. I told her that her plain Greek yogurt tastes like glue."

Aubrey shook her head. "You're hopeless. Should I be concerned about the fact that you just admitted you know what glue tastes like?" Turning a sweet smile on Mia, she asked, "How's your mom, Dr. Frasier?"

"Please, call me Mia. And she's doing great. The doctor says she might get to come home in a day or two. Nothing broken. They're still not sure why she was unconscious for so long." She shrugged. "The MRI didn't show any subdural hematoma or significant swelling. But she's had this headache, so I don't know…"

They visited for a while until Aubrey glanced down at her phone. "I have to get going, but I'll stop by to see your mom again. I'm surprised we haven't met before. Do you ever do yoga with your mom?"

"Um, occasionally. I don't share my mom's passion, or ability level, but I know it's good for me so I try."

"I love it," Aubrey said. "Your mom is an awesome teacher. I've been trying for like a year to get Jay to try a class. My boyfriend has been going with me for a while now and he can't believe how much it has enhanced his overall fitness level."

Jay scoffed. Because the idea of Aubrey's boyfriend, big, strong, tough guy Eli Pelletier doing yoga was funny. "Did he say that? 'Enhancing his overall fitness level'? You know I have to give him a hard time now, right? Besides, now that he's going with you, I figured I was off the hook."

"Why would Eli getting into better shape preclude you from wanting to do the same?"

"See what I'm dealing with?" He shot Mia a desperate look. "This woman is relentless."

"Well, she is right about the yoga," Mia said, standing. "It does amazing things for your body."

"Ha." Aubrey slapped him on the shoulder. "See?"

Without thinking it through he said, "Since your mom teaches, maybe I'll have to give it a try."

Mia's eyes sparkled. "She would love that."

Aubrey chimed in, "I'm holding you to that."

"I didn't mean it, Aubrey," he quipped. "It's just a polite thing you say in these kinds of situations."

Mia laughed and the sound seeped into him, further improving his mood. She had the kind of laugh that made you want to laugh, too, even if you didn't know what was funny.

"Thank you guys so much for stopping by. Mom will be thrilled when I tell her you were here."

Aubrey hugged her. Not for the first time, Jay marveled at Aubrey's ability to befriend people and make them feel comfortable.

Jay managed to articulate what he thought was a suitable goodbye, and as they walked down the hall toward the elevators he wondered how big of a fool he would make of himself at yoga class. Would the humiliation be worth seeing Mia Frasier again? There had to be another way… She was a vet. Maybe he could borrow a cat? Or a dog? Aubrey's sister, Nina, had a dog. He could offer to dog-sit and then pretend the animal wasn't feeling well. Pointless fantasies, he reminded himself. Especially where a woman like Mia Frasier was concerned. He'd really enjoy getting to know her, which meant he needed to keep her at arm's length.

Aubrey interrupted his musing. "Are you going to ask her out?"

Jay wasn't surprised by the question. Now that she and Eli were together, Aubrey was on a quest to find him a partner. "I already did. We're going to Lincoln City for the weekend. We're going to practice yoga on the beach and watch the sunset."

She stopped, opened her mouth, snapped it shut, chuckled, smacked him on the shoulder and took off marching again. "Funny."

He kept walking, but let out a laugh of his own as she called him a name under her breath. "Well, seriously, Aubrey. No, I didn't ask her out. Not that it's any of your business."

"You're defensive." With a smug look, she pulled open the door leading to the stairwell. "I know what that means." She motioned him through. "You better be careful."

"Careful?"

"Yes, careful. Because, despite your best efforts, one of these days a woman is going to come along and sweep you off your stubborn bachelor feet. You do know that, right? And it's going to be someone like Mia Frasier—smart, funny, kind, beautiful, compassionate. You know she's a vet, right? I'm talking about an animal doctor here and not a military veteran."

"Yes, I know what she does for a living. What does that have to do with anything?"

Aubrey gave him that look she often did just before she called him dense. "She's one of us, Jay. She's a rescuer, a saver. It's going to be someone like her that manages to get to you. And I, for one, cannot wait to see it happen. I know the reason you don't get involved with women."

He responded with his blankest stare as he wondered what she knew.

"You're scared."

And for a brief moment, he was. He was afraid that she'd somehow found out. Not that he was ashamed of his family necessarily. It was just…a lot to explain. And Jay didn't like to explain. For his entire life, explanations had been met with judgments or pity or advice. This often led to "help" in some well-meaning form, most of which was usually not helpful. At all. A neglectful single mother made for a complicated and difficult childhood for him and his five younger siblings on the best of days. Add in the challenges of her mental illness and, well, it was more than most people could truly comprehend.

She went on, "I get that. I was scared, too. People like us, all type A and independent and stubborn, aren't the best relationship material. Before Eli, I couldn't imagine ever settling down. You don't have me fooled, though. You don't even give women a chance—one or two dates and you're done. Down deep, I think you're lonely. You need someone, and I want that for you."

His answer was a long, slow blink. "That is so sweet," he drawled in a syrupy tone. "So I can be like you and Eli, right? Long walks on the beach, holding hands, late-night talks. And eventually, when the time is right, some nest-building. You know, I want that, too." He placed one hand on his chest. "So much. And I'm truly touched, Aubrey. The fact that you care about me this much—"

She punched him in the shoulder again, hard this time. "Shut up."

"Ouch."

"I'm telling you, I have a feeling about her."

"Mmm-hmm," he answered in his best unconcerned tone that didn't at all match how he felt. Because he had some feelings, too. Aubrey was wrong about him. It wasn't that he didn't want a nest. He did. He just couldn't have one. Not now, and not for a very long time to come. But Aubrey's assessment of Mia

Frasier had only confirmed his own. That's why he could never ask her out.

"Hey, Mom," Mia said a couple days later as she bent and kissed her mom's cheek. Nora was propped up in her hospital bed, her sky-blue eyes twinkling, her short black hair stylishly mussed. Bright pink slippers on feet crossed at the ankles stuck out from the blanket draped across her legs. "You look fantastic."

"Hi, honey. Thank you, I'm feeling it. Those must be my discharge papers. Doc says I get to blow this Popsicle stand today."

"Blow this Popsicle stand?" Even though her mom had kept improving, the doctors had opted to keep her for a couple extra days for observation. They were still unsure about the cause of her prolonged unconsciousness.

"Isn't that right, Ty?" Nora looked over at the bed beside hers. It was occupied by a teenage girl with short, spiked blue hair. A cast stretched from just below her shoulder all the way down her arm and around her hand. The pastel purple cast bore evidence of visitors via an array of scribbled signatures covering its surface.

"That's it, Mrs. K. You're way live now.

And this Instagram pic of your brain scan is lit. I wonder if I can get a copy of my X-ray?"

"Sure you can, this is America. Freedom of information and all that." She looked back at Mia. "Ty's been helping me with my street lingo. We're homes."

"Yeah," she drawled. "I picked up on that. That'll come in handy with your pinochle group in Pacific Cove. But I'm not sure the Freedom of Information Act really applies to medical records."

"Are you even kidding me? That's messed up."

Mia rolled her eyes. Ty giggled.

A smiling young nurse with deep dimples, a long ponytail and colorful butterflies decorating her top came in pushing a wheelchair. Her name tag read Betsy. She stopped between the two beds and swiveled her head from one patient to the other.

"Hey, Bets," Nora asked, "wha's up?"

The nurse gave a breezy wave. "You know— same old, same old."

"I hear that."

Nurse Betsy chuckled. "We sure are going to miss you around here, Nora." To Mia, she said, "It's rare to get patients as entertaining as your mom. And these two together—" she gestured between the roommates "—could take their act on the road." She asked Nora, "You ready to get out of here?"

"You know it."

Betsy helped Nora get settled in the wheelchair while Mia gathered her mom's belongings. When they were ready, Betsy began pushing her toward the door.

"Don't forget to give me your John Hancock on the way out." Ty waved a purple marker. To Mia she said, "That lingo thing is working both ways. I'm going to take some vintage vocab home to my squad."

Betsy situated the chair so Nora could comply. Ty and Betsy both stared transfixed as her mom worked her magic with an assortment of colors. Mia understood their fascination. She had seen her mom draw a million times, yet she never seemed to get enough.

"Get. Out!" the girl exclaimed as she examined Nora's handiwork, a blue-haired girl flying through the air on a skateboard. Her arms were outstretched, an apple in one hand and a book in the other. A slice of the skate park stretched out before her.

Nora pointed to the apple and then the book. "Health and knowledge. Notice how this gal keeps her body leaning forward so she doesn't have an epic wipeout in the bottom of the skate bowl?" Nora winked at her.

"Duly noted." Ty grinned. "You've got mad skills." She looked at Mia. "Your mom is like a real artist."

Mia nodded, pride welling inside her. "I know." She loved seeing her mom using her skills. Since they'd moved to Pacific Cove, she'd been doing so more and more. It filled Nora with joy and Mia knew that her mom could have done extraordinary things with her gift. Her dad, however, had never wanted her to pursue it, believing that art was a "hobby," not a profession. According to Bill Frasier, if it wasn't military, it was neither interesting nor worth pursuing. Mia's love for animals and her choice of veterinary medicine as a career also fell into this category.

Nora squeezed Ty's hand. "Come by the shop to see me when you get sprung. I'll be competing in the Sandcastle Expo next month with my squad, the Sand Bandits. I'm serious about teaching you some sculpting if you're up for it. And you've got my Instagram."

"Sounds perfect. I love you, Mrs. Frasier," Ty said without a trace of the hip that had been previously lacing her tone.

"Love you, too, kiddo."

Yes, Mia thought with satisfaction and a bit of wonder as they made their way through the hospital, *my mom is back. And we're both alive.*

No more wasting time.

She'd already parked her SUV near the curb in the loading area. Mia wasn't surprised to see her mom had plenty of strength after her hospital stint. That, and the fact that her mom didn't weigh much over a hundred pounds, made it an easy job getting her settled in the passenger seat.

"If I never see the inside of that place again it will be too soon."

"I hear that, girlfriend," Mia said.

"That's the spirit," her mom answered with a laugh. "One quick stop on the way home?"

"Definitely," Mia said, figuring she was going to ask for a carton of her favorite organic frozen soy cream "treat" or a take-out garden burger.

"Great. You know how to get to the Coast Guard Air Station, right? I've got some thanking to do."

Mia felt a surge of nervous tension at the thought of seeing Officer Johnston again. She hadn't exactly been in the best state of mind when she'd seen him last, babbling about who-knows-what and gushing with gratitude. Not that he didn't deserve the gratitude part, but she could have done a better job of maintain-

ing her composure. As much as she appreciated his kindness, and the rest of him for that
matter, because they'd had fun and he was
pretty cute, she'd kind of been hoping she'd
never see him again.

CHAPTER THREE

"JAY? HERE YOU ARE."

Jay glanced over his shoulder to see Aubrey walking through the door. He was sitting in a chair in a storage room off the main hangar at the base trying to decide what to do with the fur-covered bundle in his arms. It had finally quit shivering but didn't seem inclined to move from his lap.

"We have visitors and—" She'd been talking as she moved but now stopped in midsentence to gasp. "Is that a dog? It's adorable! Where did it come from?" She continued toward him and the animal cuddled in a fuzzy pink baby blanket on his lap.

"We rescued her early this morning. A sailboat went down trying to cross the bar. Her owner didn't make it. Can't locate any family." As if sensing she was the topic of conversation, the dog lifted her brown-and-white head. Wide brown eyes lit with curiosity as she sniffed Aubrey's fingers.

Aubrey caressed one of her silky ears.

"That is a heartbreaker. And you have her why? Did you call Holly?" Holly ran Paws for a Second Chance, the local no-kill shelter. She was their go-to person in the surprisingly often occurrences when they rescued animals.

"She kind of latched onto me for some reason. Maybe because I took care of her in the helo? I don't know, but yeah, I called Holly. No answer. Left a message." He sighed, feeling the weight of both the man's death and the uncertain fate of the poor dog on his shoulders. "She's going to need a trip to the vet first anyway. I haven't had the heart to move her yet. Poor thing is exhausted and traumatized."

He waited for Aubrey to rib him about calling a vet they knew when a different woman's voice chimed in, "Well, it's your lucky day, isn't it? I literally brought you a vet." A chuckle followed and then, "You must be Petty Officer Johnston? The young man the doctors credit with saving my life."

He looked toward the doorway again, this time to find Nora Frasier standing there smiling. His pulse stuttered when he saw Mia by her side. Nora moved his way.

He returned her smile. "Yes, I am—the first part of that, anyway. Please, call me Jay. I'm glad to see you looking so well." He started to stand, but she waved him off.

"No, no. Sit. You've got some precious cargo there. I'm feeling great, thanks to you." She walked closer and reached out a hand.

He shook her hand and settled back into his seat because she had that kind of bossiness about her. "I don't deserve the credit you're giving me for saving your life, though. That was a team effort."

"I already thanked Aubrey when she came by the hospital for a second visit. I was awake that time. My daughter tells me you stopped by and I slept through it?" At his nod, she went on, "We met the pilot and the copilot out there in the hangar. But they all say they couldn't have done it without you."

Jay grinned. He could see where Mia got her sparkle and vitality. He also remembered that she was a teacher, and he could see that about her as well. "That's the way we work, ma'am. We're a team. I couldn't have done my job without them, either."

"What's wrong with the dog?" Mia asked, stepping around her mom and into his line of sight.

Their eyes met and Jay felt that same pull of attraction, even stronger this time if that was possible. Had she had enough time to get over the gratitude-attraction thing?

"Laceration on her back," he answered.

"Oh, I see it." She knelt beside the chair and crooned, "Hi, pretty lady. Rough day, huh?" She kept talking in the same soothing tone as she caressed the dog behind her ears. The dog let out a whimper, but not like she was in pain. More like she was in heaven.

"I'm gonna give her a second to trust me."

"Yeah," Jay commented drily as the dog licked her chin. "I'm thinking mission accomplished."

Her low chuckle made him smile. Slowly, she worked her hands around to the wound. Jay liked the way she moved, gentle yet confident and practiced. It was cute the way her brow furrowed as she examined the injury. When her hands brushed against his, a current of awareness coursed through him. Funny that he'd had this thought a few days ago, of using a dog to get close to her again. He felt guilty about that now, because this poor pup's life had just been upended in the worst possible way.

"It's not too deep, but she could use a few stitches. You did an excellent job of cleaning it up." Dipping down, she kissed the dog's forehead. "Poor baby. I can only imagine what you've been through. That helicopter ride was probably bad enough, but losing your person is beyond tragic."

She then pinned that warm look of concern on Jay. He felt his insides start to go soft and realized he was no better than the dog. This woman oozed compassion and obviously knew animals.

"Who did you say you were going to leave her with?" she asked.

He cleared his throat. "Holly Camp. She runs Paws for a Second Chance. It's an animal adoption place."

"Yes, I know Holly. She's great." She kept one hand on the dog as she talked. Small hands with slim fingers and trimmed nails, he noticed. Delicate-looking, like the rest of her. But he already knew from the rescue she was anything but. No one who demanded that their fellow airplane-wrecked passengers be rescued first was "delicate." He'd watched her plunge into the ocean after Aubrey without even pausing, seen her concern for her mom and Captain Shear during the helicopter ride. Now that he thought about it, he couldn't imagine that anyone who chose veterinary medicine as a career would be considered delicate.

"Do we know her name?" Mia asked.

"Holly?" he asked, thinking that her eyes were like the blue of the ocean on a calm, sunny day.

"I think she means the dog," Aubrey said with a chuckle. "You need some shut-eye there, big guy?"

He felt his lips twitch with a grin. *No, what I need is for this blue-eyed woman who smells like flowers and makes me forget my own name to back off so I can think.* "Yeah. Maybe. I'm beat," he said. "No, no collar. She was wearing a bandanna. I know it sounds crazy, but I feel like this dog is… It's a miracle she even survived. We spotted the guy because the dog was swimming right next to him, or rather, swimming circles around him. She was in that choppy water for a long time and she's so small, I can't believe she didn't drown."

"Dogs have the most incredible will to live. You know how you hear that dogs are the most loyal creatures on the planet?"

Jay found himself nodding.

"We hear it and say it so much that I think it's become a cliché. But last year I was finishing my residency in Colorado when this border collie was brought in. Half-starved, dehydrated— turns out, her sheepherding owner had suffered an aneurysm and died. From the condition the dog was in, my colleague and I determined that she had been waiting by his side for at least a week. Just sitting there and waiting for help to come along."

He had no idea how to respond to that. He couldn't relate; he'd never had a dog or a pet of any kind. He'd always been too focused on his own survival, and more to the point, his family's survival.

She smoothed a hand over the dog's cheek again, adding, "The dog lived through it. And the sheepherder's daughter adopted her." She added a grin, and Jay could tell the incident would stick with her forever. He knew what *that* felt like. He would never forget a single rescue, but there were certain ones, and sometimes certain people, that just grabbed your heart and never let go. He couldn't help but think that Nora Frasier and her daughter were quickly earning a top spot on that list.

"Tell you what? How 'bout I take the dog to our vet practice and fix her up? She'll need a checkup and a blood panel anyway before Holly can adopt her out. You can pick her up later?"

"Uh, sure, that would be great. Thank you." He noticed she wasn't wearing a ring. Of course, that wasn't a sure sign in this day and age that she was single. Not that it mattered, he told himself; a relationship was not in the cards for him. Not until Josie finished nursing school and the kids were older, much older. Between his financial obligations, his time and the mental energy he expended trying to pseudo-parent from a distance, he simply couldn't do it.

"You can stop by Pacific Cove Vet Clinic any time after about three. I should have her test results by then."

"Oh, I have a meeting this afternoon. I wouldn't be able to get there until this evening."

"How about I bring her home with me after work then? You can pick her up at my house."

"Any time is fine," Nora chimed in. "It's just Mia and me. She usually gets home from work about six or seven, depending on the day."

"That sounds great. In the meantime, maybe we'll be able to get a hold of some family."

AT THE END of his shift, Jay stowed his gear, feeling the stress of the last twenty-four-hour shift working its way into him. It was always like this for him. He didn't let himself feel tired until he had the time to be tired. That's when the exhaustion slammed into him like a tidal wave.

"Hey, Johnston, congratulations! I hear you got yourself a new puppy."

Removing his backpack from his locker, he shut the door and turned to find a smiling Lieutenant Commander Eli Pelletier standing behind him. Eli was a pilot and Aubrey's fiancé. He'd also become a friend in the months since he'd been stationed here, as much of a friend as Jay allowed himself to have, anyway.

"Funny, Pelletier." Jay took a moment to look him up and down before saying, "Wow, you look like you've reached a whole new level of fitness these days. Almost like you've been doing yoga."

"That obvious, huh?" Eli chuckled. "Aubrey's been talking, I see. Seriously, though, how's the dog doing? Are you going to keep it?"

They'd had no luck tracking down any of the dog owner's family. Holly had returned his call only to tell him that there was no room at the shelter right now, especially for an injured dog. Could Jay keep the dog or find someone who could until space was available? He wasn't sure what he was going to do. "I want a dog about as badly as I do a root canal."

"Uh, I don't think veterinarians do root canals. At least not on people."

Aubrey walked up to join her fiancé. "Besides, it would be much less painful to just ask her to dinner."

Jay rolled his eyes. "Has anyone ever told you how pushy and annoying you can be?"

Eli laughed and raised his hand. "I do. I tell her."

"Yes, of course. He does. As do my sisters. All the time. And I'm sorry," she said, tipping her head one way and then the other. "Sort of. 'Cause isn't this kinda like a sign? Holly not having room right now? You should seriously consider keeping that sweet dog. I think it would be good for you to have someone to think about, something to take care of, someone…"

Jay grinned. "Other than myself, you mean?" Not even Aubrey knew that his reputation for being carefree and perpetually unattached was contrived. His life was anything but carefree, and his responsibilities were daunting, to say the least.

She pushed one shoulder up into a shrug. "I'm just saying."

He fished his phone out of his backpack and, speaking of responsibility, saw that he'd received a text from Levi. He'd read it after he got out of here. Stuffing the phone into his pocket, he asked, "What do you suggest I do with the dog when I'm on duty?"

"There are dog-walking services you could hire that help with that. Or doggy day care.

Sheila Roarke has one. She calls it a doggy spa. It's nicer than my house."

"I really don't have time for a dog." Either option would be an expense he could in no way afford. Not to mention the food, supplies, vet care and medicine. All funds that could go toward items the kids needed. Although the thought of those pet-related things filled him with a nice combination of anticipation and anxiety. He was looking forward to seeing Mia again, even if looking and talking was as far as it could go. "Besides, I'm sure this guy's family is going to want his dog."

"Davis said he doesn't have any family. He tracked down someone at the marina who kind of knew him. Said the guy was a loner."

"Even loners have family." *Look at me for example*, he thought. To change the subject, he asked Aubrey, "Do you have the paperwork for the meeting?"

"Yep." She held up a clipboard. Nothing like a clipboard and a meeting about volunteer work to steer Aubrey in a new direction. The woman was all about the organizing, not to mention her passion for community service.

They headed to the parking lot and climbed into their cars. The meeting was across the Columbia River in Washington, at the Coast Guard boat station, Cape Disappointment.

The trip would take about a half hour, so he removed his phone and read the text from Levi: Mom is gone again. Josie told me to tell you. She needs to talk to you. She wants to know if you have time tomorrow?

A mix of irritation and concern settled over him. As if he needed another reminder as to why he couldn't let himself get attached to a dog, much less its pretty doctor.

He tapped out a response: Hang in there, buddy. Tell her yes. I'm off duty tomorrow.

JAY WASN'T SURPRISED, but he was incredibly pleased that so many of their colleagues, including a huge number of Cape Disappointment personnel, had shown up for this Coast Guard community outreach meeting. Most people who signed up for military service were all about helping others. Their goal was to make it a little easier for them. He kept his remarks brief, letting the list of charities that he, Aubrey and two of their colleagues had compiled speak for him.

"As the incident earlier this spring illuminated, we all know it's important to show the community that the Coast Guard cares, that we're invested here in these little towns. I know a lot of you already volunteer at your church or your kids' schools or with their sports teams. Some of you are involved in Aubrey's swim lesson program and others at the hospital in Astoria and so on. So don't feel obligated, and please don't overextend your personal resources. This outreach is all about bringing willing volunteers to programs that need them. But not at the expense of your own family's needs." He went on for a few more minutes.

Jay's motivation in cochairing this initiative was twofold. There'd been an incident earlier in the spring involving two boaters. After an altercation between them, the Coast Guard intervened. One man had been ticketed for excessive speed and boating under the influence. He'd raised a fuss with the local media and in the process, he'd attempted to make the Coast Guard look like high-handed bullies. The Coast Guard personnel involved had been vindicated, but the unfortunate episode had left people talking. This had prompted command to amp up their efforts at spreading goodwill throughout the community.

In his youth, Jay and his siblings had often been recipients of these types of charities. He was passionate and resolute about giving back. And because he knew it wasn't easy to ask for help, Jay had discussed it with his superior and suggested this hands-on approach.

He and his colleagues had gone out into the community, seeking and identifying the organizations that needed assistance and in what form.

The resulting list they'd compiled was long and included a wide variety of options: a group that built homes for the needy, the food bank, a women's shelter, two homeless shelters, the library literacy program, hospice care and delivering food to the homebound were among the many organizations seeking volunteers. Their only requirements were that the need be local and the recipients be in "true" need.

"Any questions?"

A hand went up in the crowd. "Um, I see there's a short description here, but I'm not sure what some of these places do exactly...?"

Jay had anticipated this question. "Next to every organization, there should be the name of whoever signed it up. See my name by the food bank? I can tell you all about it—who's in charge, where the food goes, what specific needs they have. Any questions, just ask whoever has their name next to it."

Another hand raised. "Does it matter what we sign up for? Is there like a scale based on need? Are there some organizations that need help more than others?"

He and Aubrey had discussed this and decided it was too subjective to rate them based on need. "Nope. Between Aubrey, Vance Davis, Terrence Oliver and me, we've vetted all these places. If they're on the list, they need help. Please feel free to pick anything that interests you."

Jay felt a welling of pride as he watched his colleagues eagerly signing up for the available spots. He mingled and answered questions, and nearly an hour after the meeting started, people began to filter out.

"I think all of the places now have at least one Coast Guard volunteer," Aubrey happily reported when everyone had departed. She frowned. "Except one."

"Sign me up for that one. I was going to take whatever was left or whatever needed more bodies anyway."

"Really? Are you sure?"

"Yeah, really. I don't care what it is. I'll do it."

"Jay, you are awesome. Have I told you that lately?" Her smile was blinding. At that point, he should have known something was up. She bent over the clipboard again as she filled in a blank spot on the chart. "Perfect. I'll get these names sent to our various organizations and we'll get our volunteers set up."

CHAPTER FOUR

MIA DROVE HOME, where Nora's friend Annie met them. She'd offered to come over and sit with Nora so Mia could go to the clinic. Mia made sure her mom was comfortable, loaded her dog George into the car along with the rescue dog, and headed to work. After arriving at the clinic, she stitched the dog's wound and gave her a thorough exam. She took a blood sample and sent it to the lab with a rush order. Finally, she got the two dogs settled in her private office and headed out to treat patients and handle the backlog waiting for her.

Two days of being out of the office had left Mia with a ton of work to catch up on. Luckily, Dr. Anthony had been available to cover for her. He'd managed to squeeze in the critical patients, but her noncritical cases and some surgeries had been rescheduled. She treated a dog with a yeast infection in his ears, a cat she'd tragically diagnosed with a bleeding tumor, and an adorable boxer puppy who'd torn off his dewclaw. She admitted a lethargic turtle while waiting on some tests, vaccinated a batch of kittens, and stitched up a laceration on a golden retriever who'd been attacked by a neighbor's dog. At the owner's request, she'd forwarded that medical report to the police.

A few hours later, she headed back to her office to check on the dog. Tail wagging, George stepped off the huge dog bed that took up one corner of her office, made a show of stretching his gigantic frame, and then trotted over to greet her. The sight of her giant mastiff-bloodhound mix never failed to make her heart swell with love. Currently ninety-two pounds of clumsy sweetness covered in brindle fur, Mia estimated he had another ten pounds to gain before he would be at his prime weight.

Her boy had suffered too much in his young life. He'd come with her from Colorado, where his rescuer had found him tied to a post in the middle of a muddy yard and brought him to the clinic where she'd been working as a resident. The collar around his neck was so tight it was cutting into the skin around it. He had no shelter. A bowl of food sat beside him but he couldn't eat it because his mouth had been duct-taped shut. Normally able to keep it together even in the worst of cases, Mia lost it with George, allowing her tears to fall as she removed first the collar and then those layers of tape from his muzzle. The dog had whined in pain but never snapped. When she finished, he'd licked her hands and her cheek, and stolen her heart. They'd been together ever since.

Mia sat. George followed suit, placing his head on her lap and slobbering on her pants.

Scratching behind his ears and caressing the scarred skin of his neck, she said, "I love you, Georgie. You're the best dog ever. How was your nap?"

He yawned and smacked his jaws.

"That's great news, buddy. Sleep is important. Scientists are telling us it's almost as important as nutrition when it comes to health and longevity. You can thank Grandma Nora for that bit of helpful trivia. Speaking of nutrition." She removed two "cookies" from the canister on her desk and handed one over. He flopped beside her on the floor and began chomping. The rescued dog, who had been napping on the sofa, was now watching Mia with alert brown eyes. Mia wheeled her chair closer and offered her a cookie. Not interested. Mia's stomach did a nervous twist. The dog had been uninterested in pretty much everything since Mia had taken her out of Jay's arms. She was worried, although her initial exam had revealed her to be in good health.

She opened her email to see if the dog's blood test results had come back. She scrolled down the list until she located the one from the lab. Clicking on it, she felt a niggle of apprehension as she analyzed the numbers. Turning again, she smiled at the dog, who, as if sensing the gravity of the situation, lifted her head and let out a whine. Mia stood, walked over and scooped her up.

"Congratulations, cutie, you are as healthy as can be. Mr. Rennick might have been a loner, but clearly, he loved his girl, huh?" The dog answered by nudging Mia's chin with her muzzle. "Now we just need to find you a new home. What are the chances that handsome Coast Guard flight mechanic will take you in? He definitely likes you. I think you'd be great together."

She looked up as a knock sounded on her door, followed by a "Hey, Mia? You got a second?"

"Sure, Ted. Come in."

Her partner, mentor, friend and fellow veterinarian, Dr. Ted Anthony, walked into her office. Medium height and lean-muscled, Dr. Anthony was in his fifties but looked at least a decade younger. His head of wavy brown hair didn't have a speck of gray, and Mia thought that helped his ageless cause as well. George met him with a lazy woof and a wet sniff of his kneecap, his signature greeting.

Ted chuckled and patted the dog's head. Nodding toward the bundle in her lap, he asked, "How's our Coast Guard heroine doing?"

"Good. Wound is stitched, tests are clear, she's good to go. She's awfully droopy, though. I'm a little concerned."

"That was quite an ordeal she went through. Probably still a bit traumatized."

"Yeah, could be." She carried the dog back over to the sofa, where she immediately settled in for a nap.

As she crossed the room, Mia noticed the fine lines around Ted's reddish eyes. He looked tired, she thought, and immediately felt silly for thinking that. Of course he was tired; his daughter was fighting a serious, incurable disease where the only treatment currently available was one to alleviate her symptoms. He and his wife were driving back and forth to Portland for doctor appointments and therapy at regular intervals. They were all handling it better than Mia could ever imagine. Mia knew he and Sara would fight till the end, and Mia had vowed to do everything she could to help, including keeping the clinic running smoothly during his absences.

"Speaking of trauma, how are you doing, Mia? Have you recovered from the accident?"

"Yes, I'm fine, Ted. Thank you. Mom is good. Ready to get back to work."

"Excellent." He sighed. "Mia, I don't know what I would have done if you hadn't agreed to join me here. I certainly wouldn't have been able to keep this clinic open without you."

Ted had invited Mia to join his practice with the agreement that he'd be gone for long stretches of indeterminate time periods. It was a part of the buy-in agreement, but she'd signed it happily. Ted was more than her mentor and friend; he was also her role model, a father figure. And definitely more like a father than her own had been.

Waving a dismissive hand through the air, she said, "I think it's working out for both of us." She made a constant conscious effort not to make him feel like he needed to continually thank her. Staying positive, she believed, was also key.

He nodded, absently massaging George's neck. George could be shameless in his attempt to get a neck rub, lying his head in the lap of anyone he deemed trustworthy. Mia imagined him reveling in the feeling of being free of a collar so tight he would likely always bear the scars.

"As you know, McKenzie was approved for that experimental round of therapy we were hoping for."

"Yes, Sara told me. It's so exciting." She added a warm smile. "She mentioned she starts next week? That's sooner than you anticipated, right?"

"It is. We're really hoping it will buy her time until the new drug is approved by the FDA."

"That would be beyond amazing." Mia didn't voice her concern regarding that particular medication. He was placing so much hope on a drug that, as far as she could discern, was still too far from human clinical trials to be a viable cure. She was fairly sure it hadn't even been approved for testing on animals yet. But she would never dampen whatever hope he could generate at this point.

"I've cut back on my patient load accordingly. I'll be back and forth, but here at the clinic as much as I can. Any concerns about working on your own? Is there anything you need from me?"

"Thanks, Ted. I think I've got this. We've had a lot of applicants for the new kennel assistant position and we'll be doing interviews as soon as Charlotte can sort through them."

"I trust you ladies to hire whoever you decide on. I don't need to do an interview or a final approval or anything."

She appreciated that he had this much faith in her and Charlotte. Ted was a perfectionist and could be a bit of a control freak. She'd worried about his ability to share administrative tasks, but so far that hadn't been an issue.

"We'll get on it then. Also, I'm reserving Saturdays for Lucky Cats. Tiffany, Carla and Raeanne have all volunteered to rotate their Saturdays to help with medical procedures."

Upon relocating to Pacific Cove, Mia had started Lucky Cats, a program to reduce the stray and feral cat problem in the town and surrounding area. Part of the "trap, neuter, return" program included free sterilization. People were encouraged to trap the cats and bring them to the office, where she would spay or neuter and vaccinate them for free. They could then keep the cats or release them back outside along with a promise to feed them. This last gesture was an effort to keep the cats healthy; reduce their predation of native bird populations, a serious and ever-growing problem in this country; as well as to decrease their presence as a nuisance to gardens and garbage cans. Alternatively, they could have Lucky Cats adopt the animals out.

"It's a wonderful thing you're doing, Mia. I only wish I could help more."

"Allowing me use of the clinic is more than enough, Ted. You need to spend your spare time at home. Sara and McKenzie are more important right now, and I'm getting some volunteers lined up." She didn't mention that so far said volunteers included her, Charlotte and Minnie Mason. Minnie was a woman from her mom's pinochle club who was more concerned with the stray cats "wreaking havoc" in her garden than their safety in the community at large. Charlotte was working on community outreach and hopefully, they'd get those numbers up soon. No matter the disappointingly small number of volunteers, Mia was determined to get the operation up and running.

"Speaking of stray cats," Ted said with a grin.

Ember the office cat strolled into the room, announcing her presence with a loud meow. Leaping gracefully onto Mia's desk, she then sauntered back and forth along the edge as if to show off her kitty sleekness from every angle. It didn't seem to faze the cat that she was partially bald, had only one eye and was missing most of her tail.

"She gives new meaning to the term cat-walk, doesn't she?" Mia quipped.

Dr. Anthony chuckled as the cat perched on the corner of the desk closest to him. She let out a soft mewl. He reached out a hand to scratch her cheek. "She's out of control. She thinks she owns this office."

George waited patiently, watching Ember with love-struck eyes. Dog and cat were tight. Mia liked to imagine them bonding over their abusive pasts as they napped together on George's massive therapeutic bed. George lifted his head and Ember stepped onto Ted's lap. She rubbed her cheek against George's giant forehead before daintily licking his eyebrow.

Everyone knew the story of how the cat had changed Dr. Anthony's life. He'd only been in town a few weeks when the severely burned kitten had been dropped off on the newly opened clinic's doorstep. She'd been "nothing but a charred little ember," Ted had later been quoted in the newspaper as saying. He and his staff had done everything they could. Dr. Anthony had stayed with her for four days and nights until she was out of the woods. Word had raced through tiny Pacific Cove about what the new vet in town would do for animals. That had been nearly two years ago.

Needless to say, his practice had been flourishing ever since. People brought their pets to Dr. Anthony from miles around.

"She's earned it. Cats are such wonderful, giving, useful creatures."

Ember concurred with a loud purr.

Mia smiled. "Yes, they sure are." Ted had an interesting way of looking at life. She'd learned more from him about life than she ever had from her father. She'd certainly learned more about love and how to treat people as well as animals.

Keeping the cat nestled in his arms, he stood and said, "I'm going to go finish up some paperwork, then I'm heading home. I'll see you tomorrow."

As he departed, a buzzing sound from her phone alerted her that she'd received a text from her mom:

Our new Coast Guard friend has arrived. I'll keep him entertained until you get here.

Mia checked the time. How had it gotten to be six thirty already? She sent back a text: Sounds good. Thanks, Mom.

Because her Coast Guard charge was unfamiliar with the office, Mia clipped a leash to her new hot-pink collar and led both dogs out into the hall. Charlotte, their office manager and the best friend Mia had ever had, was busy closing things up for the night.

"Thank you again for getting this girl all set up." Charlotte had walked down to Sandy Paws Pet Shop on her lunch break and picked up some supplies for the dog.

"You are very welcome," Charlotte answered with a grin. "Did you look at her tag?"

Mia hadn't noticed the tag attached to the collar, twisted as it was into the fluffy fur of the dog's neck. She crouched to examine it and read the name aloud. "Coastie?"

The dog let out a little bark and Charlotte added a surprised chuckle. "See? She likes it. In honor of the Coast Guard hottie who saved her. What do you think?" Charlotte had something of an obsession with the military, especially the men who served.

"How do you even know he's hot?"

"Isn't he?"

"Well, there's a lot more to a person than how they look and—"

"Come on, Mia," she interrupted. "He saved you, he saved the dog, he's in the Coast Guard."

Mia shook her head. "That doesn't even make sense."

"I'm right, though, aren't I?"

"I don't…" Mia tilted her head, trying to decide how to answer without answering.

"I knew it!" Charlotte gave George a quick neck rub and then moved on to Coastie. "Good night, Coastie. Be sure and cuddle all up next to your Coast Guard hottie, okay?" Catching Mia's gaze, she gave her a wink. "That last bit of advice goes for you, too."

"Unfortunately, that's not on the table. Unlike you, I am not enamored with all things Coast Guard." Just the opposite, in fact, she added silently.

"And one of these days you're going to tell me why that is. Let me take this stuff out to the car for you."

Mia couldn't help but laugh as they headed for the door, dogs and all. If she were being completely honest, the cuddling part sounded nice. Too bad he was the wrong cuddle partner. In spite of Petty Officer Jay Johnston's hotness and other attractive attributes, he was military. And that simple yet extraordinarily complicated fact made cuddling with him, or anything else for that matter, off-limits for her.

ROUGHLY FIFTEEN MINUTES LATER, Mia and her canine companions headed up the steps leading to the beachfront home she'd recently purchased and shared with her mom. The house was way too large for her, but since she knew she was in Pacific Cove to stay, she'd gone ahead and opted for her dream home. Ever since she was young, she'd fantasized about living in a house where she'd never have to move again—a home she could fill with special moments and memories, a place to grow old in. As soon as she'd seen the three-thousand-square-foot beachfront bungalow she knew she'd found that place.

Gambling on her future income from the vet practice, she'd only been able to purchase it by borrowing a portion of the down payment from her mom. In exchange, her mom lived with her rent-free. For now, she planned to fill the space with pets, a cat and a dog so far, but it would be the perfect place to raise a family someday.

As she opened the back door and entered the kitchen, she could hear her mom and Jay chatting in the adjoining living room. It was her favorite room in the house. Looking out the windows all you could see was sand and ocean. To Mia, it almost felt like the house was floating. She headed toward the sound with the dogs close behind. Suddenly, Coastie let out a bark and darted around her in a full-on sprint toward the sofa. The dog launched herself into Jay's arms in a pile of joyous whines and tail-wagging. George followed at a trot, looking around as if trying to identify the source of the all-you-can-eat bacon bar, because nothing short of that would incite such a level of excitement in him.

"Wow," Mia said, gaping at scene. "That's unbelievable. This dog has been downright depressed since I took her with me this morning. I thought she might be suffering from PTSD. I'm not exaggerating when I say that she's barely lifted her head off the sofa in my office all day. She wouldn't even eat a cookie."

At the word *cookie* George sniffed the air, looking for a treat.

Nora beamed at Jay. "I know how she feels. She knows you rescued her and she's not going to forget it." She added a wink while Ruby the cat let out a meow from where she was watching the silly dog display from her perch on Nora's lap. Giving her paw a lick of disgust, she then tucked it beneath her.

"I don't know about that." Jay chuckled while Coastie nibbled enthusiastically on his head. "I think she might be smelling the cheeseburger I had on the way here."

Fine. Charlotte was right; the guy was hot. Not that she'd done much to dispute that point when Charlotte had mentioned it.

Coastie continued her frenzied welcome

while he bargained with her. "If you settle down a little bit I will rub your beautiful soft cheeks. Look at your fancy new collar," he gushed. "Pink is your color, sweetheart." Sweetheart? No wonder the dog was a goner. To heck with Charlotte's assessment of him being hot. He was nice. She added brave, funny and nice to the list. Had she ever dated anyone who possessed all of these qualities in such an attractive package? Ignoring the tingle of disappointment, she reminded herself that dating him was not an option.

Examining the tag, he repeated the name with a chuckle. "Coastie?"

"Charlotte, our office manager, went out and got her some supplies today—a leash, toys, bowls, dog food and a collar with that tag. She named her Coastie in your honor. I hope you don't mind?"

His lips curled up at the corners as he shrugged. "That sounds fine for now. I'm sure whoever adopts her will want to choose their own name anyway, right? How long until this heals and she can get a new home?"

"The wound looks really good. It was a little deeper than I thought, but we'll take those stitches out in a week or two and she'll be good as new. She'll need to be brought into the office for that. So it might be a good idea to wait at least that long before putting her up for adoption."

Nora chimed in, "My daughter knows her stuff, Jay. Like I was telling you earlier, she graduated at the top of her class from vet school. You know she did that program where you get your associate degree before you're even out of high school? She had a bachelor's degree in biology and a master's in animal science by the time she was twenty-one. She's won so many awards. The—"

"Mom," Mia interrupted with an awkward laugh. "I'm sure Jay's not interested in my educational background. I think all he needs to know is that I'm a qualified vet. Right, Jay?"

All these years later and her mom still didn't see that her daughter's burying herself in her studies had been her way of coping with her nomadic existence, her innate shyness, and her dad's blatant lack of attention to her. Three years of therapy had helped her nail down and deal with her issues, or at least understand them. As she'd aged, she'd shifted that focus and determination to helping animals. That felt healthy and productive, even if it did feed into her desire for "positive affirmation" as her therapist called it.

Unfortunately, Jay was looking eagerly toward her mom. She did not trust the expression of exaggerated interest on his face as he glanced at her and then back to Nora.

"Dr. Anthony was one of her professors. He recruited *her* to join his practice. Out of all the students he's had throughout the years, he picked Mia. Don't worry, Coastie will be fit as a fiddle when she gets through with her."

"I don't doubt it," Jay said.

The teakettle began to whistle in the background. Nora shot to her feet. "Who wants a cup of tea?" Without waiting for answers, she hustled toward the kitchen. Mia grinned weakly as her gaze met Jay's. Twirling a finger after her mom, she asked, "Has she been…?"

"Talking about you the whole time?" Jay offered. "Yes. She mentioned that she has a collection of your trophies. Any chance we could take a peek at those later?"

Mia groaned softly and gripped the bridge of her nose. "Sorry about that. She's…"

"She's really proud of you. It sounds like she has good reason to be."

"Um, thanks, but—" Mia didn't say that her mother was clearly trying to sell her attributes to someone she'd identified as a potential suitor.

"I didn't even make it into the spelling bee

when I was in grade school. And there you were, a three-time champ."

She pressed a finger onto her eyebrow in an effort to stop the throbbing behind her eye. "Mortified, M-O-R-T-I-F-I-E-D, mortified. Yep, that's me."

He laughed again as Nora sailed back into the room with a tray containing three steaming mugs and a plate heaped with cookies. She set it down on the table in front of them. "You're in luck. I made some cookies today. Coconut oil instead of butter. Sweetened with agave nectar and stevia. Wait till you try them. Not a drop of sugar and you'd never know."

Terror flickered briefly across Jay's face before morphing into what Mia might describe as pained enthusiasm. "Sounds great, Nora. Thank you."

Mia brushed a hand over her face to hide a snicker.

"Oops, forgot the soy milk." Nora dashed away again.

"Don't worry," Mia whispered as her mom disappeared into the kitchen for her "creamer."

"George is always hungry." She patted the dog who, at again hearing the word *cookie*, had pushed himself up into a sitting position from where he'd been lying on Mia's feet. She took two from the tray, handed them to the dog, broke another in half and spread a few crumbs around so it would look like they'd been enjoying the treats.

"What kind of dog do you think she is?" He rubbed his chin on the top of Coastie's head, which Mia found incredibly endearing. She couldn't help but wonder why he didn't just keep the dog.

"She looks Australian shepherd, but her silky coat and coloring says Brittany or springer spaniel. There might be some border collie in there, too."

He nodded, studying the fur-ball now sprawled contentedly across his lap. Mia noticed that Coastie's cinnamon-brown spots closely matched the shade of his hair. They looked good together.

"It's so great of you to take care of her. I wish…" He trailed off as Ruby came closer to investigate the new canine invading her couch space. They both watched as she stuck her neck out and executed a pretentious sniff. Coastie didn't seem the least bit perturbed by the intrusion.

"What do you wish?" Mia asked. She found herself holding a breath.

"She was healthy," he finally said. "I wish she was healthy so we could find her a new home. I hate to drag this out."

"You could keep her—you know? If no family is found."

Mia watched his entire body stiffen with discomfort.

"Oh… No, I can't. I'm really not a dog person."

From her spot on his lap, Coastie looked up and gave his chin a lick.

"Really?" she answered doubtfully.

He winced. "I know, I'm not sure what the deal is with this dog in particular. But I can't keep her. I don't do pets."

"Huh." Mia felt her smile dim. Disappointment settled into her as she realized how much she'd been hoping he'd decide to keep the dog. It was probably better this way, she told herself. Regardless of her own rule, she was already liking the guy; if she had to add animal lover to the list it would only make him that much more difficult to resist. "Must love animals" was another deal-breaker. Jay Johnston was now in violation of her top two dating criteria.

"Hey, guess what, Mia?" Nora said, coming back into the room. "Jay has offered to take a look at our sticky back door."

Living on the beach meant constantly battling issues that could arise from the humidity. The previous homeowner had installed a custom-made back door constructed from wood. It was incredibly lovely, but unfortunately, when wood absorbs moisture it swells, which was the case with the door.

"Oh, that's really nice, but you don't have to do that."

"I don't mind. I like to fix things."

"Is that a skill you learned from your father?" Nora asked as she settled back down on the sofa. Mia gave her head a little shake at her mom's obvious attempt to vet their guest.

"No," Jay answered. "Self-taught for the most part. I worked for a carpenter for a while when I was younger. He taught me the basics. I learned on my own from there." Mia silently added "good sport" to the list as she watched him swallow a large bite of cookie-blob.

"Do your parents live here in the Northwest?"

"My mother lives in Portland."

"Oh, that's not far. You two must be close. Probably requested Air Station Astoria to be near her?"

"Uh… Not exactly. But I did request Astoria to be closer to…other family."

Other family? Mia's curiosity was piqued. What did that mean?

"Are you married?" her mom asked, taking care of the question at the top of Mia's list.

"No. These are really good, Nora," he lied, shoving another cookie into his mouth.

Not married, but obviously uncomfortable talking about himself. Mia hoped her mom wouldn't go too far. And yet she found herself irrationally disappointed when Nora changed the subject.

"Mia may have mentioned it but my husband was military, too. Navy," she said proudly. "Thirty-two years. I'm sure he still would be if he hadn't up and died on me. We saw some amazing places, didn't we, Mia?"

Mia answered with a flat, "Yep." Because they had seen plenty of the world, but as far as Mia was concerned it had not been worth it.

"I'm so sorry, Mrs. Frasier. Did he die in combat?"

"What happened to calling me Nora? And no, he didn't. Heart attack. I miss him every day, but I'm determined not to go out that way." She gestured at the cookies. Jay dutifully took another bite.

Nora went on, "My son, Mia's brother, is in the Navy, too. Kyle is a SEAL. He's overseas right now…"

Mia listened silently, painful memories battering away at her, as they began chatting about the military. This was good, she told herself. It reminded her of all the things she'd disliked about military life while growing up: moving almost constantly, having to make new friends, attending new schools, learning new languages, a dad who was more devoted to his job than his family. She'd never understood her mom's enthusiasm or Kyle's infatuation. Mia didn't share their devotion. But then, she'd essentially been invisible to her father. As a child, there'd been times Mia was convinced she'd been adopted or dropped here from another planet. In middle school, she'd gone through a phase of Googling terms like "switched at birth" and "mistaken babies" trying to calculate the odds. She wasn't about to go down that road again as a grown woman. Her path was now hers to choose.

"I think I better head home," Jay said a while later. "I'm beat." He stood, Coastie still snuggled in his arms. He thanked her mom for the tea and cookies, promised to check out the door as soon as he could, and vaguely added that he'd look into that yoga class.

Mia said, "I'll walk you out."

He followed her to the entryway and stopped. Glancing around, he shifted his weight from one foot to the other. Finally, he held Coastie out for Mia to take. "Can you hold her for a minute while I get her stuff? I don't want to trip over her while I pack all this stuff up and put it in the car." He pointed at the round fleece snuggle bed Charlotte had purchased. "Is this dog bed for her, too?" At her confirmation, he let out a chuckle. "It's going to take up half my living room."

Mia took the dog, who let out a whine as she stared longingly at Jay.

Mia laughed. "Tell you what, I'll carry her stuff. You carry the dog."

"Maybe you're right." Jay chuckled as he gently removed the dog from her arms. "What am I going to do with you?" he asked as he looked down at Coastie. She gave his cheek an enthusiastic dog kiss.

In spite of his comments, the gentle way he treated the dog spoke volumes. She wouldn't let him out of here with Coastie if she didn't think he'd treat her well. A thought occurred to her then. "Never had a dog before, I'm guessing?"

"Nope."

"Don't worry. I'm here for you. Anything you need." She kissed one of Coastie's velvety soft doggy cheeks. "Both of you."

CHAPTER FIVE

JAY DROVE HOME, Coastie happily riding shotgun beside him, wondering how in the world he'd managed to get himself so…involved. He barely knew these people yet he'd offered to fix their sticky door, agreed to consider trying a yoga class (*thanks again, Aubrey*) choked down three cookies he was pretty sure were made out of sawdust and fostered a dog. *What next?* he wondered.

He pulled into his driveway and realized that if he walked down to the beach from his cabin, hung a right, and stuck to the shoreline, it would be less than a mile to Mia's house. Geography might mean they were close, but he and Dr. Mia Frasier were otherwise worlds apart. He thought about her gorgeous home as he studied his weathered gray rental cabin, a fraction of the size with two small bedrooms, one and a half bathrooms, and an open kitchen-dining-living area. It did have a cool loft with giant windows looking out onto the beach. Well, it would be cool as soon as he repaired the narrow, deteriorated stairs leading up to it, his current project.

Even with his Coast Guard housing stipend, the only way he'd been able to afford a place on the beach at all was because it was a rat hole. The elderly man who owned it, Mr. Faraday, didn't want to expend the funds or the energy to make it habitable. In exchange for a huge break in rent, Jay had agreed to fix the place up. So far, he'd caulked and weatherproofed the exterior, replaced the roof shingles, installed some new wiring and light fixtures, repaired the dry rot in the floor, and evacuated the rats. Most of the rats; he was pretty sure they were all gone, although a couple days ago he'd heard a suspicious clawing sound coming from beneath the floor in the bathroom. The plumbing still needed some work, but overall he was satisfied with the progress he'd made. He felt confident by the time his assignment at Air Station Astoria was up, Mr. Faraday would be happy with what he'd accomplished, too.

Beside him Coastie stirred, seeming to sense they'd reached their destination. That's when Jay saw the curtain move. He'd been so distracted he hadn't noticed that the lights were on inside the cabin. Lights were expensive, and he never left them on when he wasn't home.

He looked at Coastie. "Will you be okay if I leave you here for a minute while I check this out?"

Her response was a soft sigh as she curled into a ball on the seat.

Jay patted her, got out of the car, and headed around the back of the house. He considered calling the police but held back, because what burglar would be stupid enough to turn the lights on? Reaching the back door, the top half of which was glass and currently had no curtain, he peered inside. Not a thief. Raking a hand through his hair, he let out a sigh of equal parts relief, frustration and happiness. Nope, this was much more complicated than a simple burglary. He headed back to his car.

He opened the door and gave Coastie a scratch under her chin. "Okay, girl, we're home. Do you want to check out your temporary digs? I hope you like it. The inside isn't much, but I think you'll find the beachfront setting more than makes up for it."

Coastie jumped out and trotted in a large circle, getting a feel for her new "yard," which was essentially sand with a few patches of reedy scrub grass here and there with an occasional rock poking through. Jay gathered his pack and the large shopping bag containing the dog's necessities. After she'd sniffed around and done her duty, she trotted over to him and stared up like "what's next?"

"Ready to go inside and meet my family?"

She let out a yap and then raced toward the front door. Jay shook his head and followed. He supposed he was lucky in a sense, because if he was going to accidentally foster a dog, at least he'd gotten a smart one.

With Coastie trotting beside him, they headed inside, where Jay was enveloped by the heavenly aroma of garlic, onions and spices that made up the unmistakable scent of Gran's Bolognese sauce. The smell made his heart ache with love and longing for his deceased grandmother even as it made his stomach yearn for pasta. He dropped his bags. He'd seen his little brother Levi through the window, but he hadn't been expecting Josie. She was the only person in his life, outside of Gran, who could make this sauce.

Josie's presence meant he wasn't surprised to see his little sister Laney, too, who was now throwing herself into his arms.

"Jay, hi! I've missed you so much."

"Hey there, little one. I miss you, too. So much." He hugged her close, a mix of love and affection tightening his chest. "Not so little, though, huh? You've grown since I saw you last."

"You think?" Stepping away, she beamed at him. His fifteen-year-old sister had dreams of hitting the six-foot mark, a goal she felt she needed to attain in order to get to college on a volleyball scholarship. As it was, she was only a couple inches shy.

Levi was next. "Hey, buddy," he said, pulling him in for a hug. At sixteen, Levi had recently hit the six-foot mark and Jay suspected he would eventually surpass his own six foot four inches.

And finally, his sister Josie. "Hi." She smiled and wrapped her arms around him. Jay felt his heart squeeze with a special kind of love, a love he knew that only a brother and sister who'd been through a hell like theirs could know. Aside from the surprise, and the speculation as to the reason for this unannounced visit, he was filled with utter joy to see his siblings.

A notion occurred to him then. "Where's your car?" He'd bought Josie a used van a few years ago, but it wasn't parked out front.

"Craig brought us. He's visiting his aunt in Remington." Craig was Josie's boyfriend of nearly two years.

"You got a dog?" Levi asked, a special reverence in his tone. He joined Laney on the floor in front of Coastie.

Laney fired off questions. "Is it a she? It looks like a she. What's her name?"

"It is. Her name is Coastie."

Josie lifted a brow. "Really, Jay?" she asked wryly. "You named your dog after yourself?"

Jay chuckled and shook his head. "She's not really mine and I didn't name her. It's a long story. A sailboat capsized trying to cross the Columbia River bar and her owner drowned. She was supposed to go to a shelter, but she needed some stitches. There's a vet in town who is treating her for free while we try to locate family. I'm just her foster parent."

"I like the name." Laney giggled as Coastie nibbled and tugged on her sweatshirt sleeve.

"There are some toys in that bag." Jay pointed to where he'd dropped it earlier.

"Sorry about the surprise," Josie said flatly, shifting her gaze toward Levi. "I thought Levi told you we were coming."

Levi took a defensive tone. "I sort of told him. You told me to ask if he had time tomorrow and I did. And he said yes."

"What's going on? Levi's text said Mom took off again? Where are the Ds?" Jay referred to the youngest members of their clan,

Dean and Delilah, their six- and four-year-old half siblings.

"Yes, she did. They are staying with a friend of mine tonight. We need to talk." Josie pointed to the round table that was now set for dinner. "Let's sit down and eat first. Are you hungry?"

"Yes, especially for what you're cooking." He grinned. "Hey, Lanes, you want to help me get Coastie her dinner? There's dog food in that bag, too."

A few minutes later, with Coastie happily crunching her kibbles in the corner, the four siblings sat down to a dinner of pasta with their grandmother's famous sauce, Caesar salad and crusty French bread. Despite his family's difficulties, he loved his brothers and sisters more than anything. Every single day he wished he could do more for them than send his paycheck home.

They spent some time catching up, avoiding the topic he assumed they'd come here to discuss—their mother. Since Jay had been stationed in Astoria, he tried to make the long drive from Pacific Cove to Portland to visit at least once a month, and Josie brought everyone as often as their schedules allowed, but kids grew and changed so quickly. Unlike their mother, who didn't ever change and seemingly refused to try.

As Jay had gotten older, his sympathy toward their mom had grown. In many ways, her erratic behavior was not her fault. And while he understood this, it didn't lessen their reality. Like the string of men she continually had in her life. The repercussions of which they were left to deal with. Which, Josie soon confirmed, was the specific reason for this visit.

"Mom got married again," she finally said, pushing her plate away. "She left for her honeymoon last night."

Jay rolled his eyes. He didn't have to say what he was thinking, because who took a honeymoon after their sixth marriage?

"I know." Josie gave her head a little shake. "They went to the Redwoods."

"She promised after the last guy that she wouldn't…" He stopped himself, because what was the point of bringing up one of their mom's perpetually unfulfilled promises? As he raked a frustrated hand through his hair he reminded himself that she wasn't capable of keeping promises like a normal person. "I didn't even know she was seeing anyone."

"That's because she's only known him a few weeks. But this guy is unacceptable."

"Aren't they all?" Jay asked, and in this statement he was including his and Josie's loser of a father, Jacob, whom they hadn't heard from in nearly twenty years. Their mom had six kids with three different fathers. She'd had five husbands, and too many fiancés, "special friends" and live-in boyfriends to count.

Josie inhaled deeply and said, "This guy has a criminal record, including a child abuse conviction." Her face twisted with disgust. "She's done it this time, Jay. We are free. Or at least we're going to be."

They'd been in similar situations before, thinking they had a way out, only to be disappointed. He motioned for her to continue.

"Like I said, she left yesterday and we had to act fast because who knows how long she'll be gone? We packed our bags and left. When she gets back the legal papers will be waiting for her."

"Legal papers?"

"We're taking her to court."

Jay gaped at his sister. "Josie, we've tried this before." When they were teenagers, before the Ds had been born, they'd taken Levi and Laney and fled to their Aunt Stephanie's house in California. Stephanie had tried to keep them, but the legal system had forced them to return. The police had shown up and threatened to arrest Stephanie, and lectured him and Josie on the inconsideration they'd shown their mother. The court proceedings had been a nightmare. After that, they had resolved themselves to a life of taking care of their younger siblings as best they could; Josie took on the role of day-to-day caretaker while Jay became the breadwinner.

"I know, but we're not kids anymore, Jay. I'm twenty-one now. I've retained an attorney. I've filed for custody of the kids and a restraining order against Neil. She will throw a fit for sure, but we both know that she won't choose us over him, meaning that she won't kick him out to get the kids back. And if she tries something sneaky, I have the support of law enforcement." Craig was a cop and up until now, Jay had appreciated the support he'd been giving Josie. He didn't like the idea of Josie getting her hopes up only to have them dashed once again.

"What do you...? We can't afford an attorney." His paycheck was stretched to the limits as it was.

"We can afford this one. He's a friend of Craig's. He's really, really good at this and he's agreed to take on our case pro bono."

"But then what? Even if we win, what then?"

"I've got my LPN now. I'll be getting more hours at the hospital and a big pay raise. More news—Craig and I are getting married. The attorney says that will really help our case. Plus, that means you won't have to help as much with my school expenses."

"Congratulations, Josie. Craig is a great guy. But I will help you with school until you graduate with your bachelor's degree in nursing like we've planned. I will continue to help you with everything. But what about…" The "but" referred to their four siblings, two of whom were sitting at the table listening to their conversation with great interest.

Josie knew it because she went on, "I'm filing for custody of everyone because it's easiest, but Levi and Laney want to stay with you. That's why we're here."

A combination of hope and terror unfurled in his chest. If there was any chance of getting their little brothers and sisters away from their mom he wanted to take it. But…there were so many "buts" he didn't even know where to begin.

Levi and Laney were both staring at him. He hadn't seen such hope in their eyes since their mom had taken off with a long-haul truck driver a few years ago. Abandonment would have been enough to remove his siblings from the home, but at that time foster care would have been the only way out because Josie hadn't even been eighteen. Jay had been deployed and in no position to take them. Again, they'd opted to stay together and stay put for the time being.

Laney, her dark blue eyes wide and beseeching, said, "Please, Jay. We'll pull our weight. We promise."

Jay swallowed around the lump in his throat. His fifteen-year-old sister shouldn't have to worry about "pulling her weight." She should be worrying about girl stuff like homework and boys and volleyball and…whatever normal teenage girls worried about. But he and his siblings had never had the luxury of a "normal" childhood. No one could have a normal childhood with Denise Hough Johnston Porter Merrell Hyde Whittier and whatever her last name might be now as a mother. Yes, Denise was fighting demons, too. It was just difficult not to wish that she would try harder even as he hoped that she'd get better. Jay had spoken to her doctors, all of whom believed part of her condition was medical and part was her personality. It was impossible to say how much of each accounted for her behavior. By all accounts, she knew right from wrong.

Levi sat stiffly beside him, not saying a word. But his entire body radiated with tension.

They all had their issues because of their family situation, but among them, Levi appeared to struggle the most. Jay could see the insecurity, the guilt, the helplessness, at being forced to rely on others when you wanted to rely only on yourself. He saw it because he'd had it, too, at Levi's age. Which left him wondering if he could handle this. Could he deal with a custody battle and care for two teenagers on his own? Josie was so much better at the nurturing, caretaking part.

Making him wonder, "Why? Why do you guys want to stay with me? It seems like you'd want to stay together." Staying together had always been their goal.

Laney answered, "It's embarrassing. Everyone at school knows how we live. They know Mom is…not right. Dean and Delilah are too young to really feel it yet. But Levi and I, we just want a fresh start. We want to start over someplace where no one knows us."

Jay understood. He was a grown man and he didn't talk about his family.

"Look," Josie said. "I know this is a lot to spring on you like this. But I'm done, Jay. We've been dealing with this for our entire lives. I'm leaving, and I won't leave these guys with her, especially now that she's married a child abuser. The only reason we survived to be even remotely normal is because we had Gran for the first ten years. And we promised Gran before she died that we'd take care of these guys the same way she took care of us. Dean and Delilah are still young enough to shield them from a lot, but even at four and six they know that their life isn't 'normal.'" She stopped to add air quotes. "Dean knows that he's the only one in his first-grade class whose sister comes to parent-teacher night. Delilah asked me the other day if she could call me mom when I pick her up from dance class."

Levi pushed his chair away from the table. He bent and gathered Coastie in his arms, lifting her to his lap. She snuggled into his embrace. He buried his face in her fur. Levi loved animals. Ever since Jay could remember, Levi had wanted a dog. It had always killed him and Josie that they had to say no. Pets were expensive, and Josie already had so much responsibility.

Josie had always had too much responsibility. He needed to do this for her. She deserved to finally have a life of her own, or as much of one as she could ever have under the circumstances.

"Okay." Jay looked around the table, smiled at his siblings and said, "I'm in. Let's do this."

MIA PREPARED A SPECIAL, extra-pungent breakfast of albacore tuna and ground beef. She carried it out to the porch and placed it in the usual spot, hoping the smell would carry. Even in the summer, morning air was chilly on the Oregon coast, making her glad she'd grabbed a sweatshirt. Taking a seat in a comfy deck chair, she waited, listening to the roar of the ocean. Sunlight glinted off the waves as they rolled up onto the beach. She loved this view. Normally, it would soothe her, refresh her and get her ready for the day. But not this morning, because guilt was gnawing at her.

She should have rounded up the cats when she had the chance. She shouldn't have tried to wait until they knew her better. She should have…

Her mom poked her head out the door. "No sign of Jane and Edward, huh?"

"No. No sign of any of them. I'm worried."

"Stay there. I'm coming out." At least her mom was recovering well. She seemed to regain more of her strength every day.

When Mia and her mom moved into the house, Mia had quickly realized that the area bordering her property was overrun with stray cats. Walking east from her property had revealed a cul-de-sac at the end of the county road. It appeared to be a road to nowhere. Upon asking a neighbor, she'd learned that the property had been slated for development nearly ten years ago, right before the real estate market took a hit along the coast. The project had been abandoned and the property was now grassy fields and overgrown brush, the perfect spot to dump unwanted pets.

Mia had set about rounding up as many of the cats as she could. In the process, her vision for Lucky Cats had taken root. During the few short months she'd lived there, she'd picked up or trapped, neutered and treated, and then adopted out, twelve cats. With her increasing workload at the clinic due to McKenzie's condition and Dr. Anthony's resulting absences, she'd put the trapping of the more skittish and truly feral cats on hold. She'd been feeding them on her porch until she could get Lucky Cats officially up and running. There were several regulars, including Jane and Edward, but as of a few days ago, they'd disappeared. There seemed to be fewer of the other cats as well.

Nora stepped out onto the porch, a cup of some type of steaming beverage in each hand. "I'm sorry, sweetie. It's possible they'll come back. With summer coming on and the weather so nice, maybe they're off hunting mice and critters on their own."

Nora placed a mug on the table in front of her. "Maybe."

They discussed the possibilities for a few minutes before Mia finally lifted the cup and sniffed the contents. "What is this?"

"Green tea herbal mix, new blend we got in the shop." Nora lowered herself onto the chair across from her. "You know, your dad wouldn't drink tea? After he was diagnosed with heart disease, I begged him to drink it for his health. He wouldn't do it."

"I know. What I don't know is why you were surprised, Mom. If the Navy didn't order it, I'm sure he thought it was unnecessary."

Nora sighed and looked away. Mia instantly felt guilty. William—Bill—Frasier, naval officer and Mia's father, was the one topic they didn't really discuss. Her mom had adored him, and while Mia had never disclosed the depth of her own feelings with her mother, she made them clear enough. There had been no love lost between father and daughter. Mia couldn't understand why her mom wouldn't acknowledge it. Therapy had taught her that she shouldn't expect it. Yet once in a while, she couldn't seem to stop herself from commenting, especially when her mom alluded to the notion that she could have somehow prevented his death. If only she'd taken better care of him, given him this supplement or that herb or kept him from eating so many french fries. Her mom was so strong in every area of life except where her husband was concerned. Mia couldn't stand it.

In the spirit of a subject change, Mia took a sip from the cup. And immediately grimaced.

"Uh-oh, bad huh?"

"Well, it's not…good. What's it supposed to do for me?"

"Sharpen the mind, improve memory and reduce stress."

Mia tipped her head back and drained the mug.

Nora laughed and then took her own sip. Her face scrunched with distaste. "Yikes, you're right. We won't be handing out free samples of this one." She gestured toward the dish full of cat food. "What are you going to do about these guys?"

"Nothing I can do for now, except hope they show up again."

"Maybe someone else is feeding them? You always hear about those cats that make the rounds in certain neighborhoods, eating at a bunch of different houses."

"Maybe," she answered, with a doubtful tip of her head. "I just wish they would have waited till I could get them in at the clinic. They were going to be the faces of Lucky Cats—my first official clients." Part of the program was to sterilize feral cats, and if they were deemed too wild for adoption, release them. Mia had planned to use Jane and Edward as successful examples.

"Suppose word got out on the cat street what you had planned for them?" Nora joked.

Mia chuckled, appreciating her mom's attempts to cheer her. "If that's the case they would be here right now. Because they would know that it's healthier for them to be fixed. Less chance of catching a disease. Better chance of finding a real home."

Nora studied her for a few seconds over the rim of her cup. "Speaking of finding homes for animals, that Jay is a real nice guy, huh?"

Uh-uh. No way. There was no way she was going down this road with her matchmaking mom. Mia knew very well it was one of Nora's dearest wishes to see her children married with families of their own. Especially that last part, which would land her some grandchildren. Her brother Kyle was also single. Due to the logistics that went along with a career in the Navy, including the fact that he spent the majority of his time in far-off locales unknown to them, he was mostly spared their mom's scheming. But on the rare occasion he came home on leave, he was fair game. As far as Mia was concerned, he didn't come home nearly enough.

"Uh, yeah. He seems like a nice guy. What do you have planned for today?"

Her mom had taken a doctor-ordered week off after the accident to recuperate. That had been fine for a few days, but Mia could tell she was going a little stir-crazy "taking it easy."

"Doctor's appointment. I'm hoping he'll give me some idea of when I'll be cleared for yoga. I'm getting a little bored. You should invite Jay over for dinner."

Mia stood and stretched. "I'm sorry. I'd be bored, too. I am proud of you for listening to the doctor, though. Let me know what he says. I need to get to work, but let's leave this food out for a while in case they've been spooked and they're waiting for the coast to clear. Can you pick it up before you leave? The raccoons and opossums can find their own breakfast." She softened her next comment with a wink. "And Petty Officer Johnston can get his own dinner."

Mia's recent brush with death only strengthened her resolve. Life was short. Too short to waste dating men she knew she had no future with. Plus, she was more determined than ever to make that difference. Now if only the cats she was trying to help would cooperate.

From her chair, Nora let out a little sigh of disappointment. "I'll keep an eye out in case they show up."

CHAPTER SIX

"HEY, GOOD NEWS!" Charlotte said as she strolled through Mia's open office door. "I got us a volunteer."

"A volunteer? Like singular?"

"Yes, but this is only the beginning. Remember a while back when I said the Coast Guard was looking for organizations for their people to volunteer with? I put Lucky Cats on their list. I heard this morning that we got accepted and someone signed up. He'll be here Saturday." Saturday was Lucky Cats' first official work party.

Charlotte handed her the paper. Mia stared at the name and tried to make sense of it. Jay Johnston had signed up as a Lucky Cats volunteer? Why would he do that? He'd told her flat-out he wasn't an animal lover. His resistance to adopting Coastie was proof of it.

Mia sighed. Did this mean he was harboring romantic feelings and trying to get on her good side? Even as that option warmed a tiny piece of something inside her, it was quickly overshadowed by a flash of unease. She didn't need this guy getting too attached to her. There was no future here. She would have to let him down easy.

"Thanks, Charlotte." She knew she sounded disappointed.

Her friend patted her shoulder. "Don't worry, Mia, we'll get some more people interested. As soon as the community learns what you're doing, volunteers will jump on board. Speaking of that, I talked to Mayor Cummings, and Pacific Cove's website is running a spot. Several businesses have agreed to put out our fliers. Oh, and I've contacted the newspaper. Hopefully, they'll run a story soon and then we'll be swamped with calls."

Mia smiled at her friend. "Thank you, Charlotte, for your hard work. I love your optimism. It's frustrating that people can't see how important this is."

JAY STARED AT his name on the printout Aubrey handed him. He looked up at her, trying to make sense of it. "Lucky Cats? What is this?"

"That's your first volunteer stint. You're working for Lucky Cats."

"What is it? It sounds like a casino."

"It's a stray and feral cat reduction program."

"A…what? Cats? Are you kidding me?"

"No. You're going to be rounding up stray cats. It's one of those trap, neuter, return deals."

He let out a noise of frustration and shook his head. "Who approved this place?"

Aubrey's brows shot upward. "I did. It's a valid organization. They're trying to reduce the population of stray cats in Pacific Cove and the surrounding communities. It's really—"

Jay started shaking his head before she'd even finished. "No. I can't do this. I don't want to do this. Find someone else."

"What? Why?"

"My whole purpose in starting this outreach is to help *people*, Aubrey. Needy people. Community outreach." Like he and his siblings had once been. He and Josie had counted on help from places like the food bank and programs like Coats for Kids when they were younger. He would never forget what it was like to work every crap job he could after school until late in the night surviving on four or five hours of sleep to buy diapers and put food on the table and still not have enough. They'd been grateful for the help, even though it had been difficult to accept. That was before he'd turned eighteen and joined the Coast

Guard. It was one of his proudest moments when he knew he'd no longer have to accept charity for his family.

But now Jay wanted to give back to the community. He truly believed a lot of people wanted to help their down-and-out neighbors, friends and community members, they just didn't know how or where to start. He'd planned on leading the charge with his example.

"This is outreach."

"*People*, Aubrey. Not cats. I want to help people, especially kids. I never would have approved this if I'd known it was on the list."

"Cats are people, too, Jay," Aubrey quipped. "Just spend a few minutes on social media and you'll see."

"Funny," he said wryly.

"She really needs help. You don't want to disappoint her, do you?"

"She?"

Aubrey tapped on the paper. "It's organized and run by your vet, Dr. Mia Frasier."

Jay looked back down at the name that now seemed to be glowing on the paper and felt his heart sink. "Oh, great," he said, his tone saying anything but.

"What is the matter with you?" She studied him intently. "I thought you liked her."

"That's the problem. Now she's going to think I signed up for this *because* I like her."

Aubrey's face lit up. "You *do* like her. I knew it."

"Aubrey, it doesn't matter if I like her. I can't…"

She stared at him expectantly, waiting for an explanation. An explanation he had no intention or desire to give. But one that the appearance of Levi and Laney in his life had only served to exemplify.

He blew out a breath and gave the back of his neck a firm squeeze. "You wouldn't understand. Please get me out of this."

"Well, okay… I can try. Unfortunately for you, you did a really good job of selling this volunteer thing. We've got people signed up and committed all over the place. And I told Dr. Frasier's assistant that they had a volunteer showing up on Saturday. She was so grateful, said they really need someone. I'd do it for you, but I'm booked at the pool. I'll try to find you a replacement, but in the meantime, you need to plan on showing up."

MIA WAS ON her way to exam room two to treat a cat with an abscess when she heard what sounded like a whale in distress in the reception area. They didn't officially treat whales, although she wouldn't be surprised to see that someone had brought one in. In the short time she'd been working in Pacific Cove, well-meaning but overly concerned beachgoers had brought in an assortment of fledgling seabirds, an "injured" otter, and two "abandoned" baby seals. None of which had needed human intervention or medical treatment. It wasn't uncommon for people to see a baby animal along the shore and mistake the absence of a parent for abandonment.

She rushed out to find Tiffany, the technician on duty, kneeling by what looked like a massive ball of tangled fishing line and debris with a dog inside. The whimper-moan coming from the black Lab wasn't quite like anything she'd ever heard before.

Tiffany whispered, "Oh my God! This is crazy... Where do we even start?"

"We didn't know what to do." The young woman who had presumably brought the dog in was standing and fidgeting nervously nearby. "Dave and I were walking to the jetty to go fishing when we saw him. He was crying in pain and rolling around on the beach in this pile of fishing line and junk. I think there's a fishhook in his mouth."

There were a surprising number of hazards on the beach for dogs—rotten creatures to nibble on, sand and salt water to ingest, sharp objects to step on, debris to get tangled in—including fishing line and discarded fish-hooks. She analyzed the tangle of line, grass, cloth, plastic and unidentifiable debris with a dog wrapped up in the middle. Why had no one thought to cut off all this junk? she wondered as she spoke in soothing tones to the poor dog. The line was so tightly wound around one paw he was holding it up off the ground. The whimpering slowed as his brown eyes focused on Mia and seemed to beg for help. He quieted as she gently touched him. Closer examination revealed there was indeed a treble hook stuck in his mouth, effectively keeping it closed and preventing him from being able to open his jaws more than about an inch.

She started to ask Tiffany to get some medication and scissors. "I need—"

That's when a young man, a teenager— she realized his height had initially thrown her off—appeared by the dog's side. He produced a Swiss Army knife and began snipping through the mess.

His brow creased in concentration, he began talking as he worked. "This fishing line is making it worse. It's pulling on the hook." He trimmed the line around his snout and instantly Mia could see some of the pressure was relieved. "Plus, I think it's cutting off the circulation around his paw here." As he snipped, the dog leaned against him as if grateful for the help.

"Tiffany, get me a syringe of Telazol. I need to sedate him. I'm not sure what it's going to take to get this hook out."

Tiffany went to get the medication while Charlotte showed up with another pair of scissors and handed them to Mia. Between her and the boy, they soon had the dog free of the line.

The boy held his head while Mia administered the shot. They waited, comforting the dog until he slowly collapsed into a puddle of velvety black fur and droopy eyelids.

"He's in a happier place now," Charlotte said. "Poor baby."

"Do you want me to carry him somewhere?" the boy asked as he gently stroked the lab's head.

"Yes, if you don't mind. We'll take him in the back through that door." She pointed.

Tiffany reappeared. "Dr. Anthony said he can remove the hook if you want him to. He just finished another procedure, and he's all ready to go."

Mia wanted to do it herself, but she had

a torn-up cat who'd been in a fight waiting. After that, she needed to interview the applicants for the new kennel assistant. Because school was almost out, they'd had a pile of applications from high school students seeking summer jobs. Charlotte had narrowed the field to four.

Mia led the way and let the surgical technician take over. The boy followed her back to the waiting room.

"Thanks so much for your help," she told the teen. "I—"

She was interrupted as the girl who'd brought the dog in hurried forward. "How is he?"

"I think he's going to be fine. I don't know how much damage the hook has done. And we'll want to watch out for infection. He's not yours, I take it?"

She shook her head. "No, but I'd love to keep him if no one claims him. I called my parents and they already said yes. We have another dog at home. We lost our old Irish setter a few months back. My mom said she'd come in and talk to you."

Mia felt a wave of appreciation toward these kind people. She instructed the girl to give the receptionist her contact information and turned to thank the young man. But he was gone.

"Where did he go? Was that young man with you?"

The girl shook her head. "No, I thought he was with you. The way he knew what to do and all, I figured he probably worked here."

"Huh." Mia took one last look around, let the girl know they'd be in touch, picked up the cat's file and headed into the exam room.

The appointment went smoothly. The cat was a regular patient, current on vaccines, with no other health problems. She washed its wounds, dressed them and prescribed some medication.

Charlotte was waiting for her when she came out.

"They are all ready. I'll send them into your office one at a time."

"Do you have a favorite?" she asked. As office manager and unofficial HR person, she wanted Charlotte to have a say in who they hired.

"I do, but I want to see what you think before we talk about it."

As far as Mia was concerned, kennel assistant was one of the most important jobs in the clinic. This person had the most one-on-one contact with the animals. The duties entailed walking the dogs, cleaning kennels and litter boxes, providing fresh water, and seeing to the basic comfort and cleanliness of the animals. She realized she might be slightly biased as she credited her first job as a kennel assistant with cementing her love for animals and establishing her career path. Because of her dad's no-pet rule and her desire to be around animals, she'd started volunteering at animal shelters when she was fourteen. At sixteen, she'd landed her first job at a vet clinic. They'd been stationed in San Diego at the time.

"Okay, send them in."

The first two candidates seemed adequate, the third was promising, but with the fourth applicant, she knew Charlotte had saved the best for last when the boy with the Swiss Army knife walked in.

Her face broke into a smile when she saw him. She shook his hand. "I'm so happy to see you again. I wanted to have a word with you, but you disappeared. Now I realize that Charlotte herded you away. Have a seat. I didn't know you were here applying for a job."

"Thank you. Yes," he said, lowering himself into the chair across from her desk. "I need a job."

"Well, I can't think of a better way for you to get a feel for working at a vet clinic than to jump into the middle of an emergency. Thank you again for your quick thinking out there."

He nodded like it was no big deal. "It seemed like the logical thing to do."

"It was. Very logical." She looked down for the name on his application. "So, Mr. Merrell, it says here you're only sixteen, but you have several job references listed. How long have you been working?"

"Officially, since I was fourteen. But I started babysitting, mowing lawns, watering plants, and walking dogs for my neighbors when I was about ten."

This kind of initiative in someone so young was heartening. They spoke further about his work experience and what the job would entail. Finally, Mia said, "Well, I'm going to call a couple of these references because that's what I have to do, but otherwise I'm ready to offer you a job. When can you start?"

"Now?"

"I suppose you already have, right?" She chuckled as he grinned. "I do like that enthusiasm, though. Today is Friday and I have a commitment tomorrow, so how about Monday? After school?"

"Oh, I'm not in school. I mean, I'm in school, but taking online classes right now. My schedule is really flexible."

Mia was impressed, although she couldn't help but wonder if it was need or ambition that had lit this kid's fire. She'd noticed his worn tennis shoes and ratty backpack. These days, that wasn't necessarily a sign of need. And yet there was both an eagerness and a maturity about him that suggested it and tugged on her heartstrings.

"Perfect. Then we'll see you Monday morning at nine a.m. We'll work out the hours after you get a feel for the job."

The young man stood and extended a hand. "Thank you so much, Dr. Frasier. I won't let you down."

"You're welcome, Levi, and thank you. Something tells me you won't."

CHAPTER SEVEN

JAY WAS FEELING more than slightly grumpy as he pulled into the parking lot of Pacific Cove Vet Clinic early on Saturday morning. He blamed Aubrey. Things only got worse when he walked inside to find Dr. Frasier. *Only* Dr. Frasier. Clicking away on a computer keyboard behind the counter, she glanced up. He nearly winced when he saw her face brighten. Exactly what he'd been afraid of—he didn't want her to think he'd volunteered to get close to her.

"Hi, Jay," she said with a smile. "Thanks so much for being here. I'll be ready in a couple minutes."

"Good morning." He glanced around, looking for signs of life. He'd been hoping enough people would show up that he'd be able to get out of it and spend the day with Levi and Laney. Not that they needed him. They'd bought some paint the day before and had plans to paint Laney's bedroom. The cabin had two bedrooms. The spare room already had a bed for the times when his siblings visited. Laney had moved into that one and he'd given Levi his room until he could get the loft stairs finished. He'd sleep on the sofa for now.

"Are the other volunteers not here yet? Did the day and time get messed up?"

"Nope, you're it. Unfortunately, you're my only volunteer today. Well, Charlotte will be here later to help process the cats we bring back."

"Oh, um, uh…"

Looking away from the monitor, she met his gaze and held it. "Is there a problem?"

"Look, Mia, I'm going to be honest here—I accidentally got signed up for your cat thing. Aubrey signed me up without telling me what I'd be doing. She's working on finding someone else but she said you needed someone today. So…" He trailed off with a shrug. "I guess it's just me." He immediately realized how much better that had sounded in his head.

The look of disappointment that flashed across her face made him feel about two inches tall. Especially when she composed her features, blinked a couple times and said, "Oh, I see. I'm sorry for the misunderstanding. You can go. You don't have to stay."

"No, no. I'll stay. I committed to this and

you need help." He paused, "Right?" He hoped she'd let him off the hook.

She continued studying him for a few long seconds, turning up his discomfort level several notches. He found himself shifting around on his feet like a nervous middle schooler.

"Yes," she finally said. "Actually, I do. I'm glad you're offering to follow through on the commitment you made because we've got a tough case today. I'll admit I'm relieved I don't have to tackle it myself. Although I would."

"A tough stray cat case?" he asked skeptically, with more than a trace of sarcasm. He knew his bad attitude was probably shining through, but he didn't really care. Playing with stray cats was not what he had in mind when he envisioned this volunteer program. Not when he could be helping troubled kids or building homes for the needy.

He watched her reaction; eyes narrowing, brow crinkling as if she was trying to decide if he was making fun of her.

"Yes," she answered hesitantly. "Very tough. In fact, I would even say it's a cat emergency."

"A cat emergency?" He repeated the words with a chuckle.

Crossing her arms over her chest, she gave

him a scowl that reminded him an awful lot of Aubrey. "Like I already mentioned, if you're not up for it, you're welcome to go. I'm getting the idea that you have plenty of other things you'd rather be doing with your time and that your offer to stay is out of your hyperinflated sense of duty."

Hyperinflated sense of duty? Did he have that? Okay, maybe he did. "No, I'm fine. This won't be my first cat rescue. I've plucked a few freaked-out felines off sinking ships in my time." He added a grin that he hoped would de-escalate this growing conflict. It didn't work.

Her scowl intensified to a glare. "You know what? I don't have time to explain this to you but I also don't appreciate you making fun of what I do. Sure, it might not be pulling people out of icy cold water or saving them from airplane crashes, but it is important."

He scoffed. "I'm sure it is, but surely you can see it's not as important as saving—"

He was going to say "people" but at that moment a woman came through the door, interrupting him. Jay was glad because the conversation was not going well. But he had made his point.

"Hey, Mia. Whose car... Oh." She stopped and flashed Jay a wide, pretty smile as her sparkling brown eyes lit with what looked like appreciation and curiosity. "Hi, I'm Charlotte."

"Charlotte," Mia said in an overly bright tone, "this is Petty Officer Jay Johnston from the United States Coast Guard. Aren't we so fortunate to have such an esteemed volunteer with us today? Even though Petty Officer Johnston has mysteriously and inadvertently signed up for this inauspicious tour of duty with Lucky Cats, he's opting to stay and help. Isn't it incredibly gracious of him?" she gushed sarcastically.

"That's...yeah." Charlotte's gaze flickered from him to Mia and back to him again. "That's wonderful."

Deciding it would be best not to respond to Mia's exaggerated albeit possibly deserved recap, Jay reached out a hand. "Hi, Charlotte. Nice to meet you. Please call me Jay. I seem to recall you're the one who named Coastie?"

This produced a happy laugh. "Oh! Yes, I did. You're Coastie's new dad?"

"Foster dad," he corrected. He watched Mia scowl again. For some reason, this whole ordeal was making him feel like kind of a jerk.

"Any luck locating family members who might take her?" Charlotte asked.

"Not yet," Jay answered.

Mia turned her back to pick up a box, carried it out from behind the counter and set it on a bench.

"Well, you two should get going. I'll be here to hold down the fort. Dr. Anthony is working for a few hours this morning."

Charlotte plucked a slip of paper from the reception desk and handed it to Mia. "Here's the number in case you need to call the police."

The police? Jay thought that seemed a little dramatic, but he managed to keep that comment to himself.

"Thanks, Charlotte." Mia tucked the number into her pocket and picked up the box again.

A half hour later he was no longer feeling like kind of a jerk. He was pretty sure he actually was the biggest jerk in the world.

MIA DROVE TO the end of Porpoise Point Road, Jay beside her in the passenger seat. He was different this morning from the charming guy she'd believed him to be. She was glad, she told herself as she steered the Lucky Cats van onto a narrow, graveled drive, the tires making a crunching sound as they bumped along the rutted path. She was feeling rather silly that she'd ever harbored the thought he'd signed up for this because of her. It was obvious that wasn't the case. It did make this less awkward, at least, and even better, his attitude made him much less attractive.

A flash of black-and-white fur darted across the road in front of the car. A slower orange one followed. They pulled up in front of the modest ranch-style home painted dark blue with white trim.

"Here we go," she said.

"Holy... Wow," Jay said, his head turning left and right and back again. "Sorry," he muttered, glancing over at her. "But this is a lot of cats."

"Yes, it is. Hoarder," Mia said, turning off the van's engine.

The call had come in to the newly operational Lucky Cats line anonymously. Charlotte, who had taken the call and passed the message on to her, hoped the person was exaggerating when she said there were "a ton" of cats in and around the property. Mia could smell the stench as soon as she opened the van door. She counted thirteen cats before they even made it to the front porch.

They climbed the steps, dodging cats along the way. Some skittered away, while others meowed for attention. Most looked thin and sickly. Mia crouched to study a filthy cat bed that contained a pile of kittens. She estimated them to be no more than a few weeks old.

Jay knelt beside her. "Why are their ears black?"

"Ear mites," she answered. She stood and tried to gauge the severity of the circumstances.

She was surprised when Jay picked up one tiny black-and-white kitten. Mia noted that its eyes were stuck nearly shut with crusted pus. "Are these," he said, trailing a finger through its fur, "fleas? I've never seen so many fleas…" His tone held a combination of surprise and disgust.

Mia nodded. "Believe it or not, fleas are one of the worst problems with cat hoarders. The cats get so many bites and lose so much blood they end up with anemia. It's often life-threatening. That little guy is…" Mia shook her head, not wanting to diagnose that possibility.

"Will he live?"

"I don't know. He needs medical treatment ASAP."

Brow tightly drawn, his expression was a combination of pity and horror. He cradled the kitten close and Mia thought maybe he wasn't quite as cold as he'd seemed earlier.

In addition to ear mites, a cursory inspection of the cats in the immediate surroundings revealed eye infections, skin conditions, upper respiratory infections, malnutrition and what looked like several nasty abscesses, probably from fighting.

"What do we do? Where do we even start? They are all over the inside, too," Jay said, pointing toward the window.

Torn and shredded curtains were hanging haphazardly in the large picture window. The house was dark, but cats were lined up on the windowsill, multiple colors of fur pressed against the glass. They were stretched along the back of a sofa. Curious, wary eyes turned their way.

"Unfortunately, we start with the home-owner. Often these people are very resistant to help. They think we're trying to confiscate the animals they believe they are helping. In other words, we're the bad guys."

Breathing through her mouth, Mia stood in front of the door and prepared to knock. She noticed movement between a gap in the curtains. The deliberate motion suggested it was a person. It seemed too far above the ground to be a cat, although there could be an object sitting there for them to perch on.

"I think someone is home," Jay said, confirming her thoughts.

After waiting a minute, she lifted a hand and rapped her knuckles hard against the door. Cats scattered. She could hear sounds of scuffling from within, but had no idea if it was animals or people.

Jay began speaking quickly, "What are we going to do? Where's that phone number? We need to call the police. This is just…cruel. Oh no, that one is limping." Still cradling the kitten, he began taking photos with his cell phone. Mia was struck by the wisdom of that move.

She knocked again. "Let's see what the resident has to say. Maybe they'll be cooperative."

Technically, she could call law enforcement and get some assistance. Just from the cats she could see, there was ample evidence of neglect. But animal hoarding was tricky. Often hoarders weren't trying to be cruel. The opposite, in fact. They felt like they were "saving" the animals in their care and often couldn't see the damage and suffering they were inflicting. Mia knew that going into this situation from an adversarial position could likely make things worse.

She turned around to descend the steps and noticed the porch kittens had been joined by a larger, rail-thin tabby cat. Her coat was too coarse and patches of skin were showing through where fur had fallen out. She was obviously mom, as she was busy cleaning the face of one lethargic black kitten. Mia knelt in front of the bed to gauge mom's reaction to human contact. Purring immediately ensued and Mia's throat felt tight as she blinked away tears. Even with everything she'd seen in her years of training and working, the good nature of animals in even the poorest of conditions never failed to get to her. A mix of determination and desperation propelled her into action.

"We're taking these guys right now." She picked up the mom and handed her to Jay. "Put her and your kitten in the biggest crate in the back."

"Can we do that? Just take them?" Jay asked, shifting the kitten and cradling the mom. Mia liked how their unhealthy state didn't seem to make him squeamish.

"We're going to." She scooped up the rest of the kittens, filthy bed and all. "If someone inside wants to call the police, fine. It will make our job easier in a way." *Bring it on*, she thought; it would take that chore out of her hands.

After stowing the rest of the kittens inside the crate, she returned the bed to the porch. Studying the yard, her soul felt heavy with a mix of sadness, frustration and anger. Too many cats… She wished she could take them all. With the pet crates in the back, plus the built-in one she'd installed in the van after she bought it, she quickly did some math, planning on how to make the most of the space.

She told Jay, "This isn't going to be easy. But we're going to fill the crates with as many of these guys as we can. Let's pick the ones that look the worst off and that we can most easily catch. I'll tell you where to put them."

Jay nodded, his expression grim but determined. He held a cat under each arm and Mia once again appreciated the fact that he was here. This would have been so much more difficult by herself.

She took out her phone and dialed. "Charlotte? Hey, it's me. You know how you were thinking that call you took about the cat hoarder on Porpoise Point Road might be an exaggeration?" She paused as she listened to Charlotte's response. "Yeah, uh-oh is right. Can you ask Dr. Anthony how long he can stick around? Then call the vet clinics in Remington and Tiramundi and see how many cats they can take? Dr. Foster might be able to come over and help us out, too. She offered when I spoke to her yesterday. We're bringing back as many as we can."

After firming up a few more details, she

hung up the phone and took out the paper Charlotte had given her.

"I'm going to call the police liaison and give him a heads-up."

WHEN THE VAN was full of cats, Jay looked around, overwhelmed with a combination of determination and despair. "I feel like we haven't even made a dent in this." As if to underscore his statement, a big orange cat began making figure-eight patterns around his ankles. The cat's deep purr vibrated through him and then straight into his conscience.

Mia nodded. "I know. But we have. Every cat in this van now gets a chance at a better life."

Jay leaned over and snagged the orange cat. "This one can ride on my lap. What time is the police guy meeting you?"

Mia smiled at the gesture and nodded. "Tonight at seven. We'll take these guys to the clinic. I'll be able to work on them for several hours, then I'll come back here, meet the officer, and see what else we can do. Lots of times people will open the door for the police."

As he and his orange buddy climbed in the passenger seat of the van to the multitude of pathetic mewls and howls of sick and scared cats, Jay couldn't stop thinking about his attitude that morning. How inconsiderate he'd been, how ignorant. The cat circled a couple times and made himself comfortable on Jay's lap.

Mia turned on the van, her features calm but serious. She'd more than earned his respect. She'd been incredible, gathering cats right and left, some so ill they could barely move. She'd stepped over feces, vomit, piles of garbage, and crawled under cars and old pieces of furniture to reach the cats she deemed the most in need. A quick inspection and she somehow knew which cats to put where. Most shared cages while a few got their own. Jay followed her instructions, marveling at her calm and expertise.

"I owe you an apology."

She threw a surprised glance his way. He'd obviously interrupted her thoughts. She was probably already shifting into vet mode, deciding how to proceed with the cats they'd gathered, cataloging the most critical cases in her mind. The rescue mentality, he decided, was likely the same no matter if you were saving people or animals.

"I really didn't think this through. I acted like a jerk this morning, and I'm sorry."

"Don't worry about it. People don't get it. They always think someone else will help or that it's only cats and how bad off could they be? That's why we have such a problem with stray cats in this country."

"But that's what bugs me. I'm not the kind of person to think that. I'm…" He almost said that as a person who'd been on the receiving end of charity he knew better than to take it for granted or to write it off as someone else's responsibility. That would be too much information.

"You're what?"

"I'm, uh, I'm disappointed in myself. For thinking less of your program than some of the other charities we signed up."

"Well, thank you." She acknowledged the apology with a brusque nod.

After a few seconds, she added, "But I understand. There is so much need out there. Sick kids, babies with cancer, the elderly, terminally ill people…" Jay watched her shoulders tense as her hands readjusted their grip on the steering wheel. "Animals sometimes get shifted in society's collective priorities, so to speak. I'm not saying that's wrong or right, but animals need help, too. And there are lots of wonderful organizations helping animals out there, but like with everything else, there's more need than help."

Even though she was right and her words

mirrored his own thoughts, Jay wasn't sure he deserved for her to go so easy on him. One thing was for sure, he wasn't going to quit on her. He and Josie had talked often about how important it was to set a good example for Levi and Laney.

They arrived at the clinic and began unloading their cargo. Jay felt a sense of satisfaction as Mia took the orange cat and disappeared inside. After a couple more trips back and forth, a man in a green doctor smock covered with cartoon cat faces met him at the door.

He extended a hand and introduced himself to Jay. "Ted Anthony. I'm Mia's partner here at the clinic."

"Jay Johnston."

Pointing a finger toward Jay, his face lit with a smile. "You're the Coast Guard officer who saved Mia and Nora and Captain Shear."

"I was a part of the rescue crew, yes."

"They are very modest, I've learned," Mia commented drily as she joined them. "These Coast Guard search-and-rescue people. No one will take credit for anything. They pass it around like a hot potato."

Dr. Anthony chuckled. "I find that admirable. Like a team."

"We consider ourselves precisely that."

"It's wonderful to meet you, Jay. Thank you

for your service to our country. And for your contribution in saving my partner. She means the world to me."

"Thank you, Dr. Anthony. But truly, I was just doing my job."

"I get that." He grinned, turned toward Mia and asked, "What's up? Charlotte said you've got a hoarder?"

She filled him in.

"How many cats are we talking about?"

Mia shook her head. "I don't know. So many... A lot of them are skittish and feral. We could hear them inside the house, too. And see some through the window. I'm guessing as many as a hundred."

Jay added, "There were cats scattering as we pulled up, running into the woods. I would guess that number is on the low side." Jay offered his cell phone photos for inspection.

"Whoa." Dr. Anthony analyzed the screen. "That's a lot of cats."

Mia said, "I know. I'm meeting with a police liaison this evening. He told me he's bringing a representative from the humane society. We brought back a van full, but we really need to get cooperation from the home-owner before we can do more. I probably pushed it a little as it is."

"You did the right thing. No creature deserves this. We'll do what we can for now." He reached out and gave Mia's shoulder a squeeze before picking up the carrier containing three of the sickest cats they'd brought in. "I'll get to work on these guys." He carried them through the door and toward an exam room.

"He's so great," Charlotte said as they watched him depart. "I can't believe he's even here today."

"I know. I'm incredibly grateful he is. I'll be here all night as it is."

"That reminds me, Tiffany and Stacey are both coming in," Charlotte said. "And Dr. Foster."

"Fantastic news." Mia glanced at the watch on her wrist and then up at Jay. "Well, Officer Johnston, thank you so much for your help this morning. But you are off the clock."

His shift was supposed to be from 8:00 a.m. until noon. He knelt down and opened the cat carrier he'd brought in. He removed the first kitten he'd picked up earlier. "I think I'll work a double today. Where do I put this little guy? And is there anything I can do for him right now?"

The smile she gave him went some distance toward assuaging his guilt.

"Charlotte, can you take Jay and these cats

back? Let's put mom and babies in number three. We'll treat them here at our clinic. And then put Jay to work."

CHAPTER EIGHT

SUNDAY MORNING, AN exhausted Mia rolled out of bed and went in search of the coffee she could smell brewing. Her coffee-eschewing mom must have taken pity on her and made her a pot. How sweet.

As she neared the kitchen, she heard voices. Nora must have company this morning, probably Annie checking on her. A few more feet and she realized that a male voice was mixed with her mom's. A pinochle buddy? Too late she realized she was wrong; she stepped into the room and saw the back of a man she knew immediately was Jay. She'd spent hours with him the day before and she'd recognize that back anywhere. Her face flaming, she glanced down at her baggy pj's and fuzzy blue slippers. Her hands flew up to her mass of bed head that she hadn't even bothered to pull into a ponytail. Intending to retreat, she took a hasty step backward, right into George. She'd been too distracted to realize he was hot on her heels. She let out an "oomph."

"Mia!" her mom called before she could escape. "Good morning."

Jay turned, a coffee mug in his hand and a bright smile on his face. Mystery solved about that tantalizing odor so clearly not intended for her. Why was Officer Johnston in her kitchen drinking her coffee?

"Good morning," he said. Mia watched his eyes travel up and down the length of her. Was it her imagination that he appeared to be fighting a chuckle? And was it possible to actually die of embarrassment? She wondered as she tucked wayward strands of hair behind her ears and assured herself that he'd seen her looking worse. She couldn't imagine looking more unattractive than she'd been post-airplane crash or yesterday knee-deep in filthy cats. She plastered on her best "who cares" face and sauntered into the kitchen toward the coffeemaker. At least he'd saved her some.

"Um," she croaked. "It might be after I've had a cup of coffee."

"Guess what?" Nora asked her excitedly.

Mia found a cup and poured herself some coffee. "There's a Coast Guard officer in our kitchen?"

"Yep, and he fixed our door."

Mia turned to look at him, brows scooting up onto her forehead. "Really?"

"Look at this." Her mom hustled over to the back door, opened it, closed it, and then repeated the whole process. "Smooth as glass," she reported proudly. "Can you believe it?"

Mia stared at him and answered flatly, "I really can't." Because she certainly couldn't believe that he'd reluctantly helped her save cats the day before then shown up at her house and fixed her door. What was this about?

"Thank you," Mia said, feeling a little overwhelmed. She hadn't really expected him to fix the door anyway. People said things all the time intending to follow through, but not quite ever getting there.

"You're welcome. It really was a simple fix. A little planing and sanding and it's as good as new."

"Simple for you, maybe."

Nora went on, "You know how we've been talking about putting in a pantry cabinet here?" She pointed to the empty corner adjacent to the door. "I've hired Jay to make us one. He says he can make it look just like the kitchen cabinets."

Mia blinked slowly. "You can do that? Make cabinets?"

His lips seemed to be flirting with a grin. "Yes, I can."

"Oh, um, well… Do you have time to do stuff like that?"

"Yeah, it's one of the things I do when I have time off."

"Like a hobby?"

"Yes." He kind of chuckled. "And for money. Don't worry, I gave your mom a killer deal." He added a wink and not for the first time, Mia wished he weren't so attractive. *Doesn't like animals, Mia. In the Coast Guard, Mia*, she silently repeated.

"Huh," she eloquently managed to articulate through her surprise. She wasn't sure why she was surprised that he had mad carpenter skills or by the fact that he was a man of his word. He'd proved that yesterday when he'd stuck around at Lucky Cats even after he'd made it very clear he didn't want to be there.

Apparently reading her mind, he asked, "How did it go with the police and the humane society guy yesterday?"

Mia sighed, brushing a hand across her cheek. "Not good. The homeowner did answer the door, but as I was afraid of, she was very hostile. This is going to be a tough case. She's an older woman. Classic hoarder symptoms— very defensive, self-righteous. And she demanded to know where the tall guy was that stole her kittens." She paused to chuckle.

"That was you obviously. I tried to take all the blame, but she was fixated on you. She agreed to not press charges because of the animal cruelty charges she's facing herself. Even though she can't see that she's being cruel. It's very frustrating. But the good news is that the police officer helping me out seems very determined. He's a cat lover himself, wants to adopt one of the cats. He's going to get a hold of the woman's daughter." She shrugged. "We'll see."

"Can we plan another raid? I'll never forget how you just started taking those cats. Fearless." He looked at Nora and asked, "Did you know your daughter was an expert cat-napper?"

They all laughed. Mia tried to ignore how the compliment warmed her. "Yeah, I can be a little single-minded when it comes to saving animals. I'd love to plan another raid, so to speak, but the police officer cautioned me against that. He's probably right that we need to try to keep this situation as far from adversarial as we can."

"Keep me posted. I'd like to help if I can."

Mia couldn't help the surprised expression she knew must be stamped across her face. "That's so nice of you, and I really appreciate all of your help. But you don't have to come back. I know it's not your thing."

"What? I didn't do a good enough job?"

"No, it's not that. You were great actually, especially for someone who isn't an animal lover."

Nora frowned. "Of course he's an animal lover, Mia, what are you talking about? You saw him with Coastie."

Jay looked at Nora. "It's not really that I don't like animals, it's more that I don't have much experience with them. Never had any pets growing up."

Nora flashed him a sympathetic smile. Mia couldn't help the surge of annoyance that shot through her. She gave her mom a pointed look, then half smiled at Jay. "Me either, believe it or not."

Nora fiddled with a dish towel on the countertop. She felt Jay's curious gaze bounce between her and her mom. Mia instantly felt bad about stirring up a touchy subject. George, bless him, broke the awkwardness by heading for the door and letting out a low woof.

"Looks like someone needs to use the facilities." Mia stepped toward the doorway and traded her slippers for a pair of shoes. She grabbed a jacket off the coatrack and slipped it on. She opened their newly fixed door and let out a low whistle. George trotted outside. "Wow. This is so nice," she said, keeping a hand on the door. "Thank you again, Jay. For everything." She gestured after George. "I need to follow this big guy around because he eats weird stuff. So I guess I'll see you in a couple days when you bring Coastie in for her checkup?"

"You're welcome. Yeah, I'll see you soon." He sounded casual, but his green eyes were pinned intently on hers. "Goodbye, Mia."

COASTIE STARED UP at Jay, her pretty brown eyes somehow managing to look both patient and pleading. She sat politely, gently placed a paw on his knee, and let out a soft whine, her signal for "please pick me up." He did and immediately felt a rush of affection when she nestled her head against his shoulder. She was constantly doing stuff like this, sleeping with her head on his pillow, bringing him toys, greeting him at the door like he was a superhero. Were dogs supposed to act like this?

Mia came over and sat in the chair across from him in the exam room. "Boy, she's really latched onto you, hasn't she?" She reached out and placed a hand on Coastie's head.

He could tell by the slight tremble in the dog's body that she was nervous to be back at the vet. Balancing on Jay's lap, she bravely stretched her neck out so she could snuffle Mia's ear. The sound of Mia's answering chuckle somehow managed to lighten his heart a tiny bit. This dog certainly lightened his heart. Levi and Laney adored her, too. They wanted to keep her. Ironically, if it weren't for them he might consider it.

Mia examined the injured area behind her shoulder blades. "Don't worry. She's doing great. The wound is healing nicely."

He smiled, surprised at how relieved he was by the report. He'd been doing everything Mia had instructed with regard to the wound, but hearing the news felt good.

"Stitches aren't quite ready to come out, maybe another week or so. Then she'll be good to go. How is she doing otherwise? Any signs of anxiety or behavior problems?"

"Not that I've noticed. She's actually a superstar."

"Well," Mia said with a chuckle, "I'm glad it's working out."

"Seriously, I'm pretty sure she's the smartest dog in the world. I don't have anything to compare her to, but this morning I was a little late with her breakfast, I'm talking like maybe ten minutes, she went and got her food dish and brought it to me." He lifted a brow, as if daring her to dispute his claim.

She laughed. "Was this before or after she finished the *New York Times* crossword puzzle?"

"Don't laugh. That's next. Like I said before, I never had a dog growing up—or any pets. I wanted a dog…what kid doesn't? But it wasn't, uh, feasible. I feel stupid saying this, but I think I missed out."

"Not stupid at all. Personally, I think all kids should have a pet—all kids that are interested, anyway."

"You mentioned yesterday that you didn't have pets when you were growing up, either. That seems kind of strange seeing as how you're a vet and all. For some reason, I imagine vets growing up surrounded by animals."

She nodded. "I know. My dad didn't allow pets because we moved a lot. That was his excuse, anyway. He was very…adamant about it. What's your sob story? Why couldn't you have a dog?"

"Um, mostly I suppose it was the expense."

Head tilted, she studied him carefully.

When she didn't respond, he added, "Poor family," hoping that would appease her.

It didn't.

"What about now? You're all grown-up and

gainfully employed. Have you given any serious thought to keeping Coastie?"

"Unfortunately, I can't." He ignored the ball of regret tightening his chest. What was the matter with him? Coastie would be better off with someone else, a family preferably, who could give her all the time and attention she deserved. Someone who had extra love to go around.

"Why? Dogs can enrich your life in ways you can't even imagine."

Jay tensed. *Because my teenage brother and sister have just moved in with me and I don't know how I'm going to manage to take care of them, much less a dog.* A part of him wished he could just say the words out loud. For some reason, the thought of Mia thinking he was coldhearted bothered him, especially after the way he'd acted that first morning at Lucky Cats. But saying the words meant explaining, and that he did not want to do.

"My life is not exactly dog-friendly."

Her furrowed brow told him she wasn't buying that.

He tried again. "I have commitments that prevent me from being able to give this dog everything she deserves."

Her lips parted like she wanted to comment or maybe argue. Jay appreciated when she didn't.

"Okay." She nodded slowly and said, "But since you're here I want to show you something if you have time?"

"Sure," he said, anxious for a subject change.

She stood and led him through the exam room toward the back of the building where he knew the animals were kept. Coastie was content to ride along in his arms. She'd already quit shaking, apparently sensing that her time at the vet's office was coming to a close. Mia stepped into the rectangular room where the cats were housed. Three rows of cages lined the wall on each side.

She pointed to the large enclosure on the bottom where he and Charlotte had placed the rescued kittens a few days ago. "Take a look."

Jay put Coastie on the floor and knelt to get closer. He immediately recognized the tabby-striped mom and the four bright-eyed kittens studying him curiously, even though they looked drastically better.

"Wow."

"Yep," she said. "I can't believe how well they're doing. This is the result already, after flea treatments, iron shots, and ear mite meds along with a couple other things. They've got a ways to go, but I'm really hopeful."

Where they'd barely had the energy to let out a sound a few days ago, now the kittens let loose with a concert of loud meows. Jay was surprised by the rush of joy that flowed through him.

"Look at this guy." The black-and-white kitten he'd first picked up that day was bravely pressing its nose against the wire mesh. He held a finger against the cage for the kitten to sniff. "I can't believe it. I was afraid he wasn't going to make it. Can I hold him?"

"Me, too. Sure, the more they get held the better."

He unlatched the cage and reached inside to get the kitten. "Its fur even feels different, less rough, more kitty-fuzzy."

Mia smiled. "Yep, they all had baths."

Jay cuddled the tiny ball of fluff. Who knew saving something so tiny could feel this amazing? "This is so—" The rest of his sentence was lost when a figure walked through the door. A bolt of surprise shot through him at the sight of his little brother in Mia's office wearing a light green lab coat and holding a leash in one hand.

"Levi?" Jay asked. "What are you doing here?" Beside him, Coastie let out an excited yelp and danced closer.

"You two know each other?" Mia's head swiveled from Jay to Levi and back again.

Levi went with that brows raised, shoulder-shrug teenagers liked to do as if you were crazy for asking such an obvious question. "I work here." He knelt and rubbed Coastie's neck. She licked his eyebrow.

"Since when?" he asked Levi, before answering Mia, "Levi is my brother."

"Since a few days ago. Today is my first day." Levi grinned proudly. And Jay couldn't blame him. He'd been in Pacific Cove for all of a week and he'd already landed a job. Why hadn't he mentioned it?

Jay could see the confusion in Mia's expression. She asked, "I thought you said your family didn't live around here?"

"Levi has only been here a week."

Questions were swimming in her eyes. Jay was trying to decide how to explain without explaining when he saw a little blond head peek around the doorjamb. A grinning face belonging to a girl he'd estimate to be somewhere around seven or eight appeared.

"Kenzie bug, what are you doing?" Mia asked.

"Waiting for Mom to get done talking to Dad."

She crooked a finger. "Do you want to meet my friends?"

"Sure."

The girl slowly made her way inside the room, her thin legs encased in braces. Her hands clutched the handles of the canes she used to assist her motion.

"McKenzie, this is Jay. You've already met Levi. And this is Coastie."

McKenzie moved closer. Jay marveled over the fact that the dog seemed to sense that the child needed to be treated with special care. Coastie sat, the slight wiggle of her butt as she scooted closer to the child the only indication of her usual and unbridled enthusiasm at meeting new people.

"Hi, Coastie," McKenzie said.

Coastie sniffed her hand and gave it a gentle nudge.

Jay felt himself melt as the girl removed her hand from the cane and then handed it over for him to hold. She stroked Coastie's soft fur before leaning forward and placing a kiss on the top of her head. Coastie returned the favor with a "kiss" to the girl's chin. McKenzie's giggle went straight to his heart.

She said to Jay, "I'm going to be a vet like my dad and Mia."

"That sounds like a perfect idea to me. It's never too early to start career planning. How old are you?"

"I'm eight years old. I'm in third grade. Well, I *would* be in third grade if I could go to school. But I have to miss a lot when I'm in the hospital. And sometimes I get sick. My legs won't move right."

"I see."

"My mom says I'm reading at a seventh-grade level, though. She homeschools me, my mom does. But she won't let me read books written for seventh graders, so it's kind of hard. I'm stuck with stuff that doesn't necessarily challenge me, you know what I mean?"

He wanted to laugh, but instead went with, "Yeah, that's no good. We all need to be challenged."

"Right?" she answered in a way that reminded him of Laney.

"McKenzie?" A smiling woman with blond hair twisted up on her head appeared in the doorway. "Oh, hey Mia." *Sorry*, she mouthed over the girl's head.

"Hey, Sara." Mia swiped a hand through the air as if to say *it's fine*. "McKenzie is meeting my friends."

Mia introduced everyone to Sara.

"What happened to Coastie?" McKenzie asked.

"She got cut escaping from a sinking sailboat," Jay said.

Mia said, "But I stitched her up and soon she'll be as good as new."

The girl asked a series of questions, causing Jay to marvel over the fact that she was only eight years old. She reminded him a lot of Levi when he was that age.

A short time later Dr. Anthony, wearing a gray coat covered with black paw prints, stuck his head inside the open door. "Hey, here are my girls. You two better think about hitting the road, huh? You've got a long trip ahead of you."

"Okay. 'Bye, Coastie." McKenzie took her cane from Jay and explained, "We're going to Portland. I'm having a treatment but I'll be back in few days." She smiled at Levi. "'Bye, Levi."

"Goodbye, McKenzie. Good luck," Levi said and then pointed at her. "Don't forget you owe me a rematch."

"You got it." She turned back to Jay and asked, "Are you any good at checkers?"

"Fair," he replied.

"Well, you should play with your brother.

He needs the practice. I handed his butt to him on a platter."

"McKenzie!" Sara admonished.

"Sorry, Mom." Sara shook her head while the rest of the crowd laughed. Dr. Anthony kissed his wife and daughter to a chorus of well wishes and goodbyes. He remained standing in the doorway after they'd gone.

An awkward minute stretched on and Mia finally asked, "You're not going with them today, Dr. Anthony?"

He turned around, looking almost surprised to still be standing there. Raising the fingers of one hand to his temple, he tapped it. "I'm sorry. I was thinking… No, I'm leaving early in the morning. I have a few things I need to take care of tonight."

"Is there anything I can help with?"

"No, but thank you, Mia. I will let you get back to it in here." He patted Levi on the shoulder and headed out the door.

Mia explained, "McKenzie has a rare neuromuscular condition. It's a progressive and debilitating disease."

"There's no cure?"

"No, not yet. They've been taking her to Portland for some experimental therapy that seems to help with the symptoms. There's been a lot of advances in the last few years with promising drugs in development. But I'm afraid it will be a while before McKenzie sees any benefits."

"That sucks," Levi said after a long moment.

"Yes, it does," she said. They were all quiet for another moment. "That's one of the reasons it's so important to fix what we can in this world, right? Like Coastie girl here."

"And all those stray cats," Levi added. He looked at Jay. "Dr. Frasier said I could volunteer, too. I really want to help with those cats."

Jay looked down at the kitten now snoozing in his cradled arm. He was surprised by the realization that he did, too.

"LANEY, THIS LOOKS AMAZING. I was going to make you guys tuna melts." Jay surveyed the bowls on the dining table. He pointed at one. "What is that?"

"Picadillo. It's Josie's version of spicy shredded beef," she answered, beaming at him. "She's taught me how to make a lot of stuff. And I like to watch those cooking shows."

"As long as you don't make us enchiladas out of anchovies, frozen spinach and a box of wafer cookies or whatever like they do on that one show."

She giggled. "I promise I'll stick to regular man food."

Levi said, "Girl food is okay, too. I like salads."

"Really?" she asked doubtfully.

He shrugged a shoulder. "Sure. With meat on them," Levi qualified, spooning spicy meat and onions on top of the refried beans and cheese already piled on the tortilla.

They shared a laugh. Jay said, "You don't have to cook, Lanes. But if you do, you fix whatever you want and we'll eat it."

Levi agreed and then said, "How weird is this, you already knowing Dr. Frasier? And me getting a job at the vet clinic?"

"Especially since I didn't even know you'd applied."

He grinned. "I didn't think I'd get it. I got lucky."

"Lucky?"

"Yeah, I mean the dog wasn't lucky, but I was lucky to be there. There was this black Lab…"

They sat at the table in the kitchen while Levi told the story about the tangled dog and the fishing line.

"Wow. Quick thinking there, buddy."

"It was weird. I didn't even really think. I just reacted. And then later, when Dr. Frasier offered me the job, I didn't want to say anything until she checked my references." He shoved a huge bite of burrito in his mouth.

"You'd make a great emergency responder or medical professional."

Levi swallowed. "I've, uh… I've actually been thinking about the military."

Jay tilted his head thoughtfully. "Maybe you could do the GI Bill? Go to college?" Jay had wanted to go to college, but there was no way he could have gone to school and supported his siblings. So while he joined the military and earned a paycheck, he'd insisted Josie go to school. "For the both of them," he liked to say.

"Maybe. I'd like to help out with Laney, Dean and Delilah first. Like you've helped us."

Jay felt acid burn his gut as tension gathered inside him. The idea of his little brother going without, working as hard as he had all those years, was unacceptable. After Gran had died, they'd had to live off their mom's welfare check and her discretion. She'd spent it mostly on herself, telling him and Josie that she needed the money to find them a new dad.

Which meant buying new clothes and shoes for herself and going out with friends.

This was before Jay was old enough to get a real job. Those had been the leanest times, he and Josie feeding Levi and Laney whatever they could buy after scraping money together from the odd jobs they did around the neighborhood. They often went to bed hungry. Jay remembered guiltily stealing a roll of electrical tape from a mechanic neighbor. With strips of cardboard, he'd fashioned new ends for the toes of the tennis shoes he and Josie had outgrown. Years later he'd anonymously sent the guy an entire box of tape.

"Nope. Not going to happen, Levi. I'm glad you got a job, but the money you make is for you—and for college. I would advise you to buy what you need and save the rest for a car—and for college. But you are absolutely not going to help me support this family."

Levi slowly lowered his burrito. "What do you mean? Why not?"

"Because..." Because the memories were painful and Jay didn't want to share them—not even with his own brother. Especially not with his brother, whom he had sacrificed so much for. He didn't want to add that to the weight Levi already carried on his young shoulders. Jay worked hard every day to ensure that he didn't have to. So instead of explaining, he reached over and stole a tortilla chip off his brother's plate. "Because that's my job."

CHAPTER NINE

A COUPLE AFTERNOONS LATER, Mia hung up the phone in her office, let out a whoop and gave her chair a couple of cheer-filled spins. George lifted his head from where he was sprawled across his bed. He barked his approval.

"Guess what, Georgie? We've got the green light."

She tossed him a cookie.

The police officer involved in the hoarding case had called to say that he'd contacted the homeowner's daughter. She lived out of state, but after his initial call she'd come home to check on her mom. Long story short, the poor woman hadn't realized how her mom's habit had gotten out of hand. She was staying in town indefinitely to clean up her mom's property. She'd convinced her mom to give up the rest of the cats.

Mia really wanted to share the news, but Charlotte was out of the office and her mom was at a doctor's appointment. Impulsively, she picked up the phone and dialed Jay. She was disappointed when the call went to voice mail. "Jay, hi! It's Mia. I'm calling to let you know that I heard from Officer Dunbar. We've got permission to confiscate the rest of the cats! It might be a couple weeks, but I'm really excited and I know I probably sound like a rambling maniac. But anyway, it's all good news and I thought you might want to know because you asked me to keep you posted. So… Call me back here or on my cell if you have any questions."

Sighing, she set the phone down, picked up a pen and tapped it on the desk in front of her.

Her cell phone buzzed. A combination of nerves and excitement flashed through her at the thought of Jay returning her call. The excitement part faded a tiny bit when she saw it was a text from her mom. But it reappeared when she read the news: Woohoo! Doc says I'm cleared for yoga.

She tapped out a reply: Great news!

You want to meet me at class? We can grab a bite at Tabbie's after to celebrate?

Mia thought for a second before she responded. What she wanted to do was sit here and see if Jay called back. Or maybe even swing by his house and make sure he got her message. She had his address from the forms he'd filled out at the clinic as Coastie's foster parent. Would it be weird to stop by? *Do you stop by other patients' homes, Mia?* she asked herself. *No, you do not.*

She stood and headed to the front of the clinic and was surprised to find Charlotte was back from her appointment. "You're here!" She shared the news.

Charlotte was suitably excited. "Oh my goodness, that is wonderful! Hopefully, we'll be able to get in there soon."

"What are you doing tonight?" Mia asked her.

She shrugged. "Unless a really hot guy with a decent job comes in and asks me out in the next five seconds, I have no plans."

"How about yoga? Mom has been cleared to go back to class and I kind of want to keep an eye on her. Class and then dinner at Tabbie's? My treat."

"Sure. I've got my workout clothes in the car. I hope Coby is teaching tonight."

"Really? I hope he's not."

"Are you crazy? That body of his… Those muscles can't all be from yoga, can they?"

"I find both his tight pants and his intensity off-putting."

Charlotte laughed. "You just don't like him."

"He doesn't like me. He picks on me. How many times does he have to ask if I'm sure I'm related to my own mother? It's embarrassing."

Charlotte laughed while Mia tapped out a response to her mom: Sure! Can you save Charlotte and me spots in the back? THE VERY BACK ROW, MOM, PLEASE!

Unlike her mom, Mia was hopelessly inflexible. Nora insisted that Mia just needed a spot up front where she could see better. Mia kept telling her mom there was no correlation between the front row and proper extension in the half-moon pose.

Mia helped Charlotte with the last of her tasks and then locked up for the night. They climbed into Mia's car, dropped George off at home, and a half hour later Mia was pushing her hips back and up into downward dog. Upside-down with her hands on her mat, head between her elbows and hoping her phone wouldn't fall out of her top if Jay decided to call her back.

"That's it, feel the extension," Yogi Coby went on in his melodic, soul-soothing tone that made her want to take a nap. "Palms down, fingers spread nice and wide, pushing those heels into the floor beneath you. Feel your muscles lengthen…" He kept up a string of monotonous murmuring as he strolled toward the back of the room.

He paused and she heard him sigh. "Come on, Mia, push those heels into your mat."

"I am. Heels are pushing."

"You're on your tiptoes," he said as if she wasn't aware of her terrible form.

"Thank you for pointing that out," she muttered drily.

He lingered to flirt with Charlotte while Mia's Achilles tendons screamed in agony. "Beautiful extension, Charlotte. Your calves are looking long and lovely. Have you been working on them?"

"Thank you, Coby," Charlotte cooed. "I have."

"Liar," Mia murmured after he moved on. "Stretching your long and lovely calves to reach the top shelf of the freezer for the ice cream does not count."

Coby whipped around, his stare narrowing in on her like a heat-seeking missile. Raising a hand, he pressed his thumb and fingers together in the universal symbol for "shut it or I'll shut it for you."

She flashed him a semi-apologetic expression, lifted a hand to wave and nearly fell over.

Charlotte's perfectly aligned shoulders shook with laughter.

Coby didn't take kindly to anything less than total concentration in his classes. Mia was pretty sure she was incapable of that when it came to yoga. Instead of clearing her mind, she tended to fill it. She found it the perfect opportunity to multitask—planning her day, forming extensive to-do lists, running through surgical procedures, not thinking about Jay or his little brother Levi, whom she'd hired to be her kennel assistant and who was apparently staying with him. She wondered why and for how long.

At least for the summer, but what was the deal with Jay, anyway? He seemed all carefree and easygoing on one hand, yet he was standoffish and private on the other. By his own admission, he wasn't an animal person; however, his actions spoke otherwise. He'd come over and fixed her door for goodness' sake—who does that? Either he had a romantic interest in her, he really liked fixing things or he was a nice guy. The first two explanations made her hope for his return call feel that much more ridiculous. She was going to go with the last one. She'd been a little overexcited about the cat hoarding news and she'd wanted to share it. Jay was the logical person to do that with as he'd been in on the project from the beginning. There, she was going to quit thinking about it now, about him. Because thinking about him wasn't constructive no matter what his intentions were...

Coby instructed the class to move into some kind of headstand move that she couldn't pronounce.

Mia attempted to follow instructions when she felt her phone buzzing from where she'd tucked it inside of her sports bra. Unfortunately, she *heard* it, too. And so did the rest of the class. Right before the phone wiggled loose and plopped onto the hardwood floor beyond the edge of her mat.

Beside her, Charlotte snickered.

"Surely no one in this class has been thoughtless enough to bring an electronic device into my studio?" Coby asked while the phone continued to buzz throughout the room like a swarm of killer bees.

As gracefully as she could, Mia lowered onto her hands and knees, grabbed her phone and began crawling toward the door.

"Mia!" her mom whisper-shouted from her coveted spot in the front row. "Is that you?"

"Hi, Mom! Serious meditation going on back here. Promise."

Coby's horrified glare told her that not even a tsunami warning would be worthy of this interruption to his class.

She stood up and pointed at her still-vibrating phone. "Um, sorry, Coby. Pet emergency. Very sick puppy. Poor, tiny, tiny, little Chihuahua," she lied, knowing Coby owned two of these dogs himself. "Distemper, I think."

Stepping out into the hall, she swiped at the screen, not bothering to check who was calling for fear it was Jay and she'd miss the call completely. Desperate much?

"Hello?"

"Mia?" a voice asked.

Not Jay. Disappointment settled over her. "Yes?"

"Hi, it's Sara. I have some news." Her heart sank to brand-new depths as she realized her friend was crying.

"Sara, what is it? What's the matter?"

"It's McKenzie. She's come down with an infection. They've hospitalized her. They're going to have to wait a few days before they can do the treatment."

"Oh, Sara, I'm so sorry…"

They discussed the situation for a few minutes before Sara added, "Obviously, we'll be staying here in Portland. But Ted wanted me to let you know we left Gustav with my sister Carly. But if someone could see to Tumble and Downy, that would be great. Ember will be fine staying at the office." Gustav was the

Anthonys' golden retriever mix. Tumble and Downy were their cats.

"I'll send Levi over to take care of them. Don't worry about a thing."

JAY WAS LYING on his back, his head and shoulders underneath the kitchen sink, trying to remove the piece of ancient galvanized pipe that was leaking badly. He'd planned to replace the kitchen faucet and the pipes below it, so he couldn't get overly upset about his current predicament. He just wished he had the parts to temporarily fix it. He'd sent Levi to the hardware store almost forty-five minutes ago and he should have been back by now.

Coastie sat patiently by his side as if waiting for instructions. He told her, "I feel like if I asked you for a Kongsberg wrench, you'd give me one."

She responded with what he'd termed her happy whine.

"They're made in Norway, did you know that?"

Her answer was a low woof.

"Of course you did. But why did I wait till there was a problem to work on this?"

"Woof."

"I agree. It's my own fault. I should have

done it already. But I had this grand idea that I'd do it all at once."

She stuck her head inside the cupboard, sniffed his elbow and then stared at him with her wide brown eyes.

"You know, I appreciate your support on this and you're right, no one's perfect. Where is Laney, do you know that, too? Are you also telepathic, sweet girl?"

Laney hadn't gotten home from school yet. Only a week left and she'd been hanging out with classmates and/or future volleyball teammates every day after school. Jay was glad she was making friends, but she should be home by now, too. It was getting close to dinnertime and the only rule he'd really laid down was that she be home by dinner on school nights, and if she wasn't she needed to check in. Maybe the call had been from her.

"Where is Laney, huh?"

Coastie barked enthusiastically and trotted away, her toenails making a tapping sound on the worn vinyl floor. He heard the door open.

Relief seeped into him when Laney's voice rang out to greet the dog, followed by, "Jay?"

"Right here, Lanes."

"What's going on? What are you doing?" she asked, stepping over his toolbox and tools to get to him. She crouched to peer at him.

"Taking a nap."

She laughed. "Is the water broken?"

"Yes, temporarily. I shut it off outside."

Levi's face appeared beside Laney's. "Sorry, Jay. The hardware store is in Astoria."

"Levi, what are you talking about?"

"That's what the sign in the window said. 'Gone to Astoria—back tomorrow.' So I ran over to Able's Plumbing, but they were already closed."

Jay let out an "ugh" of frustration. "Bummer. Thanks, Levi. This will have to wait until morning."

"Does this mean we don't have water?" Laney's voice sounded close to panicked. "How will I get ready for school? Can I text Elise and ask if I can stay the night with her?"

"No water until tomorrow." Jay confirmed her fear, scooting out from underneath the sink. "And yes, you can. But I'll need to meet her parents." He sat up and reached for his phone. One missed call from Pacific Cove Vet Clinic. Why would the clinic be calling him? He dialed his voice mail. As he listened to the message from Mia, he chuckled, both due to the good news and the excitement in her tone. He hit the number on the screen to return her call, but it went to the clinic's voice mail. He didn't have Mia's cell phone number, so he left a quick message of his own letting her know he'd received hers. How could he get her cell phone number? Would Aubrey have it? How could he ask for it without her thinking he wanted it for romantic purposes? When he climbed to his feet, he realized his siblings were both watching him curiously.

"Are you dating this Dr. Frasier vet lady?" Laney asked.

"What? No, I'm not." Jay wondered how she'd gleaned that from his behavior. What else had he said? He'd come home on Saturday and told them all about the cat hoarder. But he'd stuck to the facts, and they'd both been eager to sign on as volunteers. The message he'd left had been completely professional. "Remember those cats I was telling you guys about?"

"The hoarder," Levi said knowingly.

"Yeah, Dr. Frasier got permission to confiscate the rest of them."

"That's awesome. When?"

"She's not sure yet."

"I'm excited to help some cats," Laney said and then cleared her throat. "I actually have some good news, too. About me, but still, it's pretty great."

Jay picked up a towel and wiped his hands. "Let's hear it, kiddo."

"The volleyball coach came up to me today after gym class. She asked me what position I played when I lived in Portland. I told her and she said they could really use a middle hitter on varsity and that she sure hopes I'll be trying out for the team this fall."

By the time she finished the story she was bouncing up and down on her toes with a smile as bright as the sun. "I know Pacific Cove is small and everything, but can you imagine me playing varsity middle hitter as a sophomore?"

Jay felt a fresh welling of happiness and satisfaction. The very idea of watching her take on that position filled him with pride. Even with his plumbing problem, this was shaping up to be an excellent day. And so far, so good as far as having his teenage siblings living with him went. It had only been a couple weeks, but still, he was killing it.

"Congratulations, Lanes. That is awesome." He pulled her in for a quick hug.

She stepped back and Levi reached out a hand for a fist-bump. "Way to go, L-Dog. I can't wait for you to introduce me to all your hot teammates."

Laney returned the gesture with a horrified glare. "I will pretend like I don't know you.

You do know that, right? I will tell them all how gross and smelly you are."

"You'll have to. Because otherwise, they won't leave you alone trying to use you to get to me. I apologize for that in advance."

Laney rolled her eyes.

Jay laughed and stretched his aching shoulders. "No water makes it kinda tough to cook, huh? How about we go out for dinner? I'm feeling like we've got a lot to celebrate around here."

Levi and Laney exchanged grins. Eating out was expensive and not a luxury that any of them got to indulge in very often.

MIA COULD NEVER get enough of the seafood chowder at Tabbie's. Creamy and thick and teeming with shrimp, crab, clams and fish, it was served piping hot in fresh-baked sourdough bread bowls. With several "healthy options" on the menu, Tabbie's was also a place she and her mom could agree on. Charlotte liked the generous selection of Pacific Northwest microbrews, not to mention the fact that it was a popular hangout for Coasties.

"Great class tonight, huh?" Nora said as they waited for a booth.

Tabbie's catered to locals, but living on the Oregon coast, there was no escaping the tourists. And ever since Pacific Cove's participation in the DeBolt Crazy for a Coast Christmas competition last December, tourism here was on the rise.

Even though Pacific Cove hadn't won, it'd been awarded the Judge's Choice prize. The town had been featured in several media outlets, including the travel section of several newspapers and numerous popular online tourism sites. A national travel magazine had done a cover story. Tourists had responded. Then Tabbie's had gone on to win "best chowder" in *Northwest Cuisine* magazine a couple months later. In fact, business was booming all over town. The mayor, who headed up the ongoing crusade to put Pacific Cove on the map, was beyond thrilled.

"Yes," Charlotte gushed.

"No," Mia countered, glaring playfully at Charlotte. "Mom, why does Coby hate me?"

"Now, Mia, as an instructor you can tell who really has their chakra in it. And I have to say, you don't seem to be as focused as you could be."

"Mom, I am focused. I have to be focused so I don't fall over."

Charlotte laughed and eyed her doubtfully. "You did have your cell phone stuffed into your sports bra. Although I would have, too, if I was waiting on a call from that bundle of Coast Guard hotness."

"Jay!" Nora exclaimed.

"Yes, I was waiting for Jay to call me back but don't get your hopes up, Mom. He's—"

Charlotte nudged her, throwing a meaningful glance over Mia's shoulder.

Any hope Mia had that Jay hadn't heard that exchange was dashed when she turned to face him. His lips seemed to be quivering with laughter, and one brow nudged up onto his forehead in question. "Jay's what?" he asked. "What am I?"

"Here. You're here and…" She offered lamely, embarrassed yet irrationally happy to see him at the same time. Before she could formulate a reasonable response, Levi and a teenage girl walked up to join them. How nice. Had Levi managed to find a friend already?

Levi greeted her, "Hey, Dr. Frasier."

The girl reached out a hand. "You're the amazing Dr. Frasier? It's so awesome to finally meet you. I'm Laney. Thank you so much for fixing Coastie. We all love her so much. My brother has lost his mind over that dog. You should see him. He talks to her like she's a person and he has names for the noises she makes—"

Jay put a hand on the girl's shoulder. "This is our sister, Laney, who talks too much and often exaggerates. We're looking into some professional help for that. Laney, this is Dr. Frasier and her mom, Nora, and..."

He continued speaking but Mia quit listening to take in this new information. A sister, too? Jay hadn't mentioned that his sister was staying with him as well. Sweet, she thought, two teens staying with their big brother for a while. Although... It still struck her as odd that he hadn't mentioned them before now.

"Charlotte Graham," Charlotte's voice pulled her back into the conversation. "Delighted to meet you, Laney."

Easy small talk ensued until Lily, the owner of Tabbie's, came hustling over. Her eyes darted around their small crowd before settling on Nora. "Are you guys all together? Because one of the big tables in the back is open and I could seat you all there now."

"How lovely! That works for us," Nora exclaimed. "Does that work for you guys?"

Levi was nodding, but Mia thought it was nice how Jay looked at Laney for confirmation.

She chimed in with an enthusiastic, "Sure."

Lily led them through the restaurant to a large picnic-style table in the back room.

Somehow, Mia wound up sitting next to Jay. Levi sat across from him, Laney on the other side of Jay, with her mom across from Laney. Charlotte took the spot across from Mia, smiling like the Cheshire cat as her gaze bounced between Mia and Jay. Mia narrowed her eyes, warning her friend to behave.

The hostess brought menus and ice water as they settled in at the table.

"I got your message," Jay said. "I tried to call you back but I don't have your cell number. That is definitely news worthy of celebration."

"Isn't it? It might be a while before she lets us in there. Her daughter will be making a visit and they're going to clean up a bit first, but yes, definitely exciting news."

Laney said, "I'm excited to help with your cat rescue stuff. I love cats. I've always wanted a cat." She slid a hopeful gaze toward Jay.

He'd recruited his brother and sister to help with Lucky Cats? Warmth and appreciation mingled inside her.

Jay smiled. "We're out celebrating, too." He gestured at his sister. "Laney has a promising volleyball career at Pacific Cove High School next year."

"Yeah, that and we don't have any water," Levi chimed in.

"No water?"

"It's not a big deal. I've got a leaky pipe. I was fixing it but I needed a part and the hardware store is closed."

"I love a man who knows his plumbing," Nora chimed in.

Mia groaned inwardly as Charlotte nearly spit out her water. Levi was chatting with a waitress and Laney was on her phone so they didn't seem to notice. Jay grinned and gave her a wink. She felt herself melt into the bench. What was it about that wink? She quickly recovered.

"You guys are going to school at Pacific Cove next year?" Mia asked Levi, her brain now spinning with questions.

"Laney is," Levi explained. "I'm taking online classes."

Jay interrupted, "He'll start his junior year there in the fall."

"Maybe," Levi said. "They have an online program I could do for the rest of high school."

"Not maybe," Jay said, and began a discussion with Levi about school.

Mia quit listening. Obviously, her assumption that the kids were just visiting wasn't accurate. What was going on? She remembered Jay mentioning a mom that day at her house.

She thought back, trying to recall if he'd mentioned any other family. Nothing came to mind. Come to think of it, it seemed a little odd that Levi hadn't mentioned in the interview that he'd moved here to live with his brother. Didn't it? Where was their mom?

At the first break in conversation, she asked, "Is your mom moving here, too?"

Beside her, Jay went still.

Levi looked down, studying his menu.

Laney froze for a long second and then pointed at Nora's nails and asked where she got them done.

Charlotte watched the exchange and Mia knew she caught on to the awkward moment as well.

Jay cleared his throat and answered with a vague, "Um, no, she's not."

She'd have to be completely dense not to pick up on an off-limits question when she asked one. She felt bad about making them all uncomfortable even as her curiosity increased. She hoped that everything was okay with their family, even as she sensed that it wasn't.

The waitress showed up to take their order. After she departed, Mia leaned over to look at Laney. "Congratulations about the volleyball."

"Thank you!" Laney gushed. She went on

to describe her plans and her desire for a volleyball scholarship. She ended with, "I really want to go to college. And I mean going away to college and really having the university experience. Do you know what I mean?"

Mia assured her that she did. She'd been ecstatic to go away herself. Getting away from her father had been at the top of her list. "I'm sorry about the water. Are you going to be okay going to school tomorrow without water? You're welcome to come over and use our shower if you need to."

Laney perked up. "Really? Are you sure?"

"Yes, of course. We have three guest rooms. If you want to stay the night I can give you a lift to school in the morning."

"That would be beyond awesome, Dr. Frasier. Jay, is that okay? Elise said I could stay there, but her entire family has the stomach flu."

"Um, I don't know… It feels like a lot to ask—"

"Nonsense!" Nora piped up. "We'd love to have her."

"Pleeeaaase, Jay," Laney pleaded. "I can't go to school without water."

Mia wanted to laugh. Only a teenage girl could make a lack of water sound like a life-and-death situation.

"Okay, then," Jay acquiesced. Mia wondered if she was imagining the flatness to his tone and tightness around his jaw. Surely he didn't have a problem with her helping out his sister, did he?

AFTER DINNER, JAY drove Laney home to get supplies to stay the night and then brought her to the house. While Nora gave Laney a tour, Mia took the opportunity to talk to Jay.

"You're okay with her staying here?"

He nodded, but she could hear that same tension in his voice as he answered, "Yeah, sure. Thank you for offering."

"But… I probably should have asked you first before I suggested it."

He paused as if considering the question. "No, it's fine. I'm… I hate to put you out."

"But you didn't ask. I volunteered."

One side of his mouth pushed up like he was trying to smile but couldn't quite get there. "Help is kind of a tricky thing. I'm not good at accepting it. I'm used to taking care of things myself. My siblings and I are a very close-knit unit."

This was odd. He seemed uncomfortable with the conversation, with any discussion that revolved around his family. They were "close-knit" yet he hadn't mentioned them?

Mia thought about that. Curiosity mingled with concern and she had to bite her cheek to keep from asking more questions.

"Jay!" Laney said as they came back inside from their tour of the deck. "They have a hot tub."

Jay smiled. "Very cool, Lanes. Levi is going to pick you up and take you to school on his way to work, okay? Call or text if you need anything."

"Sounds good. Thanks, Jay." She hugged her brother goodbye.

Mia showed Laney to one of the guest rooms upstairs.

"Wow," Laney said as she walked over to the window and looked out at the view. She circled around the room and then sat on the fluffy sea-green comforter adorning the bed. Mia headed into the bathroom to make sure it was stocked with the essentials. Laney followed and Mia pointed out where the towels and other toiletries were stored.

"This bathtub! Holy cow!" There was a six-foot cast-iron claw-foot tub enclosed in a cave of pastel-colored tiles set in a mosaic pattern against a dove-gray background. Brightly colored fish, a mermaid, anemones and other sea creatures formed an under-the-ocean scene.

Mia laughed. "It's pretty, huh?"

"Pretty? It's gorgeous! Delilah would freak out."

"Delilah?"

Laney looked up. "Yeah, my little sister. She's four and thinks she's a mermaid."

Another sister? Mia was realizing how little she knew about Jay. "That's adorable. Feel free to soak as long as you'd like."

Laney turned questioning eyes on her. "Are you sure?"

"Yep. That's what it's here for."

"But… That wouldn't be wasting too much water?" And that's when Mia knew for sure something serious was going on with this family.

"No. I have plenty of water. I'm thrilled for the tub to get used."

"Thank you so much. This is totally gorgeous. It's like a fancy hotel. Or what I imagine a fancy hotel would look like. I've never stayed in any room this nice. I've never even had my own room, until now, with Jay."

"Really?"

Laney nodded. "I've always shared with at least one of my sisters. First Josie, then there were three of us once Delilah came along. After Jay left I thought that was kind of unfair, three girls having to share, but only two boys." She added a laugh. "Of course, I get it now that I'm older."

This brought the total to six Johnston siblings while the level of mystery surrounding this family heightened exponentially. Where were the younger ones? Mia now knew that they didn't all have the same last name, so maybe some of them lived with their dad? Curiosity swirled through her. Keeping her voice casual as she leaned a shoulder against the door frame she asked, "You have three brothers?"

Mia watched Laney's expression go from happy-dreamy to startled to shuttered in the space of a few seconds. "Um, yep. Another little brother, Dean. He's six. Three brothers and two sisters and me. Is there any certain time I need to be in or out of the bathroom?"

It took her a second to realize Laney was not only changing the subject, she was probably asking this question because she was likely used to a bathroom schedule. Mia's best friend for a year in middle school had been one of eight children. One bathroom and a house full of people meant finding enough time for everyone. What was the story here? As interested as she was, she didn't feel right quizzing a fifteen-year-old.

"Nope, there are two and a half bathrooms downstairs, too. This one is all yours."

"This will also be a first," she said. She added a bright smile, but Mia could see the trace of sadness in the child's expression. She so badly wanted to ask questions, help in some way, but sensed that further inquiries would only cause her to clam up.

Mia placed her hands on her hips and returned the smile. "Well, then, enjoy. And you're welcome to stay over anytime. If those brothers of yours are getting you down, come on over and we'll have a girls' night." She added a wink. "Let me know if you need anything else."

CHAPTER TEN

"IT SOUNDS LIKE an alien," Laney said.

"Or some kind of possessed creature," Levi offered.

Jay couldn't dispute either description. His skin tingled along his arms and across the back of his neck at the sounds coming from beneath the shed's shale rock foundation. It really was otherworldly.

Jay, Levi and Laney gaped at the ancient but sturdy outbuilding behind Minnie Mason's old but perfectly kept house. According to Minnie, the small rectangular structure had once housed chickens but was now used for storing her garden supplies. Its coat of yellow paint was fading to gray, giving it that worn patina people were paying big bucks for these days. She'd proudly informed them that the house had been in her family for 152 years, so he was pretty sure Minnie's shed had come by this state naturally. Her immaculate grounds, on the other hand, clearly took countless hours of hard work.

"How are we going to get it?" Laney asked.

Jay shone his flashlight into the darkened crevice again where the beam met a pair of startled greenish-yellow eyes. They were attached to a cat. Its mangy, buff-colored fur puffed out like a blowfish while it uttered low-pitched growls interspersed with bouts of spitting, hissing and mewling.

He lowered the flashlight. "Let's go with possessed alien. And I have absolutely no idea."

It was Saturday morning, and the Lucky Cats team had managed to catch two strays so far. Besides Jay, Levi, Laney, Mia and Nora, two other volunteers had shown up, Ty, a high school girl with blue hair and a cast on one arm, and Minnie, the woman who owned the shed with the creature currently cornered.

Mia had taken the first two rescues to the clinic. Nora and Ty were at a property across town scouting the possible location of a stray female with a reported five kittens. Jay, Levi and Laney were at Minnie's trying to catch this particular tomcat that Minnie insisted was a menace to the entire neighborhood, and her yard in particular.

"How's it going?" Minnie asked as she shuffled over from where she'd wandered off to pull an errant weed in one of her flower beds.

Mentally sharp and clearly spry, Minnie was about a hundred and three years old, Jay estimated. There was no way he could ask her to crawl under the shed. Unless... Maybe she had experience from the fur-trapping days.

"Do you have experience with this cat-trapping business, Minnie?"

"Nope. Just tired of the neighborhood cats doing their business in my flowers. Decided to be part of the solution. And while this one has pretty much moved in uninvited, I'm feeling kind of bad about sending him to kitty-cat heaven."

"Oh, don't worry," Levi piped up. "He won't be euthanized. We take the cats to the vet clinic to be spayed and neutered."

Minnie placed a hand on her hip and peered at Levi thoughtfully. "And then what?"

"Well, depending on how wild he is, he'll either be adopted or released..."

Minnie's wrinkles evolved into a scowl.

Too late Levi realized his mistake. "But I'm sure—"

"Released?" she barked out. "You mean to tell me I'm helping out with some kind of catch-and-release program here? You're gonna fix 'em up only to turn them loose into my flower beds again?"

"Sort of... I mean, the cats will be so much

healthier and better off and they won't be re-producing or spreading diseases—"

"What about my cosmos? You think they'll be better off?" She threw her hands up in a gesture of helpless frustration. "Go ahead and catch that thing, but I don't want to see him around here again." With that, she stalked off toward her rose garden.

"And then there were three," Laney joked.

"This is ridiculous," Jay said. "What's the worst that could happen?"

"Well," Laney said, handing him a pair of safety goggles, "I feel like getting your eyes scratched out would be the worst. But I wouldn't want to get bitten by that thing, either. Judging from its teeth it's part shark."

"I think it's more scared than anything else," Levi offered as he passed Jay a pair of Kevlar gloves.

Jay figured Levi was probably right. In spite of its bravado, he could see the cat had a tattered ear and a weepy eye. Sympathy tugged at him. He knew what it was like to fight and scrap for everything you had. Mia had said that farmers or ranchers would often adopt not-quite-tame cats to live in their barns or stables to help with rodent control. Even regular folk would often feed a stray living on their property. In other words, as long as they were healthy and neutered, they stood a chance for a better life. This guy deserved to have that chance.

He pointed. "Laney, put one trap at that end of the shed. Levi, you put the other one down there. When it bolts, it's only got two ways to get out. Right into one of the traps. Boom, and we've got it."

The kids put the cages into position. "Make sure the hole is firmly over the opening."

Levi braced his cage with a wooden block he found lying nearby while Laney held hers tight against the shed with her foot.

"Here we go…"

Levi held the flashlight while Jay crawled toward the cat. Not a comfortable endeavor, he thought, as he inched his big frame toward the corner where the cat was now curled into a hissing ball of fur. He wasn't exactly crazy about tight spaces, and this one smelled strongly of mold and that cat "business" Minnie had been complaining about.

Oddly enough, the closer he got to it the less noise the cat made. Maybe that's why he figured he had it made. Later he would chastise himself for getting overconfident. Because, unfortunately for him, it didn't bolt. It fought. And it fought like a, well, like a hellcat.

"OH MY GOD, Jay! What happened?" Mia showed up just in time for a groaning, bloodied and cat-less Jay to emerge from underneath the old shed.

"Cat fight," Levi supplied, although he could barely get the words out between guffaws. He pointed at his brother. "Boom, and you definitely got it, right, Jay? You look like..." He couldn't finish the thought because he erupted into a fresh fit of laughter.

Laney had more sympathy. But it was mostly for the cat. "He got away. Poor thing was terrified. And limping. His paw is messed up. It looks twisted."

"These ferals can be rather slippery, I'm afraid. But Jay, I'm more concerned with your, uh, wounds. Unfortunately, these cats can carry a lot of diseases as well."

Levi pointed at his brother. "Your face looks like the guy from that cheesy slasher movie we watched last night."

"Thanks, Levi. You look like his sister, the psycho ax murderer. How did it get away? We had both ends blocked."

"I'm not sure," Levi replied.

"I think there's a hole under this side of the building," Laney said. "I saw him come out from somewhere around there. He disappeared into those blackberry bushes." She pointed across Mrs. Mason's yard to the fence line that presumably marked the border of her property. "Jay, you're bleeding all over. You need to go to the hospital."

Levi snorted.

Jay glared at him. "How is it that our sister has all this compassion and you have none?"

Levi, still chuckling, shrugged helplessly. "I'm sorry, but if you could have seen yourself. And the cat… It was like a cartoon…" The rest of his words were swallowed by more laughter.

Laney let out a giggle and then slapped a hand over her mouth. "I'm sorry, Jay. But it is kind of funny."

Jay chuckled and Mia couldn't help but join in. There might be problems with their parents, but these guys shared a closeness that warmed Mia to the core. She'd never had this with her brother. They'd had little in common as kids, and even less now. Kyle was as obsessed with the Navy as their dad had been.

But she was still worried about Jay's scratches. "He's probably going to be too skittish to trap today. We'll have to try again a different day and hope that foot isn't broken. In the meantime, my mom just texted and said she and Ty have that mother cat and her kittens in sight. All they need to do is take apart a wood pile to get to them. Levi and Laney, I'm going to drop you guys off to help them while I take Mr. Horror-Film-Face here back to the clinic and get him fixed up."

They all piled into the van and approximately fifteen minutes later, after dropping Levi and Laney off, Mia was leading Jay into the clinic.

"You're not giving me a rabies shot, are you?" he joked. "I've heard those are brutal."

"We'll see how good of a patient you are and then decide."

She directed Jay into an exam room and had him sit up on the stainless steel table. She found herself eye to eye with him. He winced when she dabbed disinfectant on his neck.

"Sorry," she said. "But I want to make sure I get these really clean. They seem the worst on your neck."

"I'm not surprised. He used that area for traction. Like some kind of psycho-cat launching pad."

"A couple of these… Wow, I didn't know a cat could scratch this deep. What was your plan exactly?"

"My plan was for the cat to either come with me willingly or bolt out one of the ends of the shed and into one of the cages we had positioned there. Whereupon I would be your hero."

"But you're already my hero," she teased. "Saving my life, saving my mom and Captain Shear. Fostering Coastie, helping me with a cat hoarder and now just…helping. You were thinking this would top that?"

He shrugged. "I don't know, maybe. You are a vet and all. And a cat rescuer."

"I am impressed with your efforts. But since you're going to be volunteering, there are a couple things you should know. Cats are predators and they will fight."

"Ohh," he drawled, "is that what he was doing? That's where I went wrong, I thought we were having a kitty snuggle."

She laughed and placed a bandage on his cheek and two on his forehead. She used two big square gauze pads on his neck. "That ought to do it for now. There's blood seeping through your shirt, though. Can you take that off?"

The second he did she wished she hadn't asked. She knew he was in good shape. That was obvious when he was dressed. His profession demanded it, but yowza, he was ripped. Wide, sculpted shoulders, biceps of steel, and his abs looked like they'd been cast from concrete. His muscles made Coby's look like the second-string quarterback's from the losing team. And now she had to treat the scratches. How to do that without ogling him, she had no idea.

She opted to just put it out there. Point out the elephant in the room, so to speak. "Wow. You know, you really should think about working out sometime. All this subcutaneous fat is gonna kill you. You know what they say about a spare tire? Heart attack waiting to happen."

He leaned back like he'd been stung, looking surprised by her comments. She felt her cheeks grow warm with embarrassment. Would she ever learn to tame her nervous babbling habit?

His lips formed a half grin. "Thank you for the warning. I'll see what I can do."

He was teasing her. And that made it worse. Of course he knew how good he looked, and he obviously knew how it was affecting her.

She doused him with disinfectant.

"Ouch," he chuckled. "That stings. You were much more gentle with my face."

"Sorry," she mumbled. "But your face I can handle."

"What?"

"I said I was sorry I hurt you."

"Are you?" he asked.

"Yes. No. Honestly? I'm sorry I asked you to take your shirt off. Look, Jay, here's the thing, I find you very…"

"Sexy?" he supplied.

"Obviously," she shot back. "Who wouldn't? But that wasn't the word I was looking for. I was going to say attractive. But I shouldn't say that, right? Because who cares how you look? Not me, that's for sure. Doesn't even matter. I mean it matters right now because it's distracting. But the problem here is that I think you're…nice. And really…"

"I like you, too, Mia," he interrupted. His eyes were filled with amusement, but his voice was soft and low and full of heat. His lips curled up slowly. Her heart, already pounding out of control, seemed to be attempting an escape from her chest.

"Oh…okay. Well, that's…" She stopped and inhaled a breath but it didn't seem to help her nerves.

"Good?"

"No. The opposite of that, in fact. It's not good at all."

He reached out and wrapped the fingers of one hand around her wrist. His touch felt hot and she stared at the contact point, struck by how his long fingers took up so much space on her arm. He removed the cotton swab from her other hand, tossed it into the pile with the others. Entwining that hand in his, he pulled her closer until she was standing between his legs. He smelled so good, like citrus and leather and something else she hadn't yet been able to identify…

After a quick scan of her face, his eyes latched onto hers. "Really? 'Cause it feels kinda good."

He caressed her palm with his thumb, which somehow made her skin tingle all over. "Um, this isn't…"

His voice was soft and low; she felt the words as much as she heard them. "My life is very complicated, Mia."

"Because of your family situation?"

He squeezed his eyes shut, but not before Mia saw the flash of pain. When he opened them again she felt a hitch in her chest. There was so much raw emotion there—hurt, regret and a sadness that made her own heart ache. "I can't be what you need."

"How do you know what I need?" she managed.

His lips played with a sad smile. "As much as I'd love to find out, I'm not the man to give it to you, to give you anything."

"Jay, I'm not asking you for anything. I don't think this—"

His gaze lowered to her lips. "This is such a bad idea," he whispered.

"I know. That's what I'm trying to tell you."

"We should do it anyway."

"Okay." She barely managed to breathe the word before his mouth covered hers. His lips were warm and soft and they fit against hers so perfectly. Sliding the fingers of one hand into her hair, he cupped the back of her head. She brought her hands up, feeling his hard muscles beneath her touch. His other hand slipped around her shoulders and urged her closer until she was brushing against the bare skin of his chest. She felt hot, but the contact somehow made her shiver.

She deepened the kiss. He moaned, low and deep in his chest, and after a time he pulled away slightly, just enough to look her over like he was memorizing her face. He whispered her name and then kissed her again. And that's when something changed, clicked into place inside her. In that moment she knew that every bit of her wanted this man. Not his body. Well, she wanted that, too, but what she really wanted was to spend time with him, to ease some of the pain she could see dwelling inside him but that he took such great pains to hide. She wanted to know where it came from. She wanted to know everything about him even as a voice inside warned her that she'd never be privy to that information.

Not to mention that she had plenty of her own reasons to keep her distance.

She hated what she had to do.

JAY HAD CONVINCED himself it would be okay to kiss her. Just one kiss—or two. Because he could do that. He'd always been able to do that, kiss and keep it casual. Usually, he could even stay friends with the women he dated after breaking it off. It was never difficult to convince them that it was his issue, his hang-up, or his inability to commit due to the mobile nature of his job or whatever, and not theirs.

But as soon as his lips met Mia's, sooner than that really, the moment he'd put his arms around her, he'd known. Maybe even before that. Aubrey was right; this woman could unravel the image he'd worked so hard to build. The one where he didn't need anyone. He couldn't need anyone. There wasn't enough of him to care about, or to take care of, anyone else. He was already spread too thin as it was.

He wasn't sure he had the power to resist her, though. And he certainly couldn't stand the idea of breaking her heart. That's why he had to stop this before it went any further.

Pulling away, he rested his forehead against hers while he caught his breath. It would be a while before his heart stopped racing, and he was pretty sure it would be forever before he could think about her, about this moment, and not have it take off racing again.

"Wow," she whispered.

"I know," he said, lifting his head to look at her. He trailed a finger across the scar still showing above her temple from the accident. Then he slowly lowered his hands. "I'm sorry. You told me this was a bad idea."

"Actually, you're the one who said that. But you were right."

"I—" He was getting ready to give her his spiel when her words sank in. "I was?"

"Yes. I really like you, Jay. I do. And even though I'd love to see where this could go, I know that ultimately it could never go anywhere, not where I'd like for it to possibly go."

This wasn't the way he'd expected this conversation to go. He'd planned on letting her down easy and now she was the one giving him the speech?

"Why not?"

"I can't date you."

When she didn't explain, he asked, "Are you going to tell me why?"

"Because…" She inhaled a breath and then

blew it out. "Because you're in the Coast Guard. I don't date guys in the military."

"You…what?" He barked out a laugh because surely she was joking? *This* was her reason? His profession? "But your mom said your dad was in the military, and I believe your brother is currently serving as well?"

"Yes, and that's exactly why. I know the lifestyle very well. It's not conducive to steady, long-term relationships. Not the kind I want, anyway. And at this point in my life, that's what I'm looking for. Or at least I'd like to know the potential is there before I get involved with someone."

"Your parents were married for thirty-six years, Mia. It sounds like it worked pretty well for them." Why was he arguing with her when she was giving him the perfect out? Because her reason made no sense, that's why. He was the one with the perfectly sane explanation for why they couldn't get involved. If it wasn't for his family situation, his responsibilities, he would prove her wrong. In a heartbeat, she would be changing her tune. The way she'd responded to his kiss gave him all the confidence he needed.

"It did." She sighed. "But not for me. I grew up a military brat and I hated it. I more than hated it. It…damaged me." She added a sad smile. "Look, I know you're not proposing marriage here or anything, but I promised myself a long time ago that I would have a stable life one day. Now I have it, I've worked really hard to get it, and this is what I want for myself. And for my mom, my dogs and cats, and my kids, when I have them. I have responsibilities and commitments here in Pacific Cove that are set in stone. Like I said, I really like you, but it would be better if we just let this—" she gestured between them "—go."

It took every ounce of his willpower not to pull her back to him and kiss some sense into her. Did she not realize that you couldn't just let this kind of attraction go? This wasn't like some butterfly you caught in your hand. That you could appreciate and admire and enjoy, and then let go. It didn't work like that. Not when this…force of nature existed between two people.

A noise sounded from somewhere in the building. "Anyone here? Jay? Dr. Frasier? Where are you guys?"

Unless, he realized as Laney's voice interrupted both their conversation and his thoughts, one of the people had six mouths to feed, a college education to pay for, a custody battle to fight, and now two teenagers to somehow keep alive, in school and off drugs. All the while hoping that no one, him included, ended up scarred for life. In that case, it was probably a good idea to let it go. And yet the idea of doing the sensible thing was twisting his insides into knots.

Keeping an even tone he asked, "You think we should let it go, huh? Pretend this didn't happen?"

Her lips parted as if considering the statement. She whispered, "I believe that would be best."

"Okay," he finally said. "We'll let it go."

"Good." She sounded relieved, but her blue eyes were wide and cloudy, and Jay thought he saw a flicker of disappointment before she busied herself by putting the cap back on the disinfectant bottle. He was glad; at least there was some regret on her part, too. She was right. Even if their reasons were different, the result had to be the same. And yet her logic irritated him. On that at least he could set her straight.

As she turned to go, he reached out and slipped his fingers around her wrist. She swiveled toward him, silently asking what he was doing.

"No," he countered softly. "It's not good at

all. I will let it go. But this conversation—"
He released her wrist. "Is to be continued."

She looked baffled. "What is that supposed
to—"

"Look!" A smiling Laney appeared in the
doorway proudly hoisting a cat carrier in one
hand. "We've got kittens. Can we have a kitten, Jay?"

CHAPTER ELEVEN

THE NEXT MORNING Mia stared at the full dish of cat food on her porch and let the disappointment seep into her. No cats. No Jay. She never should have let him kiss her. Or kissed him back. What had she been thinking? Because now she had a taste of what she couldn't have and it was pure torture. She'd finally found a guy she really thought she could like and he was off-limits. And apparently, not only according to her own criteria, but to his as well. That bothered her, too. Even though she knew it wasn't fair for her to care. He had every right *not* to want to be with her just like she *didn't* want to be with him.

The best thing to do would be to maintain some distance. But somehow, along with her growing attraction for the guy, avoiding him was now officially impossible. His little brother was working for her, and Levi was doing a better job than she could have even imagined. He and Dr. Anthony were hitting it off as well. Levi was now doing additional work for him, and taking care of their yard, house and cats during Ted's trips to Portland.

She would just have to find a way to keep things friendly, platonic. Which shouldn't be all that difficult seeing as how he intended to do the same. Except for that comment about continuing their conversation. After what happened yesterday, that made her heart race.

If only this distracting chemistry between them didn't exist, she knew they could be great friends. The problem was, it was there. And she liked him. A lot. She wished they could be more than friends. But they couldn't. So...

So here she was about to spend the day with him again. She was converting a storage room at the clinic into a "cat room" for Lucky Cats. Jay and the kids had volunteered to help. She couldn't very well turn down his help. Uh-huh.

Mia stood, picked up the dish and carried it inside the house.

"Still no sign of Jane or Edward?" her mom asked from where she stood in front of the sink washing kale for their breakfast smoothies.

"I know. Me, too."

"What? Mia...?"

Mia slowly became aware that Nora was giving her an odd look.

"I'm sorry, Mom. What?"

"Are you okay, honey?"

"Yep. Fine."

Nora looked unconvinced as she turned on the blender. Mia covered the dish and put it in the fridge. She'd try again later.

"You know what else is weird?" Mia said when the blender stopped rumbling.

"I don't know the first weird thing, but I'll bite. What's weird?"

"In the last few weeks, we've logged calls from people reporting stray cats hanging around. In the last couple days, Charlotte and I have been calling back to get details to set up traps. Now some of the callers are saying that the cats are gone or they haven't seen them for a while."

"Hmm." Her mom poured smoothie from the blender into two glasses, placed a paper straw in one, and handed it over. "That is weird."

Mia took a sip, then held the glass up for examination. "Mom, this is delicious."

Nora chuckled. "Don't sound so surprised. Coyote?"

"Sorry, but sometimes your concoctions taste better than others. I thought about that.

But it seems unlikely to me that a coyote would get both Jane and Edward at the same time, doesn't it? And what about all these other cats?"

"Sounds like you've got a mystery on your hands here. Too bad you couldn't get the surveillance video like they do on those TV crime shows, huh?"

THERE HAD BEEN very few times in Jay's adult life when he'd seriously misjudged a situation. Being forced to take on so much responsibility at such a young age meant that he'd made plenty of mistakes early on. The role he'd taken on within his family ensured that he learned from them—he couldn't afford not to. But he could now count the act of kissing Mia Frasier among the worst of his missteps. Because now he couldn't stop thinking about her, fantasizing about ways he could let her into his life, all of them impossible. And underlying it all was her ridiculous assertion about military men.

In his experience, the old adage held true about women loving a man in uniform. In fact, he was used to it being an advantage where women were concerned. Why wouldn't it be? Military men were brave, loyal, skilled, smart, fit. At least... He was. Or he liked to think he was. He tried hard to be all of those things. For some reason, the fact that he wasn't relationship material kept shifting to the back burner in his thoughts. Because he could be, if he tried, and that's what mattered here. Except, it didn't really.

He knew he should just let it go. He couldn't have her, and yet a part of him wanted to pursue her. Not only to prove her wrong in general, he realized, but to make her see that just because *he* was in the military that did not exclude him from being what she wanted—

"Earth to Jay," Laney bellowed from beside him on the passenger seat.

"Whoa." He glanced her way. "Why are you yelling at me, Lanes?"

"Because I've said your name like five times and you haven't responded."

"Really? Sorry, kiddo. What's up?"

"I need to have my registration form in by Friday for volleyball camp."

"I remember and I think I have everything ready to go. Josie emailed the form this morning with her signature on it, I have a copy of your last physical, and I already made out the check." Josie had been signing the kids' parental consent forms for so long no one ever questioned it.

She'd also called to let him know that their

mom and Neil were back in town. Instead of the dramatic scene they'd anticipated, Neil had immediately retained an attorney. This was even better than they'd anticipated, Josie informed him, because it meant they'd be in court sooner. Jay wished he shared Josie's confidence. He still couldn't quite bring himself to believe that this was going to work.

She flashed him a bright smile. "Thanks, Jay."

"Of course. How's it going at school?"

"Good," she chirped brightly.

"Any new friends?"

"Yeah, lucky for me we've been playing volleyball in PE for the last two weeks of school. I met a couple more girls from the team. And you already know Elise from my math class. I really like her."

"That's awesome, Lanes. Good for you." Jay was happy to hear it, but not surprised. Laney was such an engaging girl—intelligent, outgoing, kind and confident. He was sure her beauty and athletic ability didn't hurt, either. Laney was going to be fine. He glanced in the rearview mirror at the backseat where Levi sat with a pair of earbuds connected to his phone. Levi, on the other hand, was causing him concern. He needed to get out and meet some people, kids his own age, not coworkers at the vet clinic or fur-covered buddies with four legs.

Out of the corner of his eye, he saw Laney brush her palms against the knees of her blue jeans. She glanced his way for a moment before staring ahead again. She did it again, but this time, she inhaled a deep breath and asked, "Have you talked to Josie? Is there any news about the custody thing?"

Clearly, she was nervous. It pained him to see it. He wanted to ease her mind, to shelter her from as much of this as he could. "I spoke to her this morning. It's all going fine." He hoped he sounded more confident than he felt.

"Fine?" she repeated. "What does that mean? What's going on? What's the status?"

"Not much to report yet," he lied. "These things take time, Laney. Besides, it's not anything you need to be worrying about."

"When do we go to court? When do Levi and I get to testify? I asked Josie and she said to ask you."

"You're not."

Her voice went up several octaves and decibels. "What do you mean? Why?"

"Because you're a kid, Laney. I don't want you exposed to this kind of thing."

"Wait a minute," Levi chimed in from the backseat. Jay hadn't thought he was listening. "You're not letting us testify? Does Josie agree with you?"

"Yes," he lied again. Feeling guilty, he clarified, "Now she does."

The fact was, he and Josie had argued this point. Josie thought they should consider it. Testimony from Levi and Laney, she argued, would be compelling enough to help their case. Jay agreed that it would be compelling all right, but not enough to make them go through the trauma. He'd been there. After he and Josie had been forced to return to Oregon there had been a hearing. The attorneys had been cold, uncaring and vicious. They didn't care that you were just a kid trying to survive in a home with an incompetent parent. They made you look like you were selfish and lacking compassion. He wouldn't allow his little brother and sister to go through what he and Josie had. Josie had finally, reluctantly, conceded that she would take the matter of them testifying off the table. For now. Jay hoped he'd find a way around the option.

Laney was glaring openly at him. Levi seemed to be waiting for more information. Jay didn't have time to follow up because he pulled the car into the lot of the vet clinic. He went with a simple, "I don't want you guys thinking about it and worrying about it. Just leave everything to me and Josie, okay? It will work out."

Were things going to be weird between him and Mia now? If he was smart, he would do whatever it took to ensure they weren't. He needed to accept the fact that a relationship with her was impractical if not impossible. Then again, he realized as he climbed out of his car and spotted Mia packing a box that he hadn't added "smart about women" to his list of attributes.

MIA WAS FEELING GOOD. She'd been afraid things were going to be strange between her and Jay. But as the day wore on she thought maybe he'd reconsidered his assertion that their conversation wasn't over. What did that even mean? she wondered again. They'd established that there was an attraction between them, yet they both had reasons why a relationship wouldn't work. He hadn't said what his reasons were, but it didn't matter because they were on the same page. And that was a good thing, she kept telling herself, even as the memory of that kiss played over and over in her mind.

In a couple hours, they'd cleared the storage room of boxes and given it a thorough cleaning. Dr. Anthony had offered to let them use a portion of his garage for storage. While she and Levi took a second load of boxes there, Jay and Nora started assembling a large kitty play structure. Laney went to work setting up litter boxes, putting together toys and assembling nylon play cubes.

They were busy adding the finishing touches on the kitty condo when she and Levi returned. Laney, her tasks completed, walked over to admire the fuzzy newborns they'd brought in the day before. She reached a gentle hand to the mama kitty along with some words of comfort. Considering what she'd already learned about Jay and Levi, Mia wasn't surprised to see that Laney was good with the cats. She was, however, concerned about Laney. She seemed a little off, like she was trying a little too hard. Mia recognized insecurity masked with bravado because it had been her way of coping as a teenager as well.

"I love kittens. It was so sad to see them lying in the dirt under Mr. Jergen's porch."

She was certain the mother cat had belonged to someone in the past because of her friendly disposition. Nora, Ty, Levi and Laney hadn't had any trouble collecting the cat and her kittens. They'd had to disassemble Mr. Jergen's wood pile to get to them, but he'd been a good sport about it. The kids had managed to get the pile restacked according to his specifications. Mia was proud of her little Lucky Cats team. After the kittens were weaned, wormed and caught up on their shots, they could be put up for adoption. What she really needed was someone to spend time with the kittens during this period to make sure they were used to human contact. Which gave her an idea.

"Hey, Laney, how would you feel about a part-time job at Lucky Cats?"

"What kind of job?"

"I need someone to manage this cat room, emptying litter boxes, feeding, watering, and playing with the cats. The more people-friendly and cuddly the kittens are, the more apt people are to adopt them. If you could round up some volunteers, like kids from school or whoever, and schedule some time for them to spend with the cats..."

She continued to explain, but Laney was already agreeing before she even had a chance to finish. "I would love it! School is out in a couple days and I'll have even more spare time. I know my friend Elise will do it. And probably Brianna and a couple girls from the volleyball team."

"Perfect."

Charlotte stepped inside the room to announce that she'd ordered lunch to be delivered. The weather was lovely, with patches of blue sky poking through scattered clouds. She suggested they go across the street to the city park to eat. It was a popular gathering place in Pacific Cove and several groups of people were scattered around. Picnic tables dotted the grassy space. A family had taken up residence at one and two little girls were playing a game of tag nearby. A flock of ducks and geese glided in the water near the shore of the pond. A group of teenagers were tossing a football.

"Hey, I've got a sack of lettuce and greens in my car," Nora said. "Levi, will you run back and get it? Inside the cooler on the backseat."

"Sure."

The park was set on the edge of a small lake and home to a variety of waterfowl. Nora often scored left-over produce from the health food store and came here to feed the birds. She handed over her keys and Levi jogged across the street to retrieve the goodies. Laney and Jay headed toward the water while Charlotte and Nora settled at a table in the shade of a large maple tree.

George and Coastie wandered off toward the shore behind a line of flower bushes. Mia followed. Coastie brought her a stick and laid it on her shoes. She picked it up and tossed it near the water's edge for her to fetch. George pawed at the ground, digging for who-knows-what. She was certain that bloodhound nose of his could find a single bacon bit in a haystack. When his head came up, his jaws held a mud-covered, unidentifiable chunk of crud that looked suspiciously like a bird carcass.

In a firm tone, she said, "Leave it." Then added a quiet, "Georgie, please don't eat that." He dropped it. "Good boy!" she cried, giving her hope that he'd eventually abandon this tendency to ingest anything that would fit inside his mouth.

"Hey."

She turned to find Jay standing behind her. "Hi. Thanks for all your help this weekend."

"No problem. Thanks for offering Laney a job. You didn't have to do that."

"I know. But I realized I need someone and she's great with the cats."

"She's thrilled. Getting paid to play with cats."

"And empty litter boxes and brush and groom unwilling cats and clean up hairballs. She'll earn it, I promise."

Flashing her a grin, he then bent and picked up a rock. With a flick of his wrist, he sent it skipping expertly across the pond's surface. Coastie ran up to him and let out an excited bark as if congratulating him on a job well done. She sat, staring up at him, tail wagging enthusiastically. Jay reached down and rubbed her ears.

He tossed the stick for her again and she took off. "I wanted to talk to you."

"Sure," Mia said, even as her pulse executed a nervous flutter.

"About what happened yesterday in your office?"

"Okay." She felt her cheeks go hot. Unfortunately, they were going to continue the discussion. Just as he'd promised.

"I feel like I owe you an explanation."

She shook her head. "About what?"

"About why I don't… Why I can't get involved with you."

She waved a casual hand through the air. In direct opposition to the burst of nervous chatter that followed: "No, you don't owe me anything. Don't worry about it. It doesn't matter, does it? Obviously, we're on the same page, so…" She shrugged and told herself to shut up.

"But I don't think we are on the same page and that's what has me bothered."

"What do you mean?"

"My reason doesn't have anything to do with your profession."

She grinned. "Why would it? Veterinarians make great partners."

"As do military personnel."

She scoffed. "Trust me. They don't."

"That is totally false."

"Really?" she asked wryly.

"Yes."

"Okay, why don't you tell me why you don't want to get involved with me?"

"My reason is…complicated. And complex. And really important."

She waited, studying him with narrowed eyes. When it appeared he wasn't going to explain, it dawned on her. "Wait a sec, are we having this conversation because you want me to know that *your* reason is *better* even though you won't tell me what it is?"

He opened his mouth to speak, closed it and then shifted his feet. "It sounds bad when you say it like that, but yes."

"Does it have to do with your family?"

"It has a lot to do with Levi and Laney, yes. And other…stuff."

"Stuff? That's it?"

"That's all I'm going to tell you."

"Mmm-hmm. Well, I'm not up for a game of twenty questions. My reason is good, too."

"No, it's not."

"Unbelievable…" she murmured, squeezing her temples. "Here's another reason why I don't like military guys—you always think you're right."

"No, I don't. I don't always think I'm right. But when I am right, I like for it to be acknowledged. And when I'm insulted because of my profession, I feel compelled to defend myself and my honor, and the honor of all my brothers and sisters in uniform."

She gaped at him. "Insulting your profession? That's what you think I'm doing?"

Tilting his head, he crossed his arms over his chest, clearly intimating that yes, he believed that was the case.

"My feelings don't have anything to do with your profession, Jay. Like I told you in the hospital after you rescued us, I am incredibly grateful for what you do. I'm grateful for you, for my brother and for every single person who chooses to serve in the military, even my dad in the sense that he was truly devoted to his country.

"I love the military. I support the military. I give to veterans organizations and send gift boxes to the men and women fighting overseas. Around Memorial Day, I offer a Pets for Vets program, where I give free veterinary care to the pets of servicemen and women. It's not that I don't like the military. It's that I don't want the military in my personal life. It dictated nearly every aspect of my life for eighteen years and I hated it. I didn't have a choice then. Now I do. I don't want that anymore. What's wrong with that?"

He looked startled by her response. She hoped she didn't sound too bitter. Clearly, he hadn't thought about this from her perspective. That was fine. People rarely did. She didn't talk about it much for that reason, for fear that it sounded selfish. But she didn't think it was, or mean for it to be. The hallmark of her childhood had been instability. For most of her life, she'd been working to overcome the ramifications of her upbringing. Where the military had seemed like the most important thing to her father, more important even than his wife, certainly more important than his daughter.

She wanted, needed, consistency; a house, a family, friends, animals, a "home" town and a life where she was free to make her own decisions. A relationship with a man in the military would make that life impossible. Was it selfish to want to be first on her eventual husband's list of priorities? She didn't think so. After all, the concept was included in a lot of traditional wedding vows. Right up there with sticking it out through "richer and poorer" and "sickness and health," you promised to put each other first, "forsaking all others." Mia couldn't wait to make, and keep, that vow someday.

He peered at her carefully and Mia knew she'd probably blown her chance at remaining friends with him. Some military men, like her father, did not abide anything but complete loyalty to their cause.

She sighed. "How about this, you go ahead and tell me your very important and vastly superior reason, and then we'll take a vote?"

He scowled. "Mia…"

"Exactly," she said, letting her irritation show, too. "You're not going to tell me, so let's just let it go. We both want, or don't want in this case, the same thing. I don't want you and you don't want me. Why don't we agree to disagree about the reason… Or disagree about agreeing or whatever…" She stopped talking and nibbled on her lip. He stepped closer and the look on his face sent a jolt of nervous energy rushing through her.

"But that's not true."

He was only inches away now, and she was glad they were shielded from the others by a row of blooming rhododendron bushes. Bees buzzed loudly as they flitted among the bright flowers. A hummingbird zipped by, but the buzz inside her head coupled with the beat of her heart seemed to drown it all out.

"What's not true?" she whispered, because for some reason her voice had become trapped inside her chest.

Dipping his head so that his lips were almost touching hers, he said, "I do want you. I want you so much that I'm almost ready to set my good sense and my really, really great reason aside and kiss you again. It's torture for me to be around you and not flirt with you and touch you and kiss you. And I think, deep down, that you feel the same way. Do you feel the same way?"

Mia couldn't have moved away if she'd wanted to. She did feel the same and she wanted him to do all of that. But they couldn't. He just didn't understand. He would never understand because he'd never lived her life. She had no interest in living it again, either, not even for five minutes. Not even for this kind, thoughtful, funny, man-of-his-word closet animal lover, as tempting as he was.

Slowly, she shook her head even as she stared at his mouth, thinking about how his kiss made her feel desired. How his arms around her made her feel safe and special and… And how miserable her military-dominated childhood had been.

"No," she somehow managed to squeak out the word. "Uh-uh. Nope. It doesn't matter how I feel or how you feel. We can't do this. So stop it."

His lips brushed her cheek just below her ear. "Stop what?" he asked softly.

Breath officially stolen and her senses completely rattled, she took a wobbly step back. Struggling for words, she gestured between them. "Stop getting into my comfort zone and trying to make me admit something that will make *you* feel better. Co-volunteers or maybe, possibly, if you'll keep your distance, friends. That's all we can be. Let's just forget about the reasons, accept the facts and deal with it the best we can."

The bushes shook as a football parted the branches. It thudded on the ground next to them and managed to do what she couldn't. Coastie let out a woof. George went over to inspect it, his uncharacteristic speed leading her to believe that he hoped giant cookies were now falling from the sky. Mia stepped away.

Jay bent and picked up the ball. "Deal with it?"

"Yes. Get over it. Get over me, Jay. You

can't have me." Mia pointed in the direction the ball had come from. "We should get back. Lunch is probably here by now."

CHAPTER TWELVE

JAY HAD NO idea what exactly possessed him to start searching for Duke. Duke—that's what he'd been calling the cat who had eluded capture and used him as a human scratching post in the process. Minnie reported seeing him several times since that fateful Saturday. She'd given Jay permission to stake out her shed and otherwise come and go on her property as he pleased. He'd been back several times now to see if he could find the cat.

But it was as if the cat knew Jay was looking for him. However, this time, he was back with a plan—a plan and a box trap. He retrieved a can of cat food from his pack along with a small stainless steel bowl. Coastie scouted the area while he deposited the food into the bowl, slid it into the trap, and arranged it near one of the openings beneath the shed. This time, he wasn't going to try to force him into a cage. He wanted the cat to enter the trap on his own terms. With a little help from Tasty-Vittles cat food.

He chose a spot in the shade of one of Minnie's oversize hydrangea bushes a few hundred feet away from the shed. He removed a pair of binoculars, a fat bone-shaped treat and a frosted marionberry scone, the latter two items he'd purchased from Bakery-by-the-Sea. Clever of June, he thought, to bake treats for canine customers in addition to those for their humans. Tourists loved to bring their dogs to the beach. Most of the shops in Pacific Cove were dog-friendly and many kept bowls of water outside their doors on the sidewalk for thirsty canine tourists.

He gave the treat to Coastie. She sniffed it in that ladylike manner that brought a smile to his lips and more joy to his soul than he cared to admit. Lying down next to him, she began nibbling on the edge. Mia had removed the dog's stitches and she seemed otherwise recovered. It was probably time to find her a home. He ignored the jab to his heart as he thought about Coastie no longer being a part of his life. He didn't want to think about it right now. He bit into his scone, immediately wished he'd bought two and settled in to wait. Why, he wondered, did people like Aubrey and Nora eat sawdust blobs when they could have a scone like this? On that, at least, he and Mia agreed. Mia.

The woman was so frustrating. He'd almost kissed her again. She'd wanted him, too, he could tell. Instead, she'd backed off and told him to "deal with it." Ha. He could deal with it fine if she would admit that… That what? The realization hit him like a ton of bricks; he was the one being ridiculous here, selfish and immature. What good would it do if she admitted anything? Other than make them both feel worse. He rubbed a hand over his chest where this ache had formed, flaring up whenever he thought about Mia, about the impossible circumstances keeping him from pursuing a relationship with her.

Drawing out the inevitable was pointless; he needed to let this go. It wasn't a pleasant realization. Letting it go would mean letting her go for real. That's what hurt. Mia was right; he did need to get over her. For the first time in a really long time, he let himself feel the tiniest bit of resentment for the life he'd felt he had to lead. He was used to putting his own needs aside and focusing on the people whose lives depended on him doing that very thing.

Jay knew he was in for a struggle. Never, not in all the years that he'd been supporting his family, could he ever remember wanting anything for himself as badly as he wanted Mia. That's why he was going to have to stay away from her.

As THE TWO-WEEK mark approached without any direct word from Jay, Mia told herself it was better like this. This is what she wanted. Yeah, right. But she'd basically told him as much. Although she certainly hadn't meant to imply that she didn't want him around at all! As the days wore on, her emotions vacillated among relief, anger, disappointment, sadness and pretty much everything in between. Interspersed with this wild ride were fantasies about her and Jay somehow making a go of a relationship. Then the Coast Guard would pop into her head, along with the mysterious "reason" he had for not being able to commit to anyone. Round and round and, in a word, she was making herself crazy.

When he hadn't shown up the next Saturday for the Lucky Cats work party, she nearly folded and sent him a text. The only thing that prevented it was Laney's telling her he was on duty. That word *duty* conveniently reminding her of what she sought to avoid and strengthening her resolve.

In spite of how things had unfolded between them, she didn't let that affect her relationship with Levi and Laney. She was grateful that Jay didn't, either.

In addition to his responsibilities in the kennel, Levi had become her right-hand man.

With Ted out of the office so much, she'd begun to depend on him for myriad tasks. Ted, in turn, was relying on him as well. Mia knew how highly this spoke of Levi, as Ted was a perfectionist who could be difficult to please. Levi's maturity, intelligence, sense of responsibility and conscientiousness continually astounded her. It was easy to forget he was only sixteen years old.

Mia was rapidly becoming attached to both kids, although Laney's behavior was becoming increasingly troubling. She seemed to be reveling in her first summer in Pacific Cove, but her moods ran the gamut. Some days she chattered nonstop while others she seemed downright blue. Teenage girls could be moody, but this felt different. Mia was careful not to ask too many questions. And yet she sensed that she'd never really understand any of them, Jay included, unless she got the full story. It was frustrating, to say the least, wanting to help but feeling like her hands were tied.

Laney had begun to confide in her somewhat, sharing details about her hopes, dreams and social life. She talked about the volleyball camp she was attending while Mia filed away tidbits about the friends she was making and where she was spending her free time.

She asked a million questions of Mia, about her life, college (Laney really wanted to go), travels, cats, cooking and where she got her hair done.

"I've never had my hair done," Laney told Mia one day after complimenting her after she'd come into work with a trim.

"What do you mean?" Mia asked, surveying Laney's long golden locks. Laney had beautiful, thick, neatly trimmed hair.

"Josie always cuts it for me. I've never been to like an actual hair salon, you know what I mean?"

Huh. It wasn't the first clue Mia had received about the state of the family's finances. Levi always brought a lunch to work. Several times Laney's friends had come to play with the cats carting fancy iced drinks from the coffee shop. Laney never had one. Their clothes were always clean and neat, but she'd noticed the kids wearing the same items again and again. At first, she'd written this off to the fact that they'd recently moved, but lately she'd wondered. Levi's backpack looked like the cats had used it as a scratching post.

A few days later they were cleaning the cat room when Laney asked about things to do in Pacific Cove. "Is it really legal to have a bonfire on the beach?"

"Yep."

"Wow. That's what Flame said. But I was like, no way! So, what, you can just like light a huge fire in the sand?"

"Well, there are some rules about making sure it gets put out properly, but yes. Did you say Flame?"

Mia watched Laney's face light with that dreamy teenage girl smile and thought, *uh-oh*.

"Yeah, Flame. It's a nickname. I guess he really likes fire or whatever. He's a guy who's been hanging around and asking me out and stuff."

Mia desperately wanted to ask what "stuff" meant, but went with, "Does he go to Pacific Cove High?"

"Um, no. Well, he used to. He might be starting there again in the fall." Laney's eyes bounced around the room for a moment. Mia appreciated how she always made sure everything was in order before she left for the day. "You can meet him if you want. He's picking me up in fifteen minutes." She poured fresh litter into a cat box. "He has this awesome pickup. It's really high off the ground. A bunch of us go out on the beach and we go four-wheeling. It's so fun."

Mia fought hard not to respond, to lecture, to ask if Jay knew she was seeing this guy.

How old was he? Was Laney allowed to date already? Thank goodness for Charlotte, she thought. Charlotte had been born and raised in Pacific Cove. She'd know about this kid, and if she didn't she would find out.

"I'd love to meet him."

JAY DECIDED TO drive by Mia's house on his way home from the base. He needed to take some measurements for that cabinet...

Who was he kidding? He wanted to see her. He hadn't in two weeks and three days, to be exact. He couldn't stand it. A glimpse would do, he told himself. That would be enough to ease the achy knot now lodged in his chest. Instead of getting better it was getting worse. A lot worse.

Even though he'd been busy—working and making sure Levi and Laney were adjusting to their new lives, tending to the Coast Guard volunteer outreach, puttering away on the house, spending time with Coastie, trying to catch a rogue cat—Mia always seemed to be lingering in his thoughts.

School was done for the year so Laney was working out, playing on the beach and hanging out with friends. She'd just finished a week of volleyball camp and was now practicing with a beach volleyball team. She was also taking her new role at Lucky Cats very seriously, devoting at least a few hours there every day. She loved having some spending money, even though Jay had noticed that, like Levi, she seemed to be saving most of it.

Levi was working more hours at the clinic. He was also taking care of Dr. Anthony's cats and yard, and running miscellaneous errands for him. Jay supposed after the years of watching him and Josie scrimp and save, the habit had worn off on them.

As he rounded the corner near Mia's house, he saw her in the yard by the bushes that lined her property on one side. Without thinking twice, he pulled his car over. She looked beautiful with her black silky hair up in a ponytail. She held an object in her hands and turned in his direction as he got out of the car. She smiled. He loved her smile, especially when it was aimed at him. He felt himself relax, conscious of how much his anxiety level was already receding, the chest knot loosening.

"Hey, stranger," she said. "I've missed you."

"Hi," he said, trying not to read too much into her words, even as they pushed his pulse into overdrive. "You have, huh?"

"Yeah," she teased, "trying to round up stray cats isn't the same without your mad skills. Looks like you're all healed, though."

"Mostly." He grinned and touched the remnants of the scratches on his neck. Missing his clumsy cat-herding skills was not what he was hoping for, but it was better than nothing. "What are you doing? Is that a video camera?"

She followed his gaze down to the object in her hands. "No. It's one of those motion-activated ones that takes still shots."

"You're installing security?"

"Um… Not exactly."

"Someone is stealing your newspaper and you want to catch them red-handed?"

She laughed and he immediately wanted to hear more of the same. Unbelievable, how much he'd missed her.

"Sort of. It's more like I want to catch someone in the act. But not really."

He tipped his head in question. "Now I'm officially lost."

She explained about the stray cat situation, how she'd rounded up a lot of the cats but knew there were still many more to get. "I was feeding these stray cats—two were very regular. I was really attached to them and hoping to bring them in with Lucky Cats. But they disappeared. Some nearby strays seem to be disappearing, too."

"What do you mean they disappeared?"

"I mean, about a month ago, they stopped showing up for breakfast."

"You said they were strays. Isn't that what strays do? Go astray?"

She rolled her eyes. "Not when there's a guaranteed meal."

"Maybe someone adopted them?"

"You know, I've already had this conversation with my mom. And all the things you are thinking are possibilities. But none of them really make sense. I'm most worried about coyotes. Or even a cougar."

"Huh. But…" He paused to choose the right words. "I don't mean to sound insensitive here, but if some kind of predator did get them, then what good is a camera going to do now?"

She grinned. "That's not insensitive. That's a good question. I've kept putting food out and now, finally, there's a couple new cats coming in. If there is some kind of predator hanging around out here I want to know. But now, by feeding them I'm afraid I'm making it easier for it to get the cats. But really, everyone's pets will be in danger—strays or not. Anyway, Mom made this joke about surveillance video and that got me thinking…" She trailed off with a one-shouldered shrug. "I want to see what's out here."

"Do you want some help?"

"Yes, please!" She practically shoved the camera at him. "I'm having a terrible time figuring out where to hang it to get the view right."

Jay held the camera in place while Mia studied various angles via her laptop and directed him "up, down, right, left." After several attempts, she finally decided on the one that placed the camera on the porch facing out and down with a view of the side yard and a portion of the street. She pointed at the bushes that bordered her yard. "This is usually where they would come from and disappear into."

Her house was the last in a row that fronted the beach and on this side, the ground sloped upward. Traveling along the beach you would eventually arrive at his house, but the ground between the beach and the road was brush- and tree-covered and sparsely populated. It made sense that stray cats, and probably a variety of other wild animals, would utilize the area for refuge or for hunting grounds.

After some discussion and trying out different angles, Jay bolted the camera in place with a bracket that was included with the purchase. They tested it out and after a few more adjustments, Mia was finally satisfied.

She thanked him and began cleaning up

the packaging material from the camera. "So, what do you know about this kid Laney has been hanging around with?"

He glanced up from the instruction manual he'd been studying. "Who? Elise?"

"Um, no, not Elise. I'm talking about an eighteen-year-old pyromaniac with a giant tattoo of a sword and fire on his arm who goes by the name Flame."

"Flame?" He shook his head. "I don't know any Flame." He wasn't worried. If Laney hadn't mentioned him, then he wasn't important to her.

"On the day I met him he stared at his phone the entire time. Zero eye contact. In fact, his entire greeting consisted of 'dude, it's nice to meet you.' When I asked where he lived he said 'around.' Plus, Charlotte says the kid is bad news."

"How so?"

"He's been in trouble with the police, busted a few times."

"For what?"

"Vandalism, battery, trespassing. And this part is kind of gossipy, but I feel like I should tell you anyway…?" She trailed off with a question.

"What?"

"Rumor has it he got a girl pregnant."

"Rumor?"

"Charlotte knows a friend of his aunt's who lives over in Remington. That's where she got this information."

"I don't put much stock in gossip. Having been the object of more than my share for my entire life, I know that most of it is flatly untrue or blown out of proportion."

Mia gave a tentative nod. "That's probably true. I agree. And this might not be any of my business, but have you considered getting Laney on some birth control?"

He instantly felt defensive. "Birth control? She's fifteen."

"She looks like she's eighteen."

Jay sighed and leaned against the railing on the porch. The implication rankled him. He and Josie had both talked openly to the kids about being smart and making good choices. They had educated themselves about early symptoms that might indicate any inherited aspect of their mom's condition. Mia was right, it wasn't her business. And yet he knew she was only trying to look out for Laney. She didn't know anything about their history. But he didn't need someone telling him how to take care of his family. That's what he did.

"Look, Mia, I appreciate you trying to help, but Laney is a smart kid."

"Smart kids don't get pregnant?"

"Not ones in Laney's situation, no."

Tossing to one side the trash she'd collected, she then faced him and asked, "What exactly is Laney's situation? And Levi's? And yours? And from what Laney tells me there's six of you? Why are Levi and Laney living with you exactly? Do you guys have a father in your life? Where is your mom?"

MIA KNEW SHE'D gone too far. She could see him shutting down right before her eyes: jaw clenched, eyes averted, hands slipped into the back pockets of his jeans. Dang it. Things had been going so well. She hadn't seen him for two weeks and she didn't want to argue. Why had she brought this up? Because, she immediately answered, she cared about Laney and Levi. She didn't know how to be a part of their lives without having some understanding of their circumstances—or his either, for that matter.

With a tight smile, he said, "Please don't take this personally, but it's not a subject I want to talk about. It's not you. I just don't… Our situation is…unconventional. I know you're only trying to help, but you don't need to worry about it. Really, I've got it handled."

Mia knew she should shut up, but she'd

gone this far. If Jay couldn't see that Laney was heading for trouble, she needed to make him see it. "Are you sure?"

"What do you mean?"

"Are you sure you've got it handled? I don't mean to interfere and you're right, I'm only trying to help. It's obvious you guys don't want to talk about your family, about your mom especially, but if there's anything I can do, I want to do it, believe me. I'm worried about Laney and—"

"Yes," Jay interrupted, scrubbing a hand across his tense jaw. "I am sure I have it handled. Don't try to help us. We don't need help."

His words carried a bite and Mia waffled for a few seconds before speaking again. "But I care about you guys. I care about Levi and Laney. Something is bothering Laney. It's in my nature to try to help people. And I…" She trailed off as she stared up at his icy expression.

"Mia." His tone was gentler as he reiterated, "Laney is fine. We're fine, okay? I've got this handled. We don't need your help or anyone else's."

That stung. But she might have deserved it. He had warned her. She needed to be done with this conversation before she made a comment that really angered him.

"Okay." She held her hands out, palms down and out. "I'm sorry. I didn't mean to upset you. I will do my best to mind my own business. Thank you for giving me a hand with the camera. I really appreciate it." She turned to go inside the house, but he stopped her with a hand on her shoulder.

"Wait, Mia… Don't go, please. I'm sorry."

She faced him, wanting desperately to ask what could possibly be so bad that he couldn't share it with her? But the look on his face stopped her: pain, sincerity, regret. And she was struck with the thought that maybe he wanted to share but that it was too painful or…something. Maybe, she realized, he'd tell her when he was ready. But what was she supposed to do in the meantime? It was like walking across a minefield. And it was difficult not to intervene where Laney was concerned.

"I don't know what you want from me, Jay."

He made a fist, placed it over his chest and rubbed a small circle as he looked toward the ocean. "I don't know, either. I mean I do, but I can't…"

She waited.

After a moment, he faced her again and in a rush of words said, "I do know that I can't stop thinking about you. I am jealous of Levi and Laney because they see you and I don't. I almost called you yesterday to say that Coastie wasn't feeling well so I could bring her in for an appointment she doesn't even need. How messed up is that? I know I want to spend time with you, but I'm scared. I'm scared because I already like you. And the more I'm around you the more I like you. But I can't have a relationship, Mia. Not with anyone. I'm already maxed out—emotionally, financially, mentally and even physically lately. I'm not sleeping, and my appetite seems to have deserted me. Although the not-sleeping seems largely to be because I can't stop thinking about you. I lie awake half the night staring at the ceiling with your image in my head."

Mia stared back at him, both warmed and shocked by his confession, her heart pounding away in her chest like a jackhammer.

She didn't know what his issues were, but she knew they involved his family and it was obvious they were deep. She saw it in Levi and Laney, too. She wished she could make him understand that whatever it was, it wouldn't scare her. She had plenty of her own issues. What was killing her was the notion that she knew she could help but he wouldn't even allow her to. Regardless of her own rule, in spite of the danger of getting her heart broken, she realized she had to try. She already cared about them all too much not to try.

"Wow. Great speech. Apology accepted. Well, Mr. Tough Guy, I'll have you know I'm scared, too. I'm afraid of getting attached to you. Because in addition to whatever you have going on in your life, my issues include the fact that I know you'll leave eventually. I know you have less than two years until your assignment is up here. And I'm not going anywhere. I can't. I also recognize that the military demands more of you than I'd be willing to share. But you know what? Maybe we can do this. Maybe, since we're both determined not to get too close, we can. Spend time together, that is. You know, as friends or whatever."

He scoffed, his expression clearly conveying his doubt. "You think you could do that? Just be buddies or *whatever* with me?"

Rolling her eyes at his cocky response, she said wryly, "Um, yes. I'll have you know that you're actually not that great."

His lips twitched with laughter. "Really? I'm not great?"

"No, I'm sorry to disappoint you, Mr. Thinks-Very-Highly-of-Himself." She frowned and shook her head, feigning disappointment.

"All I have to do is remember your faults and I'll be fine."

He shook his head, but she was heartened by the smile playing on his lips. "What faults?"

She began ticking items off on her hand. "Not only are you out of shape and ugly and useless as a handyman, you're mean to animals and a terrible big brother."

He tipped his head back and laughed before meeting her gaze again. "When you put it like that, it's really nice of you to bother with me at all."

"I know." She shrugged a shoulder. "I do know that. I have a soft spot for the unfortunate and downtrodden. It's who I am. Plus, I love your brother and sister, I need your help with Lucky Cats, and I am your dog's doctor. Thus, I'm willing to overlook your huge stack of faults and give this a shot."

"Okay, but how am *I* supposed to do this when all I can think about is kissing you?"

"Um, duh. Think about my faults."

He quirked a brow. "Which are?"

She grinned. "Hmm. Aside from my overly philanthropic habits, my annoying tendency to chatter uncontrollably when I'm nervous and what Mom refers to as my 'out of control' sugar addiction? I'll guess you'll have to find out for yourself."

MIA SPENT A long time that night second-guessing this truce she and Jay had reached. She was half-tempted to do some research and find out what the Johnston-Merrell family "situation" was on her own. It was obvious their financial state was tight. She'd begun to suspect that Jay was probably supporting them all. Why would he need to do that? she wondered. What was the big mystery here? His mom was in prison, she was a spy, she was ill, she was in the witness protection program? Whatever it was, Mia couldn't think of a single reason why he felt he needed to keep it from her. But the fact was that he did feel that way. She could only hope that time and patience on her part would change that.

Even though he believed things were "fine" where Laney was concerned, Mia knew she was struggling. The girl was a stunningly good actress, but Mia could tell. She knew because she'd spent her childhood acting like everything was fine, too.

Then there was Levi who was so determined to do everything right. She wondered what would happen when his quest for perfection fell short. And it would. No one could be perfect all the time.

Not even Jay.

They all three needed her help and support.

She didn't believe by any means that she had all the answers, but she had some. She wanted to be a part of their lives and she knew Levi and Laney wanted to be a part of hers.

Although Jay's reaction did tell her something, she realized. It told her a lot, actually. No matter what he said, and in spite of what he probably believed, some part of Jay wanted her help, too. The notion sparked a kind of joy she hadn't felt in a long time. Maybe forever. All of which left her terrified, because how close could she let herself get to this family and still help them without breaking her own heart?

CHAPTER THIRTEEN

MIA AND GEORGE headed into the clinic early as had become their routine with Dr. Anthony away. She unlocked the side door and George loped inside, heading toward the kennels. He seemed to feel it was his duty to spend some time each morning visiting any canine guests who had stayed overnight. Mia followed. Her first order of the day was to shadow George, checking the animals over and administering any meds or care they may need.

She was surprised to find Dr. Anthony already making rounds. "Ted, I'm so glad you're back. I bet McKenzie is thrilled to be home."

He turned to face her and Mia was relieved to see the smile lighting his face. In fact, she was encouraged to see that he looked better than he had in months, content and, if not quite rested, then not entirely exhausted, either. His dark hair had been trimmed and he was sporting a new tie.

"Hey, Mia. It's great to be here. Yes, she and Sara both are. McKenzie is doing much better after this last round of therapy. We've got a short break before the next round starts."

"That's wonderful news. I'll call Sara and set up a time when I can stop by and see her."

"She would love that. They both would. Seems as if you have things handled around here. And Levi has been great taking care of the cats and the house. He's been watering all of Sara's plants without even being asked. It totally slipped both of our minds, but he did it anyway. She's ready to give him a medal."

She smiled. "He's that kind of kid. We powered through your absence, barely. I'm sure you noticed the new cat room?"

He chuckled. "Yeah, we should have anticipated that need, huh?"

"Probably."

"I have some good news in that regard. I found a place in Portland and they've offered to take some of the cats from Lucky Cats."

"Really?"

"Yes. It's a really special place. They're doing wonderful things there. I've arranged for thirty of the hoarded cats to be moved there."

"Thanks to Charlotte putting the word out in the Pacific Cove community bulletin, some of them have already been adopted," she said. Many of the cats were still at the clinics, while the rest were in foster homes waiting to be adopted. "But if you want to give Charlotte their contact information we'll gather what we can and get it set up."

"Uh, actually, I volunteered to take some cats to them in a week or so when I head back for McKenzie's next treatment. I'll put them in the SUV and drop them off on my way. If it works out, then I'll set up more for later."

"Okay." That surprised her. It seemed like the last thing he'd want to do under the circumstances. But Ted was generous, and above anything save his family, he loved animals.

JAY WAS DRIVING home from the base when his cell phone rang. Recognizing the number, he pulled over and answered the call.

"Minnie? Hi, it's Jay."

"Jay? Hello, it's Minnie."

Jay squelched a chuckle—same opening every time. In the last weeks, he and Minnie had spoken frequently. After camping out at her house on several occasions and catching only glimpses of Duke, he and Minnie had devised a plan. A few days a week when Minnie was home, Jay would come over and set up the box trap. They chose these days so that if they managed to catch the cat he wouldn't have to stay in the trap for long. But they'd encountered problems with this plan, catching a variety of other creatures over numerous attempts, but not Duke.

"What did we get this time? Squirrel or raccoon?"

As soon as she started speaking again, Jay knew they'd finally succeeded. "We got him. We got the cat. He's boiling mad and that paw of his looks infected. I'm sure that's the only reason we got him. That paw is slowing him down."

"Hang tight, Minnie. I'll be there in a few minutes." He clicked off his cell and detoured to her house.

Minnie was waiting in the driveway when he pulled up.

"Levi's right. I think the cat is a demon."

Jay chuckled and followed her to the shed, where he discovered Minnie hadn't been exaggerating the cat's bad mood. The ball of scruffy tan fur huddled in the trap, that ungodly growl reverberating through him like a roll of thunder. It made the hair stand up on the back of his neck. But as he stared into the cat's yellow-green eyes, a mix of sympathy and pity welled up within him. Poor cat. Jay knew that so much of his behavior was based in fear. He recognized this depth of terror, the kind that made you so defensive you'd take on an adversary many times your size. If anyone could relate to that feeling it was Jay.

After promising he'd return the next day for a celebratory glass of lemonade and shortbread cookies, he loaded the cat in his car and headed to Pacific Cove Vet Clinic. Ten minutes later he was carting the cat inside. He saw Charlotte behind the counter.

"Hey, Charlotte, is Mia here?"

"Yep, she's in her office. I'll get her."

Charlotte disappeared into the back. Jay set the trap on the bench in the waiting room. He crouched to peer inside. He felt so sorry for the cat he could barely stand to look at him. But he did. Because he knew how that felt, too, to have someone pity you so much that they couldn't even make eye contact.

"Hey, buddy," he said to the cat. "I'm sorry about this, but it will only be temporary, I promise. Dr. Frasier will get you fixed up and then we'll find a place for you to live."

"Jay?" Mia appeared by his side. "What's going on? Who is this?"

"This is Duke," he said, patting the cage. The cat let out a low growl as if protesting the mention of his name. "Minnie and I finally caught him."

Mia bent to take a look. "The one you tangled with?"

"Yep. It is. Minnie and I have been on a mission the last few weeks." Jay explained how he and Minnie had been trying to capture him and finally succeeded.

Mia shook her head. "Why didn't you tell me you were trying to catch him?"

He grinned. "I don't know. It was just… I felt like it was something I needed to do."

"What have we got here?" Dr. Anthony asked as he stepped out into the reception area.

"Jay trapped an elusive stray cat."

Dr. Anthony bent and took a good long look. "He's got some bumps and bruises, doesn't he? No overt sign of disease." He stood upright and looked at them. "Good work, Jay. I'm between appointments. I'll take him back."

"That would be great," Mia said.

"He's got a bum paw," Jay said as Dr. Anthony took a hold of the trap.

"We'll get it patched up," Dr. Anthony said.

But as Jay watched them head toward the back, he was struck with an odd feeling. A sense of loss mixed with foreboding; a part of him wanted to go with the cat, reassure him again that everything would be fine. Another part of him wanted to grab the trap and take off, find a safe place and give him his freedom. The feeling was so strong the only thing holding him back was the fact that the cat needed medical treatment. Mia must have sensed his unease.

He felt a squeeze to his arm. "He'll be all right, Jay. Dr. Anthony will take good care of him."

"Okay," he said, but knew he sounded unconvinced. What was the matter with him?

THIS IS NOT a date. Mia kept telling herself as Jay drove them south along the rugged Oregon coastline. Lush green forest greeted them from the east, while the vast expanse of Pacific Ocean stretched out to the west as far as the eye could see. None of it looked as good as Jay did in his jeans and faded red T-shirt that brought out every bit of the green in his hazel eyes. She needed to quit stealing these glances, but it felt so intimate to be riding in his car. She wondered if he felt it, too, this awareness that seemed to have settled in around her. She distracted herself by taking a good look around. His car was older, but in immaculate condition and a million times cleaner than hers.

"Your car is really clean."

"Ugh, not anymore. Can't you see the Coastie fur-balls all over? And Laney's gum wrappers? I thought teenage boys were supposed to be the slobs. Not in this family."

In the backseat, Mia heard the jingle of Coastie's collar as the dog stirred.

Jay reached an arm behind him to give her a pat. "Sorry, sweet girl, I did say your name, didn't I? At least you're not throwing your fur all over the car on purpose."

Mia felt herself melt into the seat. Something about big strong guys sweet-talking animals... And Jay in particular. He was like a two-sided figurine—all responsible, stoic, military on one side and sweet, funny, soft on the other. She tried not to think about which side would prevail when it came down to the wire. Instead, she focused on the day stretching out ahead of them.

She'd already planned on going to Laney's first beach volleyball tournament, so when Jay had called the night before to see if she and George wanted to go with him and Coastie, it had only made sense for them all to go together.

Summer tourist season was in full swing, so traffic was a mess. The coastline was dotted with RV parks and campgrounds, so pickups pulling giant travel trailers and motor homes bigger than Mia's first apartment clogged the two-lane highway along with motorcyclists, bicyclists with apparent death wishes, hikers hefting giant packs and pedestrians of all sorts. She liked how none of it seemed to bother Jay. She remembered more than once her father's lack of patience—with drivers, doctors, crowds, even daughters.

They arrived early, but Tiramundi, the little beach town where the tournament was being held, was already overrun with people. Charlotte had warned her, but she'd also said not to be intimidated. Beach volleyball was a big draw up and down the West Coast. Tiramundi had been hosting this tournament for years, and while it drew competitors from all over the country and swelled the town's numbers exponentially, they had the logistics down to a science. A man wearing a bucket hat and a reflective vest held a sign directing volleyball spectators to the elementary school's parking lot.

An attendant there directed Jay into a parking spot. He turned off the car and texted Laney to see if she knew when and where her first match would be. His phone chimed almost immediately.

"She says ten a.m. on court thirteen."

"Perfect timing."

They leashed the dogs, grabbed their cooler and a blanket, and headed toward the beach.

Oregon's coastline was rugged in places. There were miles where the beach was nothing more than a pile of rocks at the bottom of a sheer cliff. There were spots where rocks jutted out at irregular intervals from the sandy shore and where the most spectacular tide pools formed, trapping various sea creatures during low tides and leaving them on display like nature's own aquarium. But there were also stretches of soft sandy paradise. The town of Tiramundi was one of these, having been founded on a rise above a wide expanse of fine-grain sand.

Perfect for beachcombers, kite fliers and volleyball.

"This is really cool," Jay said as they approached the array of courts that had been roped off for the occasion. The tournament consisted of teams of two or six spanning several age brackets. Laney was competing in the youngest division, ages thirteen to eighteen, on a team of six.

Navigating through the crowd was slow as George seemed to form a fan club wherever he went. Mia knew it was the combination of his size, his mellow personality and his seeming interest in every single human he met. She didn't reveal to the kind and curious people that the latter was largely due to the even slight chance he might come away with a snack.

"There it is." Jay pointed. "Court number thirteen."

Laney ran up to them, her face an endearing picture of happiness and excitement. "You guys made it!" She looked around. "Where's Levi?"

"He's working for Dr. Anthony today but promises to be at the next one." He handed her the small cooler he'd brought stocked with cold water, snacks and sports drinks. They visited for a few minutes before a voice near the court announced her impending match.

She smiled. "I'm so excited. And nervous."

"You're my sister. You're gonna be awesome." Jay wrapped an arm around her shoulder. "Go get 'em, kiddo."

Mia gave her a quick hug and a "good luck."

Laney went to her knees and wrapped her arms around George and Coastie. "Group hug from my favorite pups."

Later that afternoon, Mia was pretty sure Laney's dreams of going to college on a volleyball scholarship were going to come true. The girl was an athletic wonder. If anyone hit the ball harder in her age division, Mia didn't see it.

Their team wound up a respectable third

place. A very strong showing, especially since it was their first tournament playing together.

An ecstatic Laney opted to ride home with some of her teammates, who were stopping for dinner on the way. Jay and Mia loaded the dogs in the car and took off for Pacific Cove. They rounded a bend that opened out onto a stunning view of the ocean and the rock-dotted coastline below. He pulled over into a turnout designated "scenic viewpoint."

"Would it add too much romance to this thing to stop and watch the sunset?"

This thing? Mia felt her heart flip over inside of her chest. Yes, she thought, because this "thing" was already getting away from her. "Nah," she answered softly. "We can handle it. Just don't take your shirt off." She added a wink and climbed out of the car.

He joined her. "You wanna hike down to the beach?"

"Sure."

She leashed the dogs and headed for the trail leading to the beach while he rummaged around in the trunk. When he joined her he had a blanket thrown over one arm and a small cooler in the other. Sure was feeling like a date, she thought as they took off walking.

After they reached the beach, Jay studied the ground and finally spread the blanket out on a low rise. George immediately flopped down and covered half of it. Coastie curled up beside him.

She and Jay shared a laugh.

He commented drily, "You know your dog is tired when you take it to the beach and it opts for a nap instead of a roll on a dead fish."

"We probably wore them out today. Volleyball watching is exhausting, what with all those people to greet and things to sniff."

Jay sat and patted the blanket next to him. Mia swallowed. Feeling pretty romantic, too. She lowered herself next to him and he immediately leaned back, propping his long arm behind them.

"You know I grew up a few hours from here, but only came to the beach one time during my childhood."

And this was the crux of the problem for them, Mia realized. Because what did she say at this point? He didn't talk about his childhood and she knew if she asked he would just shut down. And they'd had such a perfect day.

She went with, "I grew up on so many different beaches I don't even remember them all."

"And yet you decided to settle in a beach town?"

Mia grinned. "It wasn't the beaches' fault

my childhood was miserable. That's one thing I did realize growing up. I do love the ocean."

"Your dad was not a nice guy, huh?"

Mia shot him a startled glance. Had she ever said that? "No, he wasn't."

"He was good to your mom and your brother, but not to you?"

She shook her head. "Nope. Pretty sure he hated me."

A piece of hair had escaped her ponytail to blow across her face. He tucked it behind her ear. His touch was incredibly gentle as he then reached over and picked up her hand. Using his thumb, he caressed the skin of her wrist.

"Pretty sure that's impossible. No one could hate you, Mia. Have you ever talked to your mom about this?" His voice was soft and low and sent shivers down her spine.

She gave her head a little shake. "Not in any meaningful way. It's a touchy subject between us. I get snarky, she gets defensive. Mom is so wonderful, but when it comes to my dad it's like she has blinders on."

"Ever talk to anyone else about it?"

She turned her head, rested her chin on her shoulder and batted her eyelashes. "About my daddy issues, you mean?"

He tilted his head, brows raised.

Mia chuckled even as she felt a tug of

dreaded melancholy. Facing the horizon again, she tried to soak up some of the magic. The sun was a bright orange ball dipping into the water. Wispy tendrils of clouds laced with pink and blue promised a spectacular sunset.

Finally, she answered, "Yes. A couple years of therapy revealed that I'm all screwed up because of it." She smiled and tried to lighten the statement. "It's a good thing we're doing this distance thing. You wouldn't want to be tied to a woman like *me*. So many issues."

Beside her, his body shifted and stiffened. He threaded his fingers into hers. She looked over to find his green eyes blazing with an intensity she'd never seen before. Anger, she thought, but why would that make him angry?

He closed his eyes for a few seconds, and when he opened them he exhaled a long breath. His tone was calm but felt like a cold fog steeling over her skin. "Did someone seriously tell you that?"

"Jay, no. I was kidding. I did go to therapy. I learned that I didn't like my dad. I also learned that it's okay not to like him. Just because you're related to someone doesn't mean you have to like them. Like I said, I'm a little messed up because of it, but I've learned to deal…" Her explanation hadn't seemed to help. "Are you all right? What did I say?"

"Mia." Her name came out on a painful-sounding sigh. He reached out and cupped her cheek with a gentle hand. "Don't ever talk that way about yourself, okay? Don't even joke about it."

She stared into his earnest green eyes and was pretty sure she'd promise him whatever he asked of her. "Okay."

He tipped her chin and lowered his mouth to cover hers. This kiss was different from the first one. That one had been all heat along with a whirlwind trip of her senses. And while the heat was still there, this one was tenderness and exploration and feelings that he couldn't seem to say. Her heart clenched inside her chest as she was overcome with the fear that he might not ever be able to say them.

THEY DECIDED TO keep the details of their relationship under wraps. It would be difficult to tell other people when they weren't even sure where it was going themselves. But they soon discovered that being together without being together was not easy.

Jay was doing his best to spend as much time with his siblings as possible. In the two weeks that followed the volleyball tournament, they managed to get together to take Levi and Laney bowling. They visited nearby

Remington's seafood festival and took a shopping trip to buy Laney some new volleyball shoes.

Nora and Mia had them all over for dinner, a fun night that also included a few other friends including Charlotte, Eli and Aubrey. They were all thrilled when Ted, Sara and McKenzie were able to attend as well. McKenzie charmed everyone with her wise-beyond-her-years humor and spirit of adventure. Jay and Levi accompanied her around the beach looking for crabs and collecting shells.

Another night, they built a fire on the beach, chaperoning five of Laney's friends along with a seemingly nice group of high school boys. Mia was impressed with how vigilant Jay was in his duty as sentry. She wanted to point out to him that when Laney was out with her friends there was no one watching them, but she kept that comment to herself.

She was both disappointed and relieved when Flame didn't show. Laney had mentioned him a couple more times since the day Mia had been introduced to him. Her reservations about the kid had grown and she thought Jay should meet him.

The kids roasted marshmallows and made s'mores. Jay had managed to finish the stairs leading to the loft, so six girls slept overnight in the space. He texted Mia throughout the evening, good-natured in his complaining about how loud teenage girls could be.

But they hadn't had a chance to be alone and Mia was relieved that it seemed to be getting to Jay as much as it was her.

After a frustrating number of attempts to connect, he called her at work one day. "Hey, what are you doing after work?"

"Um, I promised George a walk on the beach. Other than that, no plans. Why, what's up?"

"Do you guys feel like having company? It just so happens that Levi and Laney both have plans."

No surprise that Laney had plans; she had too many plans as far as Mia was concerned— too many questionable, ambiguous plans. In direct opposition to Levi, who didn't ever seem to have any plans that didn't entail him working in some capacity.

"What's Levi doing?"

"Helping Dr. Anthony again."

Jay cleared his throat. "So, how about if Coastie and I start walking north and you and Georgie head south? We can meet in the middle."

"Sounds good," she said, a sense of longing filling her at his words. If only he meant that in more ways than this one.

"I FEEL LIKE if you painted a sky this blue, no one would believe it was real," Jay said a couple hours later. He removed his sunglasses to check that the color was really as rich and vibrant as it appeared.

Beside him, Mia laughed. "I know what you mean. I can't stop looking at it, either. Since I've lived here I've gotten up every morning to find that the beach looks different—there's thick fog, or thin fog, or a haze on the horizon. Or storm clouds or white fluffy clouds, or there's a mist in the air or it's pouring down rain. Whatever it is, I love how the weather makes it look different every day, even if it's only slightly. But I have to admit this, these summer days are super special."

Jay couldn't remember the last time he'd felt this kind of contentment. For his entire life, happiness had always been fleeting, rarely here and too soon gone. Which, he supposed, was part of what made it feel so precious. Like this blue sky.

Reaching out, he took Mia's hand and led her to large drift log. They sat and the dogs immediately huddled up and began sniffing for treasures.

"So," he said, "I was wondering what was going to happen to Duke? I called last week and Charlotte said he was doing really well."

Mia blinked a couple times. "Oh, he is. His foot is pretty much healed. Now that he's feeling better he's much less angry, tolerable even. He's going to be put up for adoption."

His lips curved up into a tentative smile. "What do you have to do to adopt a cat? I was thinking where I live is far enough from the highway I could let him go there and—"

Her shoulders fell. "Oh, Jay, I wish you would have asked about him sooner. Dr. Anthony already took him to Portland to a shelter there."

Disappointment surged through him, surprising him with its intensity. At least the cat was going to be okay, he told himself. He was healthy now and no longer injured and hungry. He had a chance, and Jay felt good about that.

"That's probably better anyway. I don't know anything about cats. Never had one of those, either."

Mia squeezed his hand. "Cats are easy. I wanted a cat so much when I was a kid. My dad hated cats. There's something wrong with people who don't like cats, if you ask me."

"What was he like, your dad? I know you

told me you guys had problems. But it's so odd knowing your mom to imagine her being with someone who wasn't just as nice."

She peered at him intently and he knew she was trying to decide how to answer. He couldn't blame her. What right did he have to ask about her family when he wouldn't talk about his own? He'd understand if she didn't tell him.

"My parents were polar opposites. You never would have guessed they would make a good couple. Where Mom is all free-spirited and easygoing, my dad was totally rigid and uptight. His life was all about work and self-discipline. Except where my mom was concerned. With her he was different. And with my brother."

Coastie brought a stick and dropped it on his feet. He picked it up and gave it a good throw. George was busy digging a hole in the sand.

"What was he like with you?"

"Odd, looking back on it now. It was like I didn't exist. The only time he spoke to me, which was rare, was to criticize me. I went out of my way to avoid him. Only later, with therapy, did I realize that my overachieving stemmed from that. It was how I gained the recognition and accolades I supposedly wanted from him."

"Your mom never intervened?"

"No. I didn't give her any reason to. I mostly stayed out of his way, which wasn't difficult really. We had nothing in common. He spent all his dad time with Kyle, fishing, scuba diving, sports. I wasn't interested in any of that stuff, anyway. My mom loved me. I know she did her best to make up for it."

"And you've really never talked to her about this?"

Mia pushed up a shoulder, clearly uncomfortable with his questioning. "No, not in any detail. I'm sure she knows how I feel in a general sense… What would be the point? It would only make her feel bad."

"But Mia, you feel bad. You've spent your life feeling bad about this. It shouldn't be your job to make everyone else comfortable when you're in misery."

"I'm not miserable. I'm fine now. The past is the past."

Jay could feel the pain behind her words. She seemed so confident, so outgoing, so together. He'd seen snatches of this vulnerability before, and he couldn't help but wonder how much of what she chose to show to the world was real and how much she worked hard to create.

He wanted to wrap his arms around her. He planned on it soon. "Do you think your resistance to falling in love with someone in the military is due more to your dad than the military itself?"

Mia froze, her face a blank slate as she stared back at him. Nervous that he'd offended her, he was trying to think of what to say when she finally let out a chuckle. She nudged his shoulder and said, "Nice try. I went to therapy, remember? Sure, it's about him. Partially. But it's also about stability. I'm the kind of person who needs that. I crave structure and continuity. It's also about reassurance and acceptance. It's about *not* feeling invisible."

"Hmm. So you want to marry a building?"

"As long as he's home for dinner and doesn't make me move every year, it would be a step up from my father."

CHAPTER FOURTEEN

THE FIRST TIME Laney came home late, Jay let it slide. After all, she was the new girl in town, busy making friends and wanting to fit in. The second time he wrote it off to a miscommunication. So he'd established some ground rules, including a clearly defined curfew and restrictions on where she could spend her time. The third time warranted a call to Josie. He hated to bother her, as he was determined to handle this transition on his own. But he needed some advice.

"What do I do? She's an hour late."

"Well, what would you have done if I had done that?"

"You never would have done that."

She paused. "Only because I couldn't. Believe me, I wanted to sometimes. But if I had, what would you have done?"

"I would have gone looking for you."

"There you go."

"I don't want to humiliate her in front of the new friends she's making."

"If she's making the right kinds of friends, they will understand. This situation tells me she's not. Because if she was, those parents wouldn't be letting their fifteen-year-olds stay out this late, either."

"Good point."

Jay hung up the phone and asked Levi, "Do you have any idea where to find her?"

Levi shrugged. "Not really. She doesn't tell me much."

Jay suddenly realized how much she wasn't telling him, either. He knew the last names of exactly two of the girls she'd met here in Pacific Cove, Elise and Brianna. Maybe Mia was right and he needed to keep a closer eye on her. Concern welled inside him as all the worst scenarios played out in his mind.

"I'm going to go out and look for her."

"Where?"

"I have no idea. I guess I'll drive around and ask…"

Levi answered with a skeptical look. "That seems pointless. Do you want me to help?"

"How?"

"I could see what she's doing on Instagram. Those girls put everything they do on Instagram."

Why hadn't he thought of that? "Yes. Do that."

Ten minutes later Levi had pulled up photos of Laney and Elise from earlier in the evening at a place called Radio Beach. "I have no idea where that is," he murmured. There wasn't enough background detail in the close-up photos. How many selfies could a person take? It looked like a million other beaches.

"I'll call Aubrey." She'd grown up in Pacific Cove and seemed to know everything about the place. He explained the situation, then forwarded her a few photos.

After a few moments, she said, "I don't know, Jay. Kids find these secluded spots you have to hike into or maybe because of the cliffs you can only get there at low tide. They give them these nicknames thinking other people won't know where they are. Word eventually leaks out and they find a *new* place. I mean, there's only so much shoreline and accessible beach. You need to talk to a teenager. Someone who goes to the high school. See what's popular right now. What about Levi?"

"He doesn't go to the high school yet. And he hasn't really met that many people."

"I'll ask Eli and my sisters and call you back if we can think of anything. Keep me posted."

"Maybe call Dr. Frasier," Levi said when he hung up with Aubrey.

"Why would Mia know?"

"Well, you should call Nora, actually. I'm friends with her on Instagram. I know it sounds weird, but she's friends with that girl Ty. Ty knows everyone…"

Twenty minutes later Jay, Levi, Mia and Ty were driving toward a secluded stretch of coast known as Radio Beach.

"TAKE A RIGHT up by that cedar snag," Ty instructed from her spot in the backseat next to Levi.

Mia steered her SUV off the highway and onto a rutted dirt and gravel drive.

"This is it," Ty said when they reached a tree-lined dead end. "You have to hike down that trail through the Scotch broom. It's pretty steep but I can show you—"

"We're not letting you go," Mia said. "Your mom was nice enough to let us steal you for this trip. I doubt she'd appreciate me bringing you back broken. Especially when you haven't quite healed." The girl was still wearing a brace on her arm.

"I'll stay here with her," Levi volunteered. "I don't think Laney will appreciate me showing up down there. She's already going to know I ratted her out."

Mia asked Jay, "Do you want me to come?"

He looked up from where he'd been rummaging around in his backpack. "I do. If you don't mind."

She'd been hoping he'd say that.

They got out of the car and he handed her a headlamp and a flashlight. She slipped it over her head and adjusted the strap to tighten it. He reached over and turned it on. She was surprised by how well she could see with it.

"This is great," she said, tipping her head up and down and back and forth.

"SAR necessity," he said.

Mia spotlighted his face in time to see his amused half smile. Of course. Search-and-rescue was a huge part of his Coast Guard work. Mia felt vaguely nauseated at his use of the term. She was nervous about what they would find down on the beach. Best-case scenario was a bunch of kids having fun around a campfire. Worst case… No point in thinking about that yet. Ty had told them that there was no cell service once you dipped over the hillside and descended about halfway down. Memories of Flame and his hostile attitude kept running through her mind. *Just because Charlotte had heard that he uses drugs and*

*had a child with a sixteen-year-old doesn't
mean he did...*

Mia followed Jay down the hillside, grateful for the light. The trail was definitely one that had come about from use and not strategic design. It was steep and covered in loose rock with shallow roots protruding at irregular intervals.

They could hear the kids long before they ever got to the beach. As they moved closer, Mia could make out comments and questions from the group: "Do you think it's Justin? What if it's the cops? This is private property, man! Can the cops come down here? Cameron, what are you doing? I'm not sure this is private property, moron. Don't run. There's nowhere to go…"

Jay stopped. He turned toward Mia, placing a finger over his lips indicating for her to stay quiet. He reached over and flipped off her headlamp. She followed his lead and did the same to her flashlight. Then he strode purposefully toward the group huddled around the fire. She was almost startled when his voice rang out.

"United States Coast Guard. Stay where you are. No one is running anywhere." As he spoke he lowered a large flashlight to the ground and Mia was impressed by how effectively it spotlighted the crowd. She quickly counted twelve bodies, but none of them appeared to be Laney. Or Flame.

A boy's voice responded, "Hello, sir. What can we help you with this evening?"

"The Coast Guard? He can't arrest us," a boy with a backward baseball cap said, and then spit into the fire.

"Yes, he can, you dipwad."

Jay interjected. "Tell me your ages?"

A couple brave voices spoke up with "seventeen" and "eighteen."

"Is there any underage drinking going on here tonight?"

Silence.

Jay walked toward the fire. The voices became quieter as Jay began to question the kids.

That's when Mia heard a weak voice off to the right. "Dr. Frasier?"

She moved toward the sound. "Laney?"

"It's Elise, but Laney is—"

"I'm here, too..." Laney's voice trailed off with a quiet sob.

Mia turned on her flashlight and found the girls sitting on the sand leaning against a large rock. Mia hurried over and knelt beside them. "Laney, are you okay?"

She shook her head with that floppy back-

and-forth motion that only small children and drunk people did. "Jay is going to kill me."

"No, he's not," Mia said quietly. "He's going to be happy we found you. Are you okay, Elise?"

Elise nodded. "Yeah, I'm fine. Laney had a little too much to drink. She wanted me to call you, Dr. Frasier. But there's no cell service down here. And I didn't want to leave her and climb up the hill by myself. We were getting ready to try to head up when we saw your lights. We decided to wait here and see who it was first. I'm so glad you're here."

"Did you guys have anything besides alcohol?"

"No. Laney had three beers, but I didn't have any. It tastes so disgusting."

Mia prayed the girl was telling the truth. She stood, shone her flashlight in the direction of the fire and called out, "Jay? Over here."

In a matter of seconds, he was beside them. "Laney? Thank God! Are you okay?"

"I'm sorry, Jay." Laney began crying quietly.

Mia explained, "She appears to be fine other than being a bit intoxicated."

Handing Elise a flashlight he said, "Elise,

you follow me, okay? Stay between me and Mia."

He bent, scooped Laney into his arms and carried her up the hill like she weighed nothing more than a bag of chips. He was barely breathing hard when they reached the top, where he set Laney on her feet beside the car. She swayed and Elise put an arm around her.

Jay said, "Mia, I hate to ask you this, but is there any way you can take the girls home? I need to call this in. It's not that I want these kids to get into trouble, but I don't want any of them driving home."

"Yesss," Laney slurred. "I wanna go with Dr. Frasier anyway. Maybe sheel keep me since you don' wanna."

"Laney, what are you talking about?" Jay asked.

She flailed a finger in his general vicinity. "You won't lemme…test and fry. Tha's be cuz you don't really want me."

Jay scrubbed a frustrated hand across his jaw. It was the first time all evening he'd shown anything but his usual calm. His voice was low and menacing as he told her, "Okay, drunk girl, we are not going to have this conversation right now. Get in the car. We will talk tomorrow."

MIA DROVE LEVI and Ty home before heading to her house. Between tears and apologies, Mia and Elise managed to get Laney into bed. It took about twelve seconds before she was snoring softly. Mia was incredibly relieved that it didn't appear she was going to be spending the night cuddled up next to the toilet. Elise had said she'd only had three beers. She was beginning to think the count was probably accurate, which hopefully meant this wasn't a habitual thing.

Elise opted to stay the night, too.

"Thank you for your help, Elise."

"This isn't like her, I promise. She told me tonight that she's never drunk before. She's very antidrug and alcohol. She wants to get a volleyball scholarship and she wouldn't do anything to screw that up. She was really upset and she kind of lost it…"

Mia could only hope this was true. "What happened?"

Elise looked down, fiddling with the seam of the bedspread. "Um, I know it has to do with her family. With her brother and stuff…" She met Mia's gaze and Mia could see the anguish in the girl's eyes. "She talked to her sister Josie today and she got bad news. Laney asked me not to tell anyone, but you…"

"No, no." Mia held up a hand, palm up and out. "Don't tell me. I'll talk to Jay. I don't want you to break her confidence. Aside from Laney's hangover, things will be better in the morning. Good night, Elise."

Elise puffed out a loud sigh of relief. "Thanks, Dr. Frasier. Good night."

Mia smiled at the girl. "I can see why Laney likes you so much. If you keep up this kind of loyalty you two will be friends for life."

Tears sparkled in her eyes. "Laney is really great to me, too. I know we've only known each other a couple months, but she's already like the best friend I've ever had. I've had some problems with my boyfriend and she's been there for me. I just know she always will be." Elise fluffed her pillow and put her head down. The next words were spoken so softly Mia barely heard them. "If she gets to stay."

If she gets to stay? Why wouldn't she? Mia pondered those words, suspecting that simple statement might hold the answers to a lot of Laney's troubles.

JAY WOKE UP the next morning grateful for the fact that it was Sunday and he was off duty. Telling himself not to overreact, he tried to analyze Laney's behavior. Kids did things, stupid, impulsive things. But they also acted out. Jay had been doing everything he could to make sure Laney was happy here, spending time with her but also allowing her plenty of time to get out and socialize. He thought about how Mia had intimated that maybe he was allowing her a little too much freedom. Yet she appeared to be thriving. She was outgoing, talkative, cheerful—usually. Teenage girls could be moody, he knew. And she hadn't abused her privileges, except for those couple times… Was she struggling and he wasn't aware of it?

In the other room, he heard the door open. The tapping of Coastie's paws and then the lapping of water from her dish suggested that Levi had taken her out.

Walking into the kitchen, he found Levi cracking eggs into a bowl.

"Hey, good morning, you want an omelet?" He picked up a whisk and went to town on the eggs. "I walked Coastie already because I figured you were going to be occupied with Laney. I'm working for Dr. Anthony today."

"Thank you. Yeah, but I'll pass on the omelet. You know, you don't have to take every extra hour that comes your way. You could go out and do some fun stuff."

Levi shrugged. "I like working. I'm saving for a car like we talked about."

Jay nodded. Levi had definitely adopted his work ethic, which was a good thing, he thought. He just wished his little brother would see that he didn't *have* to. A conversation for another day.

"Okay, I'm going to head over to Mia's and pick Laney up in a few minutes. You have any idea what's going on with our sister?"

Levi paused for a beat, his gaze flickering upward to meet Jay's before focusing on his breakfast again.

A twist of his gut told Jay that something was going on. "If you know something, Levi, you need to tell me."

"I know she's scared."

"Scared? Of what?"

Levi's eyes latched onto his and the anguish there made Jay's breath catch.

"Of the future. We're both worried about this custody thing. We don't want to go back, Jay. I *won't* go back."

"Oh." That was a relief. Fear, he understood. Fear, he could deal with.

LANEY AND ELISE didn't sleep in nearly as long as Mia thought they would. They showed up downstairs, chatting away and looking surprisingly chipper, giving further credence to their story from the evening before.

Mia told Laney, "I talked to your brother and he isn't planning on picking you up until ten. Do you want me to call him or do you girls want to hang out here for a couple hours?"

They opted to stay. After Mia fixed them a huge breakfast of pancakes, bacon and eggs, they took George for a walk on the beach.

"Thank you, guys, for taking George," she told them after they returned. "He loves the beach."

"He's the sweetest dog ever, Dr. Frasier." Elise was scratching his neck. "Laney was telling me about how you rescued him. I totally cried. Will he have this scar on his neck forever?"

"Well, he's still growing, so we'll see. But I have a feeling that hair might not ever grow back."

Laney gave George another pat and asked, "Is it okay if we walk to the clinic and see the cats?"

"Absolutely. Mom can drop you off if you want. She's heading to yoga class soon. You can either walk back here or I'll send Jay to get you at the clinic."

"I'll call my mom and grab my bag, Laney. I'll be back in a few minutes."

As soon as Elise was out of sight Laney

moved closer. She stood in front of Mia, her fingers twisting nervously together. "Did you talk to my brother? I mean, I know you talked to him, but did he *say* anything?"

Mia didn't know what she was referring to exactly, but it could mean many things. "About what?"

"Like about how mad he is or whatever? Or...about anything else?"

Mia could only wish he would talk about it, about anything that mattered. She shook her head. "No, he didn't. Your brother doesn't talk about..." She trailed off, trying to decide how to word it.

Laney rolled her eyes. "About anything? I know. But I was hoping that maybe finally, with you, that was changing. He seems to really like you." She let out a dramatic sigh. "Maybe Josie is right and he'll never get close to anyone."

Mia felt the disappointing words like a stab. Even though she'd already reached that conclusion herself, she'd been holding on to the same secret hope. But this was about Laney. "Is there anything I can do, Laney? Do you want to talk to me about what happened?"

She did; Mia could tell. It was stamped all over the poor girl's face. Laney's eyes filled with tears as she nodded slowly. "I don't know. I should probably talk to Jay first."

"Okay," Mia said, and her already hurting heart seemed to crack a little bit more. She pulled Laney in for a hug as her anger and frustration toward Jay gathered like a storm.

Nora and Elise came down the stairs and a few minutes later they all headed out. Not long after that, Jay knocked on the door.

"What are you going to do about this?" she asked after pouring them both cups of coffee and grabbing a bag of real cookies from her stash. "About Laney?"

"I'll talk to her. I think it was just a mistake." His tone was so casual, so seemingly unconcerned, Mia nearly lost it.

"A mistake?" she repeated flatly. "That's it?"

"Yeah, she's a fifteen-year-old kid. Fifteen-year-olds do things, stupid things. You know, experimenting and all that."

"Hmm." She busied herself with taking a drink so she could consider how to most diplomatically say what she wanted to say. Giving up on that strategy, she said, "Yes, they do, but often it's a sign that they're feeling angry or insecure or sad…"

"What do you mean?"

"I mean that teenage girls are very emotional. Something is bothering her. This feels like more than 'experimenting' to me."

"Did she say something to you?"

He sounded horrified by the thought and Mia felt her irritation boiling over. Laney should be able to talk to someone if she wanted. She also knew why she didn't, and he was sitting right in front of her.

"Elise said she was upset. Apparently, she talked to Josie yesterday and the conversation seemed to upset her. Then there was her little display at the beach. She didn't seem too pleased with you either. She acts like I did at her age. She's a pleaser, a peacemaker... She acts like everything is fine hoping it will be eventually. But I promise you, this issue will come to a head eventually."

Mia watched his mouth tighten into that grim line it did whenever she even hinted at issues he didn't want to discuss. Which she'd gotten used to when it came to the two of them, but she felt strongly enough about Laney that she knew she needed to push it.

"I can talk to her if you want me to. I think she wants to tell me—"

"That's not necessary," he interrupted. "Mia, look, I appreciate your—"

"No, Jay. Don't give me the 'you appreciate my concern' speech here. I know you love your sister. And I know you believe you're doing the right thing by giving her plenty of freedom or whatever, but ignoring this behavior is—"

With a sigh, he reached over and picked up her hand. "I'm sorry." He kissed her palm. "I realize you're trying to help. And you're right, but I'm pretty sure I know what's bothering her. I'm not ignoring it."

"You know what's bothering her?"

"Yes. And I'm going to fix it. You don't need to worry about it and neither does Laney. I'm going to make sure she understands that."

Mia shook her head, letting her skepticism show. "All right," she finally said. Even though she knew that where Laney was concerned, it was far from all right. The girl was headed for trouble. Mia could only hope that by the time Jay figured this out it wouldn't be too late.

CHAPTER FIFTEEN

WITH THE REST of the cats on Porpoise Point Road rounded up and treated over the previous weeks, Mia had decided to suspend work at Lucky Cats for the day. The woman's daughter had moved to town and sought counseling for her mom. They'd convinced the woman to keep only six of the cats, all of which Mia had sterilized and treated for free. Mia felt confident this instance had a good chance of having a successful long-term outcome.

Mia put those thoughts aside as she and Charlotte strolled along Pacific Cove's boardwalk on this balmy summer Saturday, gazing down at the amazing array of sand sculptures beneath them. A wide set of stairs led down to the beach below. At the top of an arch overhead, a large sign read Pacific Cove Sandtastical 30th Annual Sandcastle Exposition. Pacific Cove hosted the contest every year. And while it wasn't one of the largest held along the West Coast, it had a reputation for being one of the most fun. Vendors selling crafts and artwork were set up on one end of the venue, where attendees could purchase everything from kites and sand toys to homemade soaps and lotions to pet supplies and antiques. Food carts were selling a mouthwatering variety of delectables including funnel cakes, fish and chips, deep-fried pickles, clam strips and "the world's largest" ice cream sundaes. A beer garden at the far end of the venue offered an array of local microbrews and wines.

"Where's your mom's crew?" Charlotte asked Mia as they descended the stairs onto the sand.

"She said they were assigned a spot about two-thirds of the way down near the south end." Mia pointed even though there was no way they could see that distance. A sea of bodies was swarming the beach as the artists had already been at it for several hours. The sculptures were taking shape and generating a ton of excitement with the spectators.

"Jay is bringing Levi and Laney. So be on the lookout. Laney and Elise are sleeping over tonight, because Jay has to work and Levi is house-sitting again for Dr. Anthony."

Charlotte didn't respond. Mia glanced over at her friend to see her wearing a pinched expression.

"What?" Mia asked.

She sighed. "I didn't want to tell you this today, but since you brought him up there are some things I need to tell you."

"About?"

"I asked around a bit about Jay."

Jay? It was the first time she'd actually heard Charlotte call him by his name and not "hottie" or "Coast Guard man candy" or any of the other clever monikers she'd dubbed him. This felt like a bad sign.

"Oh, man, Charlotte, I hope you didn't say anything…" She trailed off, cringing inwardly at the thought of the entire town now thinking or knowing she had a crush on the guy.

"I was careful. I swear, Mia."

Mia gave her a hopeful, skeptical look. "And…"

"Well, I don't know how else to say this but he seems to be what I like to call a serial heartbreaker. Apparently, he dates, but… By all accounts, he's a nice guy who's afraid to commit."

Mia felt an initial rush of relief; she already knew that.

"Well, all the better for me then, huh? We're just friends." Slightly more than friends, she added silently, glad she hadn't told Charlotte any more than that. She and Jay had never defined the parameters of their relationship beyond not getting too close… Her stomach knotted as she realized, wondered, if he had "more" with other women, too? Laney's words from a few days prior came back to her again, like they had a million times already. About how he didn't get "close" to anyone.

Charlotte barked out a laugh. "Friendship might be what you have in mind, but he doesn't look at you as if you're just a friend."

"I don't think…"

"I know you don't." Charlotte stopped, grabbing her elbow and urging her around. Her brown eyes were wide with concern. "That's why I'm telling you. Be careful, Mia." She paused. "I know you don't have experience with these kinds of guys, but I do. They take what they want but they're not willing to give in return. I love you, Mia. And I don't want to see you get hurt."

Mia waved her off. "I'm not going to get hurt, Charlotte. I won't let myself get that close. He's military, remember?"

Charlotte eyed her skeptically. "I bet him being military isn't going to matter once he turns those charms on you."

"Hey, I have charms, too, you know? Why am I the one getting hurt in this scenario? Maybe I'll be breaking Mr. Coast-Guard-

Hottie's heart." Mia could hear her attempt at a casual reply falling flat.

Charlotte let out a little gasp. "Oh no… Mia, you're not already…? You've fallen for him already, haven't you?"

"Charlotte, no, I'm… We're—"

"Mia! Charlotte!" Conversation halted as they heard a voice calling for them. They turned to see Nora waving them over.

They moved closer… And stood frozen for a moment as they silently beheld the phenomenal sand sculpture before them.

Finally, Charlotte finally whispered, "Wow."

"Wow is right. Mom…"

"You like it?"

"Like it? I'm…" Mia felt joyful tears gather in her eyes. The middle of the sculpture was the shape of a woman with a cat on her shoulder—her. She was kneeling on the ground surrounded by animals; there were cats and dogs of various shapes and sizes, including ones that looked remarkably like George and Ruby and Coastie. The sign read Pacific Cove Vet Clinic because Mia had sponsored their endeavor. She gathered her mom close for a hug. "Thank you," she said. "Mom, you amaze me."

Her mom whispered, "Right back at you, daughter."

Nora sniffled and then gestured around, her smile electric. "Isn't this whole event a wonder? There are some talented, talented people on this beach today. I feel honored to be among them."

"Um, yeah, Nora, and you are one of them. I am speechless and you know that never happens to me," Charlotte said, circling the masterpiece that Nora had designed and helped create.

Nora had spent countless hours over the preceding months studying sand sculpting techniques and practicing various methods. She'd teamed up with Kendra Maddox, a local artist; her friend and fellow artist Nan; and Dennis Fulton, a potter from her pinochle club. Their group, the Sand Bandits, was hoping for a good showing in the over-fifty-five category. Mia smiled as she saw Ty off to one side talking animatedly with Kendra. From what Mia had seen so far she thought they had a solid chance of winning.

Laney came galloping over with her friends in tow. "Mia, Charlotte, hi! Mrs. Frasier, hey!"

"Laney!" Nora leaned over and hugged her.

"You are like a total genius." She introduced her friends. "You know Elise and this is Brianna. We've been following all of this on Instagram. Other kids didn't believe me when I told them I knew you." She turned toward Mia. "Oh. My. Gosh. Dr. Frasier, that is totally you, like preserved in sand or whatever! And George and Ruby and Coastie! It's so cool! Can you guys huddle together so I can take your picture?"

Laney's friends asked questions and Nora explained how they formed the block of sand in the general shape of the object they were going to sculpt using a set of wooden forms in a technique similar to pouring concrete.

"As the water drains and the sand sets, you remove the forms and start carving. It's important to keep it moist so it doesn't dry out too much. That's what the spray bottles are for..."

Mia felt a welling of pride as a small crowd gathered around to hear Nora speak. She loved her mom receiving this attention that she so deserved. She'd always believed that her mom could have made a name for herself in the art world. Instead, she'd chosen to devote herself to a husband who was only there for her part-time. She'd taught art to high school students and seemed content. Mia had made a vow to herself that she would never do that; she'd never put a man's opinions and "needs" above her own. She'd never...

Mia froze, her entire body going cold as

she realized that was exactly where she was headed with Jay. It wasn't like they were on the path to marriage or anything, but they were definitely having some kind of a relationship. But, she suddenly realized, it was a relationship on his terms—only his terms. He wouldn't even let her get close to his little sister, who so clearly needed to get close to someone. She wasn't allowed to discuss how Levi was spending too many of his precious, fleeting teenage hours working too hard. She knew virtually nothing about Josie or their youngest siblings, not to mention his parents. Lifting a hand, she placed it across her forehead as if she could calm the throb of humiliation and disappointment now pounding away there.

She'd known this was going to happen and she'd let herself go down this path anyway. Charlotte was right; she'd gone and fallen in love with him. She'd fallen for a man who could never love her the way she wanted.

Down the beach near the coffee stand, she spotted Jay and Levi. They appeared to be engaged in lively conversation with Abby Quinn. Abby was a pretty third-grade teacher at the elementary school. Her already-unsettled stomach did a flip. Was she jealous? Maybe, but that didn't matter. Charlotte was right about this as well. For that matter, Jay had been, too. It wasn't that she was going to get hurt; she was already hurt and it was only going to get worse. The truth of that, the devastation, nearly left her breathless.

JAY WAS TRYING to keep track of Laney and her two friends, Elise and Brianna. Nice girls, Jay thought, but he had to concede that Mia was right that his sister was far too pretty for her own good. Boys seemed to flock around her. And although she didn't seem overly flirtatious, he scowled at a few, feeling fine about the fact that they scuttled away like scared crabs when they noticed him. He may have growled at one of them. Not on purpose. It just kind of came out.

He fielded questions and compliments about Coastie—those filled him with an illogical pride. All of this while he argued with Levi about his latest plan to continue taking online classes in the fall.

"But Jay," Levi argued, "I could finish in a year if I did it like that."

"Levi, I don't understand why you want to finish early. You should be having fun in high school."

He was also on the lookout for Mia. He needed to see her. Okay, *needed* was a strong word, but when he went a day or two without seeing her, he felt…off. She was like some kind of a balm for the anxiety and uncertainty that seemed to be eating away at him. Hopefully, soon this custody situation would be settled and maybe they'd all feel more secure.

There was an uncharacteristic snap to Levi's tone as he answered, "The fun you didn't get to have, you mean? I'm not you, Jay."

Jay leveled an assessing look at his brother. "This is not about me. But yes, I would like for you to have at least some of the fun I didn't get to have."

"I could work full-time."

Jay lifted a brow in response, almost laughing at the expression on Levi's face as he realized he was arguing Jay's point.

"I mean I would have more time for work *and* fun. You wouldn't have to give me money for anything. I could help with the bills and even send some to Josie."

"Levi, no. We've talked about this. I don't want you to have to work full-time. I did that and it's terrible. You will have no social life—no football games with your friends, no flirting with girls between classes, no school dances—"

"I don't dance."

"You know what I mean."

"I don't want to do any of those things."

"But you might once school starts."

"Hey, there's Nora," Laney called out to them. "We're going to go say hi." She and her friends headed toward the roped-off area where Nora was huddled with her teammates. His pulse kicked it up a notch when he noticed Mia standing there, too.

Jay turned to face Levi. "You will go to school in the fall like a normal kid."

Levi was looking down at the sand, muttering under his breath, no doubt gathering his counterargument.

"Jay!" A female voice called loudly. He turned to see Abby Quinn walking toward him. He'd gone out with her a few times last winter. They'd had a lot of fun until the fourth date when she'd sprung the sneak attack. Jay had thought they were going to dinner in nearby Remington when she'd informed him they were going "home" to Astoria to meet her family. He'd broken it off as gently as he could the following week.

"Abby, hey, how are you?"

She hustled over to them, a tiny dog cuddled in her arms and one of those purse-shaped bags to carry it in over her shoulder. "Looks like we have this in common, huh?

And you told me you didn't want a dog when we were dating."

Jay would have never said they were "dating," but he let it slide. Levi's gaze bounced curiously between him and Abby. "Abby, this is my brother, Levi."

Out of the corner of his eye, Jay saw Mia and Charlotte approaching.

"Nice to meet you. You guys look alike." Abby smiled at Levi and stuck out her hand. Then she looked at Jay, her forehead wrinkling with confusion. "I didn't know you had a brother. You never told me you had a brother."

"It never came up."

"I took you home to meet my family."

"Yep, well, things change, circumstances change, right?" Did they ever, he realized, as he thought about the fact that he was now trying to devise a way to be with Mia tonight. Maybe she could drop the girls off at the movies and they could grab dinner?

Abby's eyes lit with eagerness. "They sure do. Maybe we should get these two together for a playdate, huh?"

"Um…" Jay said, because Mia and Charlotte were now standing in front of them. "I don't…"

"Sounds like a great idea," Mia chimed in

brightly and rather unhelpfully. "It's really important for dogs to socialize."

"Hear that, Jay?" Abby giggled and gave his arm a playful nudge. "Dr. Frasier thinks we should socialize."

Coastie was prancing around her feet, so Mia picked her up. The dog sniffed her neck and Mia let out a little laugh. What kind of a man was jealous of his own dog? And why was Mia trying to foist him off on Abby?

Abby addressed them. "Hi, Dr. Frasier. Hey, Charlotte."

"Hey, Levi," Mia said, putting Coastie down and positioning herself closer to him with her back to Jay and Abby. "Charlotte and I were going to grab scones and snacks for Mom's team. Do you want to give us a hand?"

Abby was waving at someone down the beach. After a quick goodbye to everyone and a "see you later, Jay," she sped away.

"Yeah, sure." To Jay, Levi said, "I'll meet you by Mrs. Frasier's sand castle, okay?"

Jay watched them walk off toward the booth that read Authentic State Fair Scones. Then he looked at Coastie, who'd plopped beside him in the sand and was gazing longingly in their direction.

"Yeah, I know, girl. We like scones, too."

SOMETHING WAS UP and Jay didn't like it. Mia hadn't smiled at him even once. Well, unless you called that closemouthed grimace a smile. He didn't. Fortunately for him, Laney and Elise were staying the night with her after the Sandcastle Expo. They were going shopping in the morning. He was incredibly grateful not to have to take two teenage girls shopping.

Dropping them off for the evening also gave him an excuse to find out what was going on. Luckily for him, the girls immediately grabbed a volleyball and headed down to the beach.

Jay took a seat on one of the stools behind the bar in the kitchen. "Your mom is really talented. First place in the over-fifty-five division and third place overall. That's fantastic."

She sort of smiled at that. "Yeah, I know. I'm really proud of her. She's new to sand sculpting, too. She's good at everything art-related. She paints, draws, sculpts…"

"What a gift."

"I know," she said flatly. "She's awesome."

"Okay, what's going on?"

"What do you mean?"

"I mean that I'm not an idiot. You won't smile at me. You cringed earlier when I tried to touch you. You're mad at me."

"No, Jay, I'm not. I don't want to be. I'm

just... I'm sad at you. And I don't like myself very much right now either."

"*Sad* at me? What is that supposed to mean?"

"It means..." She looked out toward the ocean for a few seconds and he could see her eyes cloud with tears. Had he done that somehow? Had he made her cry? The very idea made his heart hurt. When she met his gaze again Jay knew this was going to be bad.

"IT MEANS I don't think this is going to work. I thought maybe I could do this. I wanted to try. I agreed to it and for that I'm sorry. I really thought we could be friends and...a little more. I liked you so much I was willing to try to be content with as much as you were willing to give. I thought I could be satisfied with that. Keep things casual and let you take the lead." Saying the words out loud upset her, but they also strengthened her resolve. She'd been heading down the same path as her mom without even recognizing it, letting the man in her life call the shots in the relationship. And a man in the Coast Guard no less, whose assignment here would eventually end. Even if he was able to get reassigned here, then what? How had she let this sneak up on her? Because she cared about him, that's how. She'd made allowances for Levi's and Laney's sakes, too.

"I'm so sorry, Jay, but I have to break this off before it gets worse for me. I know I said I could handle this, the 'little bit more' or whatever. But it's turned into a lot more than a little more for me. I... I have...feelings for you. But I know that you can't give me what I want. And, yes, I know you already told me that." Fresh tears sprouted and this time, she couldn't quite keep them at bay. "I was afraid of getting involved with you because you're in the Coast Guard, yes. But I see how much less important that was now. I don't even care about that anymore. I mean I care, but what I should have been worried about is the other stuff. Like you not really sharing your feelings with me. Or your life. I'm thinking about how I didn't even know you had a brother and sister until I met them. Everything I know about Josie, Dean and Delilah, I learned from Levi and Laney, which is precious little by the way. You've done a bang-up job of training those two not to talk either."

"Mia, can I—"

"No." She cut him off with an outstretched palm. "Let me... Please, Jay." She tried to gather her thoughts. She needed to stay focused and not ramble.

"I want to be here for you, Jay. I do. For Levi and Laney, too. And the rest of your family, whoever they are. But I realize that I can't really be because you won't let me. You don't want me to be. And that's fine. That's your choice…but it bothers me too much to *not* be." Mia felt her already-cracked heart break into a million pieces.

Pulling her shoulders up into a helpless shrug, she went on, "You were right, Jay. Your reason was better than mine." She stared at him, tears flooding her eyes. She tried unsuccessfully to blink them away. "Your reason was better than mine and I don't even know what it is."

His beautiful green eyes sparkled with unshed tears and Mia felt a million times worse that she was hurting him in this process, too.

His voice sounded raspy when he spoke. "Mia, I told you how it was with me."

"I know." She swiped at her moist cheeks and choked back a sob. "I know that and I didn't listen. That's what I'm the sorriest about. Because I feel like this is my fault. Because I'm the one who can't handle things like they are."

At the look on his face, she nearly threw herself into his arms and took it all back.

He inhaled a deep breath and released it.

Then he nodded and came around to her side of the bar where he put his arms around her. "Okay," he whispered, and held her tight. He pulled away, his gaze on her. His fingers entwined with hers and in that moment, she nearly caved, but his next words saved her.

"It's not all your fault, Mia. In fact, it's more mine than yours. I'm the one who can't give you all of myself. I knew it wouldn't be enough for you, but I was selfish to take what I could get. I'm so sorry I hurt you. Please believe me when I say I never meant to. I understand why you need to let me go. And somehow, I need to let you go, too." He brushed a kiss across her forehead.

"I want you to understand that the Coast Guard is just a job to me. It's a job I love, yes, but it wouldn't stop me from loving you, too, and being exactly what you need. No, I can't be with you in the way that you want, or the way that I want, and it was probably stupid of me to try. But just so that I'm clear about where I stand, I tried to keep you because I've never wanted anyone in my entire life as much as I want you."

CHAPTER SIXTEEN

JAY KNEW MIA was right; they were better off ending things before they became any more tangled than they already were. Problem was, he'd done a terrible job of protecting himself from getting hurt. Even worse, he'd hurt Mia. The whole "relationship thing" had been ill-advised. Being honest with himself, he'd known that from the beginning but selfishly, he'd wanted whatever he could get. His heart felt like a painful mass of battered pulp in his chest, every beat serving to remind him of how deeply this cut.

With Mia on a shopping trip with Laney, and Levi actually hanging out with a friend for once, Jay headed over to Mia's house. Nora wasn't home because he'd seen her car parked at the health food store. Was Jay avoiding seeing them? Yes, he was. It would be too painful to see Mia right now, and for some reason the thought of seeing Nora left him with a current of guilt.

Pre-heartbreak, he'd told Mia he'd check the

camera's images because she'd been having a difficult time accessing them with her tablet. He gathered his laptop from the backseat of his car and carried it to the front porch.

After removing the card from the camera, he slipped it into his computer and downloaded the file. Scrolling through, he was surprised at the myriad animals captured on screen: raccoons, opossums, rats, mice, a family of skunks and numerous stray cats. A lone coyote showed up in three photos. There was no evidence that it was hunting cats, but that didn't mean it wasn't. It was a fact that coyotes preyed on cats and even dogs. But if, as Mia believed, such a large number of cats had disappeared, it seemed like it would have taken a whole pack of coyotes.

Then a strange shot appeared; a person wearing a stocking hat and dressed in dark clothing. A man, judging from the size and general shape of him, although he couldn't be 100 percent sure. A surge of adrenaline rushed through him as the possibilities ticked through his mind—a prowler, a burglar, some killer looking for victims… But no, the figure reappeared and left a trap at the brush line. Jay watched the events play out in a slide show; a cat approached the trap, sniffed around and went inside. Presumably, the trap snapped shut because the figure showed up again, disappearing with the trap and then returning. This happened again and again, sometimes over successive nights, and sometimes a few days would go by. He also captured various other animals, all of which were turned loose. The cats were never seen again. Was this some kind of vigilante cat rescuer? But why would this person be so secretive? Where were the cats? Why wouldn't Mia know about this person?

The slide show continued. Several nights captured more of the same; raccoons, rats, the skunk family returning, the coyote, more rats, cats... And then, the form appeared again. This time, it came closer, the camera catching his furtive glance first one way and then the other, but never fully revealing his face. He was sure it was a male, and he seemed familiar. Jay felt like he should know him...

One thing was certain, though: he needed to talk to Mia.

JAY DROVE THE short distance home from Mia's wondering what to do. There had to be a logical explanation here that he wasn't considering. Yet a weird, unsettling feeling was creeping over him. Someone was trapping cats without Mia's knowledge, but why would they do that?

He parked in the driveway and walked into his house. Instantly, he realized no one was home here either, not even Coastie. Where was his dog? Stepping into the kitchen, he saw a note on the counter: *Ty and I are walking Coastie on the beach. Levi.* That was a relief. Ty with the blue hair? Huh. Well, she seemed like a nice girl.

Feeling antsy, he moved into the bedroom he "shared" with Levi. He'd pretty much given it up for his little brother, keeping his clothes in the closet and in the bottom two drawers of the dresser. Intending to catch up with the kids on the beach and maybe take a walk of his own, he noticed Levi had put some of his socks in one of the drawers Jay was using.

When he opened Levi's drawer to put them away, an envelope fell out. He picked it up, noticed the return address and froze: State of Oregon, Juvenile Court.

A flood of adrenaline swept along his bloodstream. Levi was in trouble? What should he do here? Did he read the letter?

He fished his phone out of his pocket. Maybe Josie would have a clue. His finger was poised to tap on her number when he realized that if she knew Levi was in trouble, she would have shared it with him already. Besides, Josie had enough on her plate as it was; he needed to handle this on his own. He put the envelope back without looking inside.

SHOPPING WITH TWO teenage girls was enough to make anyone forget their problems, if only for a little while. Mia was glad that Jay didn't allow their estrangement to affect her relationship with Laney and Levi. She and Laney had planned the trip the week before along with Charlotte and Elise. They'd driven an hour down the coast so the girls could go to an open-air outlet mall. All in all, the day had gone great. Mia thought she'd done a good job of keeping her heartache to herself.

She got up the next morning to a quiet house. A combination of hope and habit had her preparing a bowl of food for her still-MIA cats. She took it, along with her coffee, out onto the porch to enjoy the ocean view. Laney joined her before she'd finished drinking that first cup.

"Hey, um, Elise and I were wondering if we could walk to the bakery this morning and meet Brianna and Kaylee for doughnuts?"

"Yeah, sure. Go for it." Mia checked the time on her phone. "You've got a few hours before Jay is picking you up."

"Cool. Thanks, Mia."

A few minutes later the girls departed and soon after that Nora came downstairs outfitted for work at the health food store. After downing a cup of tea, she headed out the door and Mia found herself alone again. She was considering a walk on the beach when she saw Jay's car pull up.

Just watching him get out of the car, she was startled by how painful a wave of longing she felt. He was so good-looking, and sure, she'd been attracted to that initially. But now that she knew him better, she realized that it was everything inside that had hooked her. His attempts to keep her out had failed in some ways because she could see his goodness—fostering Coastie, caring for his siblings, his devotion to the Coast Guard volunteer outreach, helping with Lucky Cats and refusing to give up until he'd rescued Duke. Mia had asked Dr. Anthony about the cat and he'd told Mia he would try to track him down for her. She hadn't said anything to Jay yet, hoping to surprise him if Ted was able to locate the cat.

"Hey," she said, managing a smile as he climbed the porch steps. Coastie pranced along beside him. "I thought you weren't picking the girls up until ten so I told them they could walk to the bakery to meet their friends."

George let out a welcoming woof.

"That's fine. That's good, actually. I need to talk to you anyway."

"Okay." Mia led them all inside so she could get more coffee. She offered him a cup while he turned on his laptop.

She took a seat across from him at the table. "What's going on?"

At his serious tone and expression, a ball of nerves tightened inside her. "Mia, I looked at your camera photos while you guys were gone yesterday."

"And...?"

"I don't know how to tell you this, so I'm going to show you instead."

"Jay, you're scaring me. What did you find? Is it a cougar?"

He tapped a few keys and then swiveled the screen until she could see the monitor.

"What is this? What is going on?"

"He's trapping cats. Do you recognize this person? He seems familiar to me but I can't quite…"

Mia sat back, confusion and dread clouding her brain. "Why would someone be trapping cats at my house?"

Jay shook his head. "I don't know. I was hoping you could tell me."

She leaned in and studied the photos again. He seemed familiar…

A loud crash sounded from somewhere upstairs. She jumped up and looked around. "Where are the dogs?"

"I don't know," Jay said. "Coastie?" he called. No response.

They climbed the stairs, peeking into each room as they traveled down the hall. As soon as Mia reached the guest room she could see what had happened. "Oh, George, what have you gotten into?"

Jay followed close behind as she entered the room the girls were sharing. Garbage was strewn all over the floor, trailing from the open door of the bathroom. She went there. "Ugh. He pulled over the garbage can in here."

"That was a loud crash, though."

"I know. I told the girls to keep it up on the counter so he wouldn't get into it. He found a way obviously." She glared at the dog.

An already-contrite George slunk out the door. Coastie followed, tail wagging.

Jay said, "I can see Coastie and I are going to have the 'don't jump off the bridge just because your friends are doing it' talk, huh?"

They looked around at the mess. "Please

don't ask me to trade dogs with you," Jay joked as he began picking up the garbage.

Mia laughed and went to work in the bathroom. As she knelt on the floor, she saw a small brown paper bag with Laney's name written across the front. Torn and crinkled, she figured George had been after Laney's sack lunch leftovers. She picked it up and the contents fell out. As she absorbed exactly what she was seeing she felt the breath catch in her throat. She stared down at the box, the strip of colored cardboard and plastic on the bathroom floor.

"Jay," she called with a shaky breath as a sick feeling washed over her. "You need to come here."

"What is it? Now you're scaring me."

As he walked up behind her, she pointed.

He bent and peered at it. "What is it?"

"Pretty sure it's a pregnancy test."

"Is it Laney's?"

"I can't be sure. But it was inside a paper bag with her name on it."

"Is it…? Is she…?"

"It's positive."

AND JUST LIKE THAT, Jay felt the fragile framework of this world he'd been trying to create crumble down around him. A whooshing sound pulsated through his head like the crashing of ocean waves against the jetty. A sharp pain shot through his chest as he struggled to inhale a breath. If he wasn't medically trained he'd think he was having a heart attack as a combination of panic and anxiety bore down on him hard and fast.

Everything he and Josie had worked so hard to prevent seemed to be happening all at once and all under his watch. Levi was in trouble and Laney was pregnant. He never should have agreed to take them in. They had been much better off with Josie. With weak legs, he turned and sat on the edge of the tub willing himself to breathe. Beside him, Coastie let out a whimper.

At least he hadn't screwed up the dog. But then again, she wasn't technically his. He'd been dragging his feet about officially adopting her, a good thing, he could see now. He probably would have messed her up, too...

"Jay?" He slowly became aware of the fact that Mia was talking, saying his name.

"What?" he whispered.

"You need to go downstairs in case the girls come in. I don't want them to know that we found out like this."

He shook his head back and forth slowly, her words not registering. "Why?"

"Listen to me." She stood before him and placed her hands on his shoulders. She gave him a light shake. "Because you need time to process this, to figure out what's going on and what you're going to do. You need to talk to…someone. Josie maybe? This needs to be dealt with very carefully. You can't approach this with anger or just brush it off and hope it goes away."

"Brush it off?" he snapped. "How do you brush off your little sister's pregnancy? Believe me, I know that it's impossible to brush off a baby."

She opened her mouth to comment but snapped it shut instead. Calmly she pleaded, "Please, Jay, go downstairs and get your game face on. Your rescue face, the one you use when you're on that helicopter and telling people everything will be okay. Because it will be. One way or another, it will be. This is your fifteen-year-old sister who may be pregnant. You have to handle this with care."

He sat for a few more seconds, but the only thing he could truly process was his own failure, and how badly he'd let his family down.

CHAPTER SEVENTEEN

Mia couldn't stand not knowing what was going on. She had to give Jay credit, though, as he'd acted only slightly off when Laney and Elise walked through the door. Laney had asked him if he was okay and he'd told her he was tired. That was good.

That had been more than an hour ago. She hoped the old adage that no news was good news was working here.

She added sunflower seeds to the eggs and sautéed veggies in the pan and stirred. She looked at her phone hoping to see a text that she knew wasn't there because she'd been checking it almost constantly. She carried the pan to the table where her mom was buttering toast for each of them. Mia sat and dished some eggs onto both plates. She shoved the food around with her fork as she thought about Laney.

"Your father would have hated this." Nora smiled wistfully and took a bite of the egg mixture. "But I think it's delicious."

"Yeah well, Dad pretty much hated everything, didn't he? Unless the Navy served it to him. Except you and Kyle."

Mia's bite turned to sand in her mouth as her mother stared back at her looking shocked and a little wounded. Ugh. She hated to upset her mom. Normally she avoided talking about her dad. But the words just slipped out. Or maybe not. She was brimming with nervous energy, and ever since she'd had that conversation with Jay on the beach she'd been thinking about what he'd said. Jay was right. She shouldn't have had to spend her childhood walking on eggshells. She shouldn't have to do it now. Three years of therapy had helped her accept the fact that nothing she could have done would have made her father love her or persuaded him to treat her differently. But she shouldn't have had to try. He should have loved her, too. That's what dads were supposed to do.

And she shouldn't have to avoid the topic now to spare her mom's feelings. Yes, her mom deserved Mia's respect and love and admiration, but Mia had deserved some of that from her father, too.

"Well, I don't know about that," Nora muttered, wiping her mouth with a napkin. She didn't meet Mia's eyes, so she knew she'd hit a nerve.

Mia inhaled a sustaining breath and hoped she wasn't making a huge mistake. "He was mean to me, Mom."

"Mean? Mia, that's harsh, don't you think? He never laid a hand on you."

"That's true," she returned. "Not in anger or in love. One of my earliest memories as a little girl is trying to hold his hand. He pulled it away like he'd been burned." Tears welled up in her eyes. Why did this still hurt so much? she wondered. "He was worse than mean. His total lack of regard for me was cruel. I didn't deserve it. I was a good kid."

"Oh, Mia, I know you were. He didn't mean to be. He didn't know…"

"Didn't know what, Mom? I've spent years trying to understand why he didn't love me. I still don't understand that part, but I've learned to accept that I can't change the past. I've done my absolute best to be smart and good and productive, to do things that will make the world a better place so that I'll feel valued. A lot of that is because I didn't get any of that from him."

"But I love you. I value you. More than anything in this world, Mia. More than your father even or I never would have agreed…"

George let out a woof from where he was lying beside Mia's chair. A banging sounded on the porch. He lumbered to his feet and let out a real bark. Which he didn't do often, but when he did it was impressive. Mia felt confident the deep sound reverberating through his barrel chest would scare off anyone with evil intentions.

She got up and walked toward the door. A loud knock followed before she could even get there. Standing on her tiptoes, she looked out the window that made up the top portion of the door and felt her heart leap into her throat.

She opened the door to a sobbing teenage girl. "Laney? Sweetheart, are you okay?"

The girl threw her arms around Mia. "He didn't even give me a chance to explain. He wouldn't listen. He accused me of all this bad stuff and asked me what was wrong with me. He didn't say it but I know what he was thinking. He's afraid I'm like our mom. But I'm not and it's not how he thinks… He's totally being irrational. So I ran away."

Like their mom? What did that mean? "Shh, it's okay." Mia held her and let her cry. "It will be okay." And, Mia thought, it would be. Because she was about to do whatever it took to make sure of it.

AFTER GETTING LANEY into the house, they settled on the couch. Nora made a "calming" tea that didn't taste half-bad. Mia let Laney cry, offered words of encouragement and didn't ask questions.

"Can I stay here for a while?" Laney finally asked.

"Of course you can, but I need to call your brother and let him know you're here and safe."

"That's fine, but I don't want to see him right now. He just doesn't get that Levi and I are capable of doing things, making decisions and helping."

"I'm sorry." Mia didn't ask how having a baby accomplished any of these things. "How about a bath?"

"That would be nice. I need to think."

"Come down when you're done and we'll have some ice cream. I have a container of the real stuff hidden in the freezer behind a bag of rice flour."

"I think the occasion warrants the real stuff," Nora said. "I'll join you."

Laney offered a weak smile and headed for the stairs. "Okay, thanks, you guys."

Mia texted Jay: Laney is here.

He answered immediately: I suspected as much. I'm coming over.

Steeling herself, she tapped out a response: She doesn't want to see you. I told her she could stay awhile.

That's fine. I wouldn't want to see me, either. I need to talk to you.

Minutes later he was pulling up outside her house. She stepped outside and joined him. "Hey, she's really upset. Did she tell you anything?"

"No." He raked a hand through his hair. "Probably because I did exactly what you advised me not to. I confronted her. In anger. I don't know what's the matter with me. Well, I do. I'm afraid. I'm terrified… I feel like a total failure. And I'm not sure I can do this. I don't want to do this again…"

Mia nodded, waiting, hoping he'd continue. He backed away until he was leaning against the porch railing. Gazing out at the ocean to his left, he tapped his fingers on the railing for a long moment. A breeze set off the tinkling of her mom's wind chimes and brought with it the scent of the ocean. A dog barked, the sound carrying from the beach below them.

"Our mom…" Mia noticed a tremble in his hand as he brushed it across his jaw. "Our mom is mentally ill. Over the years she's been diagnosed with a variety of conditions—depression, bipolar disorder, personality disorder, narcissism... I don't know if you're familiar with mental illness, but my personal opinion is that she has a borderline personality disorder, which falls into what they call cluster B of personality disorders in the psychological world. She exhibits behavior from both the histrionic and narcissistic categories as well.

"She's been hospitalized numerous times, committed a couple of times and been on and off more medications than anyone could ever keep track of—everything from antipsychotics to mood stabilizers to antidepressants to plain old sedatives. These prescriptions usually help for short periods of time. I say short because she won't stay on them long enough to get stable. She doesn't like the side effects. She's... It makes life really difficult for her and for us."

To another's ear, the way he relayed this information might sound cold, but Mia knew better. She'd seen the depth of his kindness and compassion, his love for his siblings. Mia tried to imagine; she'd had a friend in college whose dad was schizophrenic. It was a constant balancing act between sympathy and compassion and self-preservation. And in Jay's case, the well-being of his five younger siblings had been paramount. The implications sank into her, the reason for much of his behavior—the silence, the secrecy, the distance he maintained with people. How in the world was he so normal considering? And Levi and Laney, too?

"How did you...? I mean, how are you not...?" She didn't even know what or how to ask the million questions swarming around in her mind.

"When Josie and I were little we had our grandma, our mom's mom. We lived with her, and our mom was just this person who kind of came and went in our lives. She's never been capable of motherhood in any meaningful way. The narcissism prevents her from putting anyone else's needs above her own.

"She can be very cruel and she's always erratic, but Gran managed to keep this distance between her and us. Our mom would be gone for weeks or months at a time. Now I realize that she was either hospitalized or living with a man. Like I said, part of her illness includes this constant need for attention and reassurance, which she gets from men, or tries to. When Gran died, she was living with one of her husbands, Lyle, and had just had Levi. They all moved in with us after that, into Gran's house. Laney was born a year later and Lyle somehow managed to keep her on meds to the point that she was somewhat stable. But he was killed in a car accident and that's when things got really bad. I think she loved him, as much as she is capable of that emotion, anyway."

He went on to explain how in her grief, their mom didn't get out of bed for weeks, barely came out of her room for months. He and Josie were already taking care of their siblings so in that respect things didn't change much. But when she finally emerged from that fog, her behavior spiraled downward very quickly.

"She went off her meds and fixated on finding another husband to replace Lyle. At one point, she moved in with a guy who didn't even know about us. She was with him for six months. She left Josie and me to take care of Levi and Laney. She would come home maybe once or twice a week to drop off a few groceries and pick up her mail."

"There was no one to help you?"

"That was complicated. Over the years, we had a few social workers, our aunt, teachers, a neighbor. There were a few people who tried, but Josie and I quickly figured out that the kind of help these people wanted to give us meant foster care and we would be separated. We promised Gran that we'd all stay together no matter what. I started working whatever jobs I could find—mowing lawns, yard work, fixing things. I landed my first real job when I was fifteen. I cleaned a woodworking shop in the evenings. After school, I would do my homework, help Josie as much as I could and then head to work. I didn't get home until two or three in the morning. But the owner was good to me, taught me stuff. We did what we had to do to survive and stay together. That's what we're doing still. It became a little easier when I graduated from high school and was able to join the Coast Guard."

"What about your dad?"

"Dads, you mean? Plural. Six kids, three different fathers. Or at least that's what she tells us. Genetics seem to hold true for me and my sister, Josie. And for Levi and Laney. I'm not so sure about Dean and Delilah. She was cheating on Dean's dad with a guy who has red hair, and Delilah has red hair. But she thought it was clever to name us according to the first letter of our dad's first names. Josie and I were fathered by a guy named Jacob, so we got *J* names. Levi and Laney's dad was Lyle. And she was married to David when Dean and Delilah were born. She recently got married for the sixth time to a man named Neil. At least we can rest easy knowing that no Nancys or Neds will be born, because she had to have a hysterectomy after Delilah." He paused. "She's had a string of other boyfriends and fiancés. The only one who was worth anything and wanted anything to do with us was Lyle, and he died.

"Her latest husband has a criminal record that includes child abuse, so Josie decided to file a lawsuit to gain custody of our siblings. She's keeping Dean and Delilah, but Levi and Laney decided they wanted to come and live with me. I wanted this to work so badly. For Josie's sake especially. She's the one who has been on the front lines, so to speak, for the last several years. Joining the Coast Guard was great in that I had a steady paycheck to give her, but it also took me away from them, leaving her to raise four kids including the two baby Ds."

Mia felt hot tears burning in her eyes. This was so unbelievable. Yet she believed every word because she knew Jay. She had seen his love, his complete disregard for his own comfort and needs. She knew Levi and Laney and all the bits and pieces she'd heard from them were now flashing through her mind and snapping into place to form a picture. A picture of a brother and sister who had overcome dysfunction so severe she could barely comprehend it.

"I know how this must sound. Like we're a bunch of freaks."

His tone, his body language suggested that he expected her to recoil from the information, from him. She wasn't about to do that, but she wasn't quite sure what to do. "No, more like you and Josie are the most incredible brother-sister team ever. You give new meaning to the word *family*."

He nodded. "You can see why this pregnancy has me so shaken up. How will we manage with another baby? Josie already has the little ones and I... It's not that I don't love my siblings. I do, more than anything. I want so much more for them. But my finances are strapped as it is with Josie in nursing school, living expenses, insurance, sports, day care, dance classes for Delilah...life. I wanted Laney to go to college and have a chance at a normal life. I want that for all of them."

It explained so much. Everything. She wanted to throw her arms around him and tell him all of that was still possible. But she knew it was too soon for that. Instead, she stood rooted to the spot because she wasn't sure what to do. She knew he wouldn't want her pity. If he wanted that, he'd shout his story from rooftops because everyone would listen. He could write a book and it would undoubtedly be a bestseller. Instead, he took great pains to keep it to himself. They all did. Mia couldn't help but think that silence, that avoidance, came at a cost.

Finally, she went with, "Thank you for telling me."

He smiled sadly, catching her gaze with his own. "I've never told anyone our story. As you know very well, I don't talk about it. But I wanted you to know now because I think—I hope—maybe it will show you how much I care about you. I haven't allowed myself to get close to anyone. My family has always come first. I hope you can see how it has to." He paused to look out at the ocean before turning toward her again. "The second I let my guard down this is what happens. And there's a problem with Levi, too. He might be in trouble..." He folded his arms across his chest. "This is my fault. I never should have let myself get close to you. I knew it wasn't a good idea, but I just... I couldn't seem to stop myself. And even when you broke it off, I kept wondering whether we'd still find a way. But that was part of the problem, too. It was distracting me from my purpose."

Mia felt her already-aching heart take another hit. "Wait a minute. Are you saying you believe this happened because you weren't vigilant enough? Because you took a little bit of time for yourself and for me?"

Forcing her own feelings aside, she said, "Jay, none of this is your fault. No matter what's happened, or what you think has happened, I know Levi and Laney. They are good, wonderful kids—smart, kind, thoughtful. They are amazing human beings because of you and Josie."

"But...you were right. I should have paid closer attention. I should have... I don't even know."

"What did Laney say exactly?"

He shook his head. "Like I said, I didn't really give her a chance to explain."

Her conversation with Laney played through her mind. Teenage girl scenarios followed. "Did she confirm that she's pregnant?"

"Pretty much. She didn't deny it."

"Pretty much? So you accused her—you didn't ask her?" Mia was getting irritated now by his inability to stay focused on the bigger picture. "But she didn't confirm it?"

Jay's phone began ringing. He pulled it out

of his pocket. "It's Josie. I have to answer it in case Laney called her.

"Hi, Josie."

As he listened, his already drawn and stressed expression morphed into one of shock. His eyes widened and his face went white. "What do you know?" He listened for a few minutes. Finally, his gaze found hers, full of pain and confusion. "Yes. I'm on my way." He clicked his phone off and said to her, "We have to go."

"Jay, are you all right?"

"No. I'm not."

Mia assumed that somehow Josie had heard the news about Laney. So his next words came as a total shock.

"Levi has been arrested."

"Arrested? For what?"

"I'm not sure. Josie is in town. She said to meet her at the police station."

"Okay, well, let me know if there's anything I can do—"

"Both of us. It has something to do with you, too. With the vet clinic."

CHAPTER EIGHTEEN

MIA RAN INTO the house and told her mom that she needed to take care of an errand. Nora readily agreed to be there for Laney when she came downstairs. Mia grabbed her purse and keys. Jay was waiting by her car. They climbed in and Mia drove the few short miles to the police station in silence.

"There she is." Jay pointed across the parking lot toward the steps that led into Pacific Cove's small police station. A woman was standing beside one of the two benches there.

Mia parked and they got out. As they neared her, Mia could see that Jay's sister was also tall. She had long, dark brownish-red hair and eyes so strikingly green she had to make an effort not to stare. Her smile revealed the same dimple on the left side of her mouth that Jay had. The resemblance between her and her older brother was startling.

She reached out a hand for Mia to shake. "Mia, hi. It's nice to finally meet you. Levi and Laney talk about you all the time. Thank you so much for everything you've done for them. I wish we could have met under different and better circumstances."

"I've heard a lot of wonderful things about you as well."

"Josie, what's going on?" Jay interjected, putting an understandable end to the small talk.

Josie turned toward her brother. "The police are saying that Levi has been illegally selling cats."

"Selling cats?" Jay shook his head. "What the…? To who?"

Mia felt light-headed. The ground seemed to turn to liquid and roll beneath her. Gulping a breath, she reached for the back of the bench.

"To a company that is allegedly using them for medical research. There's apparently nothing illegal about selling cats for that purpose, except that the company buying them isn't properly licensed. And maybe doing some kind of shady research. I don't know all the details but the investigation revealed that some of the cats were coming from a vet clinic here in Pacific Cove. There's ethical violations or some such thing…"

Mia whispered, "He's been selling my cats?" Her eyes found Jay's and her heart seemed to break a little bit more. He looked like he was in pain, muscles tense, his face pale and drawn. She wasn't sure how much more bad news he could take or if he'd already reached this conclusion himself. "That's why I can't find Duke."

SHORT OF A tragedy involving dismemberment or death at his hands, Jay didn't see how he could have possibly screwed this up any worse. He turned and paced down the sidewalk, muttered a curse of desperation and came back again.

"This is a mess. My mess. I can't believe I didn't see... How could I have let this happen? I shouldn't have..." He stopped himself as he caught sight of Mia's glare.

"Jay," Mia said firmly. "You need to snap out of it. Just like with Laney, this isn't about you. Despite the way he acts, Levi is only a kid. Whatever happened or whatever he did, he needs you right now. He needs to know that you love him no matter what." She pointed toward the doors. "Go in there and be what he needs."

"You don't understand. This never would have happened if it wasn't for—"

"But it did happen," she shot back. "And you have to deal with it."

Josie stepped forward and took him by the elbow. "Jay, she's right. She's absolutely right. Right now, we need to go in there and get our little brother and be there for him in whatever way we can."

They all headed inside and were met by two police officers who explained what Josie had already relayed. He added that Levi had requested an attorney. Smart kid, Mia thought, a wave of relief washing through her. Even from the sketchy details she had, she knew he was going to need a good one.

"I'll call Craig," Josie said, already dialing her phone.

A man in blue jeans and a plaid button-down shirt joined them. He looked at Mia. "Dr. Frasier?"

"Yes."

"Hi, I'm Detective Barnes." They shook hands. "You're a veterinarian at Pacific Cove Vet Clinic and the person in charge of this Lucky Cats organization, is that correct?"

"Yes, it is."

"Good. I'm glad you're here. We're going to need to ask you a few questions as well. Can you follow me please?"

PART OF MIA wanted to run away. She wanted to go home and hug her mom and check on

Laney and pretend this wasn't happening. But she couldn't. Not yet. Levi needed her. Jay needed her. Even though he'd done his best to keep her away, she realized now that this was his defense mechanism. But this time, she was going to help whether he wanted her to or not. And her first order of business would be to find out exactly what, if anything, Levi had done. In her heart, she knew he would never do anything to harm an animal. Not knowingly, anyway.

The detective gave her a few minutes. She called her attorney and quickly outlined the situation. As she anticipated, Mia was instructed not to say anything until she arrived.

Next, she called her mom. "Hey, Mom. How's it going?"

"Good! I love this kid. We're watching *Goonies*. Remember that movie? So cute. Laney's never seen it. She's loving that it was filmed right here in our stomping grounds. I told her I'd take her to Astoria to look at the old houses."

"Great. Thanks, Mom. I'll be home as soon as I can, but it might be a little while."

"Everything okay, sweetheart?"

"Not really. Levi has gotten himself into a bit of trouble. I'm afraid it's kind of my fault."

But not in the sense Jay was clearly intimating. "I'll explain later."

"Okay," her mom said tentatively. "I don't like the way you sound right now."

Mia let out a sigh. "I don't either, Mom. I don't like the way I feel."

She was hanging up the phone as Detective Barnes stepped back into the room.

CRAIG HAD CALLED their attorney in Portland, who had gotten them in touch with the best criminal defense attorney he knew in the area. After an hour waiting for her to arrive, and another three hours of questioning, the police finally allowed them to take Levi home.

Josie made them grilled cheese sandwiches, which sat untouched as they gathered around the table.

Jay wasn't sure where to start. "Does this have anything to do with the envelope in your dresser?"

"What envelope?"

"The one that fell out of your sock drawer from the state of Oregon, juvenile court."

Levi stared down at his plate. "No."

"An envelope from the juvenile court?" Josie looked from him to Levi and back again.

"Family court," Levi clarified.

She asked, "What's going on, Levi? Does

this have to do with the custody hearing? Did you send in a statement like we talked about?"

"What statement?" Jay asked. "I don't know anything about this."

"Levi did some research," she explained. "In lieu of testifying, often the court will accept a written statement from a witness. He wants to testify, he and Laney both do. I told him he could send in a statement."

Jay glared at them both. "Without talking to me? Levi, I told you I wanted to keep you out of it. I don't want you and Laney to have to go to court."

"That's the problem, Jay!" Levi shouted, throwing his napkin down on the table. "You want to do everything! You don't want Laney and me to do anything. You want to do it all yourself. We can do stuff, too, you know? Maybe not as good as you. But we can."

"Okay," Josie said in a gentle tone. "Let's talk about this calmly and from the beginning. What is the letter about, Levi?"

Levi inhaled a breath and slowly blew it out. With a determined set to his jaw, he scowled at Jay. "I applied to be emancipated. If I get emancipated it basically means that I'm legally an adult and I can make my own decisions. I can go to court and testify for Laney, Dean and Delilah and you can't stop me. I can go to school online and work and send money to Josie, too. Like you do."

Jay buried his head in his hands as the implication of Levi's actions seeped into him. Jay realized Levi was right. Laney was right, too. He'd been completely obtuse, stubborn and overbearing. As difficult as it was, they should have a say in their futures. Jay was all about taking control of life. He'd always had to. Even though he'd only been trying to take care of them all, he'd gone overboard. In trying to shelter them from the difficulty that he knew a trial would bring, he'd taken away their control. As a result, they'd both found ways to get some semblance of that control back. He couldn't blame them; he would have done the same thing. If he hadn't been so intent on doing things his way, maybe Laney wouldn't have acted out by drinking alcohol and getting pregnant. Levi certainly wouldn't have been forced to these lengths of desperation.

"Is this why you were selling cats? So you could send money to Josie?"

Levi shook his head. "No. I didn't even know I was *selling* them. The cops told me that part. I thought I was delivering them."

"Delivering them where?"

Levi shrugged. "To an animal shelter place. That's what Dr. Anthony told me."

"Where was Dr. Anthony when you got arrested?"

"I don't know. He wasn't there. He would give me the cats and tell me where to go. This guy in a white van would meet me somewhere and we'd transfer the cats from one van to another. He totally set me up. I can see that now."

"Where's the money?"

"It was probably all in cash. Each time, the guy would give me an envelope. I would take it to Dr. Anthony. I didn't even know there was money in the envelopes. I thought it was cat inventory or whatever." Levi scoffed and Jay knew he was embarrassed at not having figured this out. The kid was always so hard on himself. No mystery where that trait came from.

Jay felt his stomach sink. No way to trace cash. The word of a poor sixteen-year-old kid from a troubled background against that of a highly educated, esteemed and respected doctor. And a medical research facility. Everyone in Pacific Cove knew and loved Dr. Anthony. The entire community was rooting for McKenzie. Levi didn't stand a chance. No one would ever believe him.

"I need to talk to Mia," Levi said. "The cops said the clinic might be in trouble if this is true, like their reputation and maybe some legal stuff. I need to explain."

This was so incredibly difficult. And Jay had been through plenty of "difficult" in his life. Levi could explain all day long, but Jay knew how much Dr. Anthony meant to Mia. He was like a father to her. He also knew the man was brilliant. If he'd set Levi up, Jay knew he'd done a good job of it. No one would ever believe that he'd done this. Not to mention that the man was a very successful veterinarian. Jay had seen the mansion he lived in and the fancy cars he and his wife drove. He made plenty of money and had no reason to sell cats. Those were the actions of a desperate person. It wouldn't be difficult to make Levi appear to be that.

Levi put his head down on his arms. "I only wanted to help."

Josie reached out and laid a hand on his back. "We know that, Levi."

Jay reached over from the other side. "We're here for you, buddy. Always." He let out a sigh. "I need to go pick up Laney."

"Let's all go," Josie said. "A family is a family even when it's in crisis mode." She shot a pointed look at Jay. "It's not the first time we've been in crisis mode and it undoubtedly will not be the last."

Jay thought about Laney and his stomach dropped. "That's true. In fact, we're about to face another."

CHAPTER NINETEEN

WHEN MIA ARRIVED HOME, Laney and her mom were practicing yoga poses in the living room.

"Mia, hey, look at Laney's downward dog. What a natural."

Mia smiled. "Seriously, Laney, that is amazing. My mom does not pull punches when it comes to yoga skills. Did she tell you how bad I am at it?"

"It may have been mentioned," Laney said with a giggle, and then added a sincere, "But only in the sense that she's concerned." They settled on the floor into matching double pigeons that had Mia shaking her head with wonder.

"So jealous. I tip over backward when I do that pose." Perching on the edge of the sofa, she clasped her hands together and asked Laney, "Have you heard from Jay or Josie, by any chance?"

"My phone is off. It's been upstairs this whole time." Her eyes widened. "Does Josie know about this, about me and us… Jay and I having a fight?"

Mia could only assume that she did at this point. "Probably. Your sister is in town."

"She is? Oh, my phone…"

"Well, she's here because of Levi."

"Levi?"

Mia wasn't sure how much to say but felt confident Jay and Josie would tell her the basics. She went with, "Your brother was arrested earlier today."

"Arrested?" A shocked Nora sank onto the sofa next to her.

"Arrested? Levi?" Laney repeated the words as if she couldn't quite believe them. "He would never…do anything wrong. You know him, he's like sixteen going on thirty. This has to be a mistake."

A knock on the door saved her from having to explain further. Jay, Josie and Levi were standing on the porch. Mia invited them in and they'd barely made it inside before Laney was throwing her arms around Levi.

"I take it you told her?" Jay asked Mia. She couldn't read anything in his expression.

"Only the bare minimum. I was afraid she'd hear it from someone else."

Josie nodded. "Thank you, Mia. That was

actually really thoughtful in these days of social media oversharing."

"What's going on? What happened?" Laney demanded. "Levi, are you going to jail?"

"I hope not, Lanes," Levi said. His gaze found Mia's and she wished she could throw her arms around him, too, like Laney had. These circumstances already hurt and they'd only just begun.

Jay said to Laney, "Why don't you get your stuff and we'll go home and talk about it. All of this." His expression seemed to beg her not to argue.

"No." Laney stepped back and crossed her arms over her chest. "I'm not going with you."

"Laney, stop being unreasonable. We've got a lot going on. Please, get your stuff. We're not talking about this here."

"Why not? Why can't I talk about stuff, Jay?"

"You know very well that we don't air our private business in this family."

"Air our private business?" Laney repeated with an eye roll. "And yet people still seem to find things out, don't they?" She turned to Josie. "He's the one who is unreasonable, Josie. Even though he says he wants Levi and me to stay with him, he doesn't act like he does. He says Levi and I can't testify at the hearing when we all know it will increase our chances of winning by about a million percent. He won't let me get a cat, he won't commit to keeping Coastie, who is the most amazing dog that has ever lived. He loves her, but he won't keep her. You see where I'm going with this? He won't even commit to Mia. He claims he wants to be a family, but he isn't acting like it."

Testify? The light went on in Mia's brain. The night Laney had too much to drink she'd mentioned that Jay wouldn't allow her to "test and fry." She'd had no idea what that had meant. A simple interpretation of that drunk rambling could easily be "testify." Couple that with Elise's statement about Laney possibly not getting to stay, and it all made sense. She was scared that she'd have to leave. Mia couldn't blame her. Could Jay really not see that this is why her behavior had been so erratic?

If Mia thought Jay looked devastated before, now he appeared completely ruined. "Laney… You know what? It's not as easy as it looks. Maybe you'll do everything right where your child is concerned but for now, I have to—"

Laney let out a groan of frustration and stomped a foot. "I'm not pregnant, Jay! I was trying to tell you that, but you wouldn't let me. You wouldn't even listen—"

"Pregnant?" Josie broke in. "Was that a possibility?"

"Yes," Jay said.

"No!" Laney cried at the same time. She looked at Josie. "My friend asked me to buy her a pregnancy test because her aunt works at the drugstore. No one knows me here yet. So I did it. George," she said, pointing at the dog who was quietly watching the drama from his spot near the sofa, "got the test out of the garbage. Mia and Jay found it and our genius brother here automatically assumed it was mine."

"It was in a bag with your name on it, Laney."

"So what? It was in my lunch bag and that automatically means it's mine? I don't even have a boyfriend. And even if I did I wouldn't be having sex. I'm too young in case you didn't notice. Did it even cross your mind that maybe it wasn't mine?"

"Okay," Mia broke in. "This is a lot for everyone to take in and—"

"Did you know?" Jay narrowed his eyes and looked at Mia. "Did you know Laney wasn't pregnant?"

She sighed. "No, but I didn't assume that she was, either. I was trying to tell you this when Josie called about Levi. But Laney is right, it should have occurred to you, too. You need to take a step back and think about some things, Jay. As much as you want to do the right thing, your lack of trust and confidence in people, especially people who love you, isn't doing you any favors. It's not doing your family any good."

Levi stepped forward, appearing to be on the verge of tears. It nearly did her in. "Dr. Frasier, I want you to know that I didn't—"

She would have given nearly anything not to have to interrupt him. "Levi, please don't say anything. I've already spoken with my attorney. We can't talk about what happened. I'm a witness and what I know could get you into more trouble."

"You're a witness?" Jay repeated.

Levi looked stricken.

She nodded. "Not just a witness. At this point, it looks like I may be charged in the case as well."

JAY SHOULD HAVE known better than to believe that things couldn't get any worse. What Mia had said was worse. What did she know about all of this? It had to be bad for her to tell Levi not to talk to her. This was all so unbelievable. He'd been so careful to keep her out of the madness that was his life and yet now she held Levi's life, his future, in her hands.

And Jay knew that she'd never believe Levi over Dr. Anthony. Why would she? She'd told him that he was a father figure to her. Family first. That was Jay's very own philosophy. He'd seen Mia execute the same belief where her mom was concerned. She'd demanded her mom be rescued first; she'd begged Jay to take care of her. She treated Dr. Anthony, his wife and McKenzie with the same reverence. She'd committed to stay in Pacific Cove as long as Dr. Anthony needed her.

He couldn't blame her. He'd do the same in her situation, had already done the same, essentially. He'd chosen his family over her from the very beginning. Why should it be any different for her?

Coastie jumped onto the sofa where he was sitting. Josie and Laney had gone to bed. Levi was in his room, but the soft light of his lamp glowing from beneath the door suggested he was still awake. Knowing Levi, he was probably studying ways to handle his own defense in court.

The dog nudged his hand and he turned to look into those brown eyes that always seemed to know how he was feeling and what he was thinking. He scratched her neck. "Laney is right, isn't she? I need to commit. It's not fair for you just like it wasn't fair to Mia."

She let out a contented sigh and curled up next to him, her head in his lap.

"I want you to stay." There, he'd said it. It felt good to say the words. A lightness filled his chest. Even under these circumstances, it managed to ease the ache in his heart a tiny bit.

Was Mia right, too? Did he need to have a little more faith in the people he loved? And he did love Mia, he realized. He loved her and yet he suddenly realized how much frustration and pain he must have caused her. And now, because of him, his mistakes might cost her her livelihood, too.

Mia PACED IN her kitchen trying to solve this puzzle. Levi claimed he didn't know he was selling the cats. His story was that he was acting on Dr. Anthony's behalf. And hence, hers too in a way, since most of the cats he'd sold had come from Lucky Cats. It was too bizarre to believe and yet she knew Levi. But she'd known Ted longer.

Wait. *Most* of the cats...

She went to her computer and pulled up the photos that Jay had retrieved from her security camera. Recognition rolled through her brain, unstoppable and every bit as dreadful as a tidal wave. She knew exactly who the figure was. What she couldn't figure out was why...? She needed to talk to him.

Closing the file, a photo of McKenzie on the desktop caught her eye. And that's when she had her answer.

"Of course!" she said, giving her forehead a smack.

"Hey," her mom said, walking into the room. "That's my daughter you're assaulting there."

Mia managed a tired grin. "I think I figured this out, Mom. I may know what happened..." She riffled through the papers her attorney had given her until she found the name of the company Levi had allegedly been selling to. An internet search added further credence to her theory. But any satisfaction she would have felt quickly gave way to a bone-deep sadness.

She ran the scenario by her mom, who agreed with her theory.

"Wow, this is really terrible."

"It is. What do I do now? How do I choose between people that I love? I understand Ted's desperation, Mom. You know McKenzie. I'd do just about anything to save her myself. And if it were me, I think you'd do anything to save me."

Nora reached out and squeezed her hand. "You got that right."

"If this gets out it will ruin him. He'll never be able to practice again probably. And then what happens to McKenzie? And to Sara? Levi will recover. The charges against him aren't that serious. I mean, my attorney said it's highly unlikely that he'll spend any time in jail, especially since he's underage."

Nora stared out the window for a long moment, a troubled expression on her face. She looked back at Mia and said, "This is a very tough decision you're facing here. Choosing one of them over the other will cause so much pain for the other…"

Mia felt a welling of sympathy for her mom.

"Mom, I'm sorry I've given you a hard time about Dad lately. It couldn't have been easy for you to be stuck in the middle between two people you loved, either. I thought I was over it, but maybe I'm not."

Nora glanced away for a few seconds, her fingers tapping on the countertop before her. "Except that…" When she faced her again, tears were shining in her eyes. "Oh, Mia. You're right about your father. It shouldn't have been that way for you. I should have left him when you were a girl. But he was a good dad to Kyle and…"

A tingle ran up her spine. "What do you mean?"

"I loved him. I did. He loved me and he loved Kyle. But you're right, he didn't love you."

Even though she knew it, Mia felt the words like a blow.

"Because you weren't his."

"What?"

"I know the timing is terrible here with all of this going on with Levi and Ted. I've wanted to tell you for the longest time, but I didn't know how."

"Words are always good," Mia said, the shock of this information still sinking in. "Or letters. Even a phone call... Who? How?"

"I had an affair with a married man before I met your fath... Bill. Bill promised he would take care of you if I married him, which he did. That was my mistake, because he never said he would love you. I believed that he would, though, I thought that would happen naturally. Especially after you were born, because you were so precious and sweet and smart as a whip, but he never..."

"Did." Mia finished for her. Questions immediately coalesced in her brain. "Who was he? Did he know...?"

"No, he didn't. And he died when you were only a few months old. He didn't have other children. Mia, I promise you I wouldn't have kept this from you had he lived. Bill and I had already agreed on that. That I would tell you someday. But when he died, it didn't seem as important."

Mia nodded, her eyes drawn to the image of McKenzie on the screen. But it had been important. This information could have changed the course of her life. The truth, she believed, was nearly always the right choice. Because the truth always came out in the end. Lying inevitably did more harm than the truth ever could. She needed to table these feelings for now. She had to do what she could for both Levi and Dr. Anthony.

"Mia, I'm so sorry, honey. I know those are just words, but..."

Her mom was staring at her with a terrified expression, tears sparkling in her pretty blue eyes, eyes that had never looked at her with anything but love.

"I forgive you, Mom. I love you more than I can say. You're the best mom in the world. Thank you for telling me. Yeah, maybe you should have told me sooner, but it'll be okay. And under the circumstances I'm facing here I think your timing is spot-on."

CHAPTER TWENTY

TED ANSWERED THE DOOR. "Mia! Hello, come in." He stepped aside to let her in. "Sara and McKenzie aren't here right now. I was just brewing some tea your mom gave me. It's supposed to boost my immune system. I've had this cold that's been lingering."

She followed him to the kitchen, where Mia found the first few minutes of small talk excruciating. But she sensed she needed to tread carefully. He set two mugs on the small table in the breakfast nook adjacent to the kitchen. The view looked out on one side of their fenced yard where Gustav was rolling in the grass with their cat Tumble.

Mia took a sip from her mug and then asked, "Have you heard about Levi?"

Ted's eyes snapped up to latch onto hers. "Levi? What about him?"

"He's been arrested, Ted."

"Arrested?"

"Yes. For illegally selling cats."

His features twisted with confusion. "Selling cats? What in the world?"

"To a medical research lab."

Mia watched his reaction carefully. He seemed truly surprised, yet she saw a slight tremble in his hand as he set his cup down.

"Do you know anything about this?"

"No, absolutely not. He's delivered cats to Portland for me, to a shelter. Or so I thought."

"What shelter?"

"Uh, the one I told you about a while back. I can't remember the name off the top of my head. They all sound alike, don't they?"

This confirmed for Mia that he hadn't even tried to find Duke. If he had, he would know the name of the shelter. Disappointment coursed through her.

A long moment hung in the air between them. Twisting his mug on the tabletop, he went on, "Levi is a very intelligent, industrious young man. He's told me a bit about his family. It's extremely dysfunctional. Their financial situation is pretty desperate. He must have seen an opportunity to make some money. This is…extremely unsettling. What kind of trouble is he facing?"

"I'm not exactly clear on that yet. But we could be in trouble, too. Both the clinic and Lucky Cats are being investigated because

Levi works for us. I've just come from our attorney's office. We need to be prepared to answer their questions. If the clinic or Lucky Cats is implicated in any way, we'll be finished. The ethical problem, even the appearance of one, will be too much to overcome. Who would want to bring their animals to a vet clinic who was selling cats for medical research? We have to be able to explain how this could have happened without our knowledge."

His face was a mask of composure as he gave his head a slow shake. "I'm not sure what to say. I'm devastated. We'll hire the best attorney in the state…"

As he rambled on Mia pulled her laptop out of her bag. She opened the photo file and shifted the screen.

"Let's start with this. Remember how I told you cats were disappearing around my place? I installed a camera on my porch because I was afraid there might be a coyote or a cougar getting them. These are the images the camera captured."

"Oh…"

She waited, noting how his complexion paled.

"Yes, I was going to tell you about this. I wanted to surprise you by trapping these strays and—"

"Stop. Ted, I'm giving you an opportunity to do the right thing here. You're about to ruin a young man's life. You have to be aware of that. He's facing serious charges, possible juvenile detention."

At that, his entire body seemed to crumple like a sand castle in the tide. He put his head down on his forearm resting on the table. When he looked at her again, she could see he wasn't quite ready to concede.

Wild-eyed, he banged a fist on the table. "What about my daughter's life? The FDA is dragging their feet and the drug company needs cats to test the medication that McKenzie needs. I had no choice, Mia. Surely you can see that. What else could I do? I didn't mean for Levi to get caught or hurt. I love that kid. He's like the son I could only imagine..." He broke off with a sob and Mia felt the weight of the world bearing down on her.

"Ted, this company used you, you know that, right? They're not properly licensed. They don't even have FDA approval for this testing..."

Mia's insides twisted painfully. How could she ruin this great man's life? She'd looked up to him, respected him, emulated him, loved him. He'd spent years trying to make the world a better place, saving the lives of countless animals, generously giving his time, expertise, advice, money to many different causes. Mia literally would not be where she was, she would not be the person she was, without him. At his core, she still believed he was a good man. A good man who'd made a terrible, horrible mistake.

She didn't know what to do.

THINKING THEY NEEDED to close ranks, Josie took time off work and brought Dean and Delilah to stay in Pacific Cove for a couple weeks. Time crept by at a snail's pace waiting to hear when Levi's trial would begin. They tried to act as normal as possible, spending hours on the beach, playing games, enjoying family meals.

One morning, a week after Levi's arrest, Josie, Levi, Laney, Dean and Delilah were all seated at the table. Jay had just placed a platter piled high with bacon in the middle. French toast was sizzling on the griddle.

A knock sounded on the back door at the same time that Jay saw their attorney, Becky Holt, through the window. He waved her in with a spatula.

"Hey, Becky," he said as she came through the door.

"Hi. Wow. Smells delicious in here. Is this everyone?"

Jay smiled proudly. "Yep, this is everyone. We've got plenty if you'd like to join us for breakfast?"

Six faces stared at her expectantly. Delilah said, "Hi, I'm Delilah. I'm a mermaid."

Becky smiled. "Nice to meet you, Delilah. I wish I was a mermaid."

Out of the corner of his eye, Jay could see Levi twisting his napkin in his lap. These days had been absolutely brutal for him as the re-alization of what he was facing had sunk in. Initially, he'd believed that because he'd been ignorant of what he'd been doing it would mean that he'd be exonerated. Gently, Becky had shown him how difficult this was going to be to prove.

Becky said, "I'm glad you're all here be-cause everyone should hear this. Levi, are you okay with that?"

He nodded.

"Good, because all the charges against you have been dropped."

A chorus of cheers rang out. Levi jumped to his feet. Laney joined him, throwing her arms around him. She picked him up and spun him around. Josie came along with Dean and Delilah who linked hands and screamed with delight even though they didn't really understand why.

Jay eyed Becky curiously. "Why?"

"Dr. Frasier has produced evidence against her colleague—evidence that effectively exonerates Levi."

Mia's phone buzzed on the coffee table in front of her. She picked it up and read the text from Jay: Can you meet me in the middle?

Staring at the words on the screen, she knew he meant that he wanted her to meet him on the beach, at the driftwood log, between their two houses. He must have heard the news about the charges. Jay's problems were over while Mia's had just begun.

"What do you think, George? Should we go hear what our Coast Guard friend has to say?"

Mia slipped on a fleece hoodie. George let out an enthusiastic bark while she tied her tennis shoes. She texted back a simple Yes. She left a note for her mom and headed down to the beach.

A short time later, she spotted Jay sitting on their driftwood log, which at some point he'd calculated was almost exactly halfway between their homes.

"Hey," he said when she'd closed the distance. Coastie gave her an enthusiastic sniff and a tail wag before scooting over to greet George. The dogs barked with their usual excitement; long-lost friends together at last.

"Hi," she said.

He gestured at the makeshift bench. "Sit?"

George and Coastie both obeyed the command, and they couldn't help but share a laugh.

Mia gave the dogs each a pat. "All right, you guys are free." They tore off down the beach, stopping to sniff a large jagged chunk of what appeared to be a broken Styrofoam cooler.

Mia lowered herself down onto the log next to Jay.

"So, I hear we have you to thank for getting Levi out of this mess?"

"Not really," she said, draping her sweaty palms over her knees. Why was she nervous? "I just passed on the information that I'd learned. It took me a while to get everything together. Well, it took my attorney a while to make sure everything was all legal and whatever. I recognized Ted in the photos. Then I called the medical lab and…" She lifted a shoulder. "It all fell into place."

"He was selling the cats to a company that researches McKenzie's disease, wasn't he?"

Mia looked at him sharply. "How did you know?"

"Levi actually put it together. You know how he is."

Mia nodded and looked toward the ocean. "I know how terrible this all sounds, how terrible it seems…is. It's such a tricky ethical subject even when it is done right and legally. To be perfectly honest, I'm not even sure how I feel about it in general… The benefits are indisputable and yet…"

"Mia," he interrupted. "I understand. And I understand Ted's desperation. I might do it, too, to save one of my siblings. I don't know… I can only imagine the feeling a parent has for a child. I feel so bad for him I can barely stand it."

His comment tightened the knot of sadness already lodged in her chest. "The company is in real trouble, so that's good. Their operation is shut down. Ted has to quit practicing for now. I don't know what will happen long-term."

"But you're in the clear?"

"Yes, Levi and me both, thanks to Dr. Anthony. I mean, he confessed to everything and he made a deal with the prosecutor's office. And the best news is that the cats are all going to be fine. There wasn't enough time and the doses weren't high enough for the drugs to do any harm."

"That's more good news then. But Mia, I'm so sorry."

"Me, too." She stared into his eyes, willing him to understand what she had to say next. "Jay, I'm going to help them in any way I can. I'm angry about what he did to Levi and to those cats, but I've been close to them... I feel for them and I have to..." She was unable to hold them back any longer, and tears began to slide down her cheeks.

He reached over and squeezed her shoulder. "I understand. Levi even understands. We all fell in love with McKenzie. If there's anything we can do to help, please let me know."

A rush of admiration flooded through her at his words. "You're serious? After what he did to Levi?"

"Mia, in hindsight, I know my devotion to my family seems over the top. To the exclusion of other things and people, even you. But I hope you've seen that I do have compassion. And that over the years, I just got in the habit of using it judiciously, so to speak. To keep from getting my hopes up and getting hurt, to keep myself together and to stay focused.

"Thanks to Levi and Laney, I'm learning that I can't control everything. Regardless of how hard I try to prevent the worst, sometimes things just happen. And I need to deal with the unexpected a little better. You're my inspiration for that, by the way. Because of my feelings for you, I've also learned that I don't have some set amount of love in my heart. Just because I love someone or somebody—" he tipped his head toward Coastie "—outside of my family, it doesn't mean that I love my family any less."

She stared, trying to absorb what he was saying while hope bloomed inside her.

"I realize this family of mine is a lot to take. But right from the beginning they didn't seem to scare you. Even when things went south with Laney and Levi got arrested, you were just…calm. You dealt with it. You helped us, even when I didn't see that you were helping. That's why Laney ran to you. And saving Levi—I'll be forever grateful for that. I know you have a deep aversion to military life, but you would make one top-class soldier. Nothing seems to scare you."

She let out a laugh as her mind replayed the thoughts she'd had before the airplane crash. She loved that she was more like her mom in this way than she'd realized. "I'm afraid of plenty, trust me."

"Really? Like what?"

"When the plane was going down all I could think about were the things I hadn't yet accomplished in my life. My biggest fear is that I'll die without making any difference on this planet, that my life and my hard work will have been meaningless. I'm afraid of being invisible."

He flashed her a look of surprise. "Well, you can rest easy now, huh? In the couple months that I've known you, you've made a difference in more lives than I could ever keep track of. Levi, Laney, her friend Elise, a cat hoarder, not to mention the innumerable cats, one perfect dog and another that is incredibly sweet even though he looks like he's about ready to eat a jellyfish…"

Mia followed his gaze down the beach. "George," she called. "Leave it." The dog flashed her a disappointed look but moved on. "Good boy!" she called happily.

"Even Dr. Anthony's life, even though he screwed that up for himself. You were always there for him and for Sara and McKenzie doing what you could to make the situation more bearable. And you're going to keep helping them, too."

He was right. And that felt good. But the mention of Levi and Laney made her heart hurt. She'd missed them these last few weeks. She missed Jay most of all.

He took her hand and placed it on his chest. Closing his eyes for a few seconds, he drew in a deep breath and blew it out. When he opened his eyes, he said, his voice almost a whisper, "It's so weird. Almost since we met, it's like I can feel you, right here, all the time…" He trailed off with a little shake of his head.

Mia's pulse fluttered and the air around them suddenly felt light.

He went on, "But you know what?" With his other hand, he gently cupped her cheek. "The life you've made the biggest difference in is mine."

His beautiful green eyes were shining with so much emotion, emotion that she'd been longing for but had given up on ever seeing. She felt his heart pounding fast and hard beneath her palm. "Oh yeah?"

"Yep. In fact, I would say that you've tipped my life upside down, shaken it, and now I'm trying to figure out how all the pieces fit back together. But I also know that nothing will ever fit right again without you in my life—in our lives. I love you, Mia. And if you're willing to give me another shot I'd like to show you how much. I'd like a chance to prove to you that a military man can make you happy."

She already knew that last part. And she was done punishing herself for the way her dad had treated her. She'd spent far too much time associating the military with her unhappiness when Bill Frasier was the only one to blame. No, she wouldn't choose to live her life with a man in the military, but sometimes love had other plans. She would definitely accept those plans if it meant she could be with Jay.

She stood and moved until she was facing him. Placing one hand on each of his shoulders, she leaned in until her face was only inches from his. "I'm more than willing to let you try."

His lips curved up into a smile while his arms wrapped around her and drew her down onto his lap. Sliding the fingers of one hand around the back of her head, he stared into her eyes for a long moment. "I love you."

"I love you, too."

Entwining their fingers together, he pressed their joined hands against his chest, over his heart. "Right here," he told her. Then he dipped his head and kissed her.

EPILOGUE

A few months later

MIA PULLED UP in front of Jay's cabin, nearly overflowing with excitement. She got out of the van and slipped on her jacket. The fall breeze brought a taste of winter, but the sun was bright in the sky. The gorgeous weather matched her mood perfectly. George hopped out of the van and she grabbed the pet carrier from the backseat. She knew Laney and Levi probably wouldn't be home yet; Laney had volleyball practice. It was Levi's day off from the clinic and he was going skateboarding with Ty. Mia loved Ty for a lot reasons, not the least of which was her influencing Levi's decision to start high school this year at Pacific Cove High.

Josie had been right about the custody hearing; their mom didn't fight it. Turned out, Neil wanted absolutely nothing to do with the Oregon court system. The judge awarded Josie full custody of all four of their younger siblings. Soon after that, Jay had officially been made Levi and Laney's guardian.

Mia heard the sound of a pounding hammer and knew Jay must be putting the finishing touches on the cabin's new deck. George knew the path and he trotted around back seeking his best pal. Coastie let out a bark and met them at the corner of the house. Mia set the carrier down where it would be out of Jay's sight for the time being.

Jay saw George first, and Mia liked that he immediately lowered the hammer, his gaze searching for her. His lips curled into a smile as his eyes found hers.

"Hey, you," he said, climbing to his feet.

"Hi." She moved closer. He bent and gave her a kiss. When he pulled away, Mia could see the love shining in his eyes. Love and joy, both of which she liked to think she was somewhat responsible for.

He said, "Your text said you have a surprise for me. Which is fun because I have one for you, too."

"Okay, do you want to go first?"

"Nope. You."

"Mia!" Laney came running out of the house and stopped in front of them. "Did you hear? Did Jay tell you?" she asked, bouncing up and down on her tiptoes.

"Not yet, Lanes. Mia actually has something to tell me first."

"Oh, sorry. Am I interrupting?"

"No, I'm glad you're here. You'll like this."

Mia was surprised to see Levi and Ty come out of the cabin, too. They were both smiling as they walked over to join them.

"Okay." She jogged back and picked up the carrier, then brought it over and set it in front of Jay.

"May I present to you, His Majesty, the Duke of… Go ahead and fill in the blank because I can't come up with anything off the top of my head."

"Duke?" Jay bent and peered into the cage. "You found him? You found my cat?"

Mia nodded and grinned. "I did. It took a while. You already know about how the police confiscated the cats from the lab. That's how I got Jane and Edward back. But some of the cats were unaccounted for. The lab didn't want them due to age or illness or whatever and they were taken to area shelters. Believe it or not, I think Duke's bum paw may have saved him." The paperwork was a terrible mess and Mia had run down one disappointing lead after another. But finally, this morning she'd received a call, and here he was.

Jay's smile was electric as he stuck a finger

through the metal. "Hey, buddy, how are you doing?" From inside the crate the cat started to purr. "Time for you to finally get your freedom, too, huh?"

"So, Lanes, do you want to tell Mia our good news?"

She blurted out the words so fast, it took Mia a few seconds to absorb their meaning. "Jay is buying the cabin and starting his own business."

"You're… What?"

"There's a little more to it than that. You know how I only have a year and a half left at Astoria and I've been trying to decide what to do?"

"Yes," Mia said, her stomach taking that familiar dip at the idea of him being transferred. He'd talked about requesting another assignment at Air Station Astoria, but she knew there were no guarantees. But she'd committed herself to trusting Jay's promise that if he had to move they'd somehow make it work.

"I'm starting my own construction business."

Laney added, "We're staying in Pacific Cove forever! Well, until I go to college. Josie and Craig are moving here, too, after Josie finishes school." Laney's volleyball season was going better than anyone could have hoped. She already had colleges expressing interest.

Mia's mind was spinning. Did that mean…?

"I'm not reenlisting. We're here to stay."

She stared at Jay and asked, "Are you sure about this?"

"Yes, I'm positive. This is my dream, Mia. You know that. I've never felt I was able to take a chance on it. But now, with everything finally stable in our lives, it's time to try."

"You're going to be great." Mia felt her heart squeeze inside her chest. She threw her arms around him as the sweetest combination of relief and happiness washed over her. They would have made it work if Jay had to leave, but she was incredibly grateful that they wouldn't have to try. She hugged Laney next, then Levi, and Ty, too, for good measure.

Jay reached a hand in his pocket and pulled out a velvet-covered box. The sound of Mia's pulse pounding in her ears was louder than a storm-tossed beach. Laney let out a gasp and slapped a hand over her mouth.

"Come on, Jay. Don't be a bum. Take a knee," Levi advised.

Jay rolled his eyes at his little brother. "Give me a second here, will ya?"

Mia said, "You don't have to do that."

He knelt and opened the box. "Mia, will you marry me?"

"Us, too?" Laney teased. "Think about this before you answer because you'll be stuck with the lot of us forever."

She reached out and gave Laney's arm a gentle squeeze. "Oh, Laney, there's nobody on earth I'd rather be stuck with." She looked at Jay and then the ring. She bent to take a closer look.

"It was special made. I hope you like it. But even if you don't, the guy said we could return it."

Mia felt tears gathering in her eyes. "Oh, Jay, I love it and I love you. Yes, I'll marry you. I can't wait to marry you all."

Beside her, Laney let out a whoop. Ty clapped while Levi grinned. Jay removed the sparkling paw-shaped ring set with tiny diamonds and slipped it on her finger.

"I never would have believed that an airplane crash would be the best thing to ever happen to me," Mia said, admiring the ring and its perfect fit.

Coastie barked excitedly and ran in a circle around Jay and Mia. George sniffed the air for a cookie.

Jay chuckled. "Who would have believed

that fostering a dog would be the best thing to ever happen to me?"

"Me, Jay. I did."

* * * * *

*If you enjoyed this romance
from acclaimed author Carol Ross,
be sure to check out the companion story,
CHRISTMAS AT THE COVE,
available from www.Harlequin.com!*

Get 2 Free Books,
Plus 2 Free Gifts—
just for trying the Reader Service!

Love Inspired

Get 2 Free Books,
Plus 2 Free Gifts—
just for trying the
Reader Service!

LIS17R

Get 2 Free Books,
<u>Plus</u> 2 Free Gifts—
just for trying the
Reader Service!